The Spaces Between Us

THE SPACES BETWEEN US

STACIA TOLMAN

Christy Ottaviano Books

HENRY HOLT AND COMPANY

NEW YORK

Henry Holt and Company, *Publishers since 1866*
Henry Holt® is a registered trademark of Macmillan Publishing Group, LLC
120 Broadway, New York, NY 10271 • fiercereads.com

Library of Congress Cataloging-in-Publication Data

Names: Tolman, Stacia, author.
Title: The spaces between us / Stacia Tolman.
Description: First edition. | New York : Henry Holt and Company, 2019. |
   "Christy Ottaviano Books." | Summary: Outcasts and best friends Serena
   Velasco and Melody Grimshaw strive together to survive senior year and
   break away from their rural factory town.
Identifiers: LCCN 2018039241 | ISBN 978-1-250-17492-5 (hardcover)
Subjects: | CYAC: Best friends—Fiction. | Friendship—Fiction. | Coming of
   age—Fiction. | High schools—Fiction. | Schools—Fiction. | Family
   problems—Fiction.
Classification: LCC PZ7.1.T6238 Sp 2019 | DDC [Fic]—dc23
LC record available at https://lccn.loc.gov/2018039241

Our books may be purchased in bulk for promotional, educational, or business use. Please
contact your local bookseller or the Macmillan Corporate and Premium Sales Department
at (800) 221-7945 ext. 5442 or by email at MacmillanSpecialMarkets@macmillan.com.

First edition, 2019 / Designed by Katie Klimowicz
Printed in the United States of America.
10 9 8 7 6 5 4 3 2 1

For Teresa

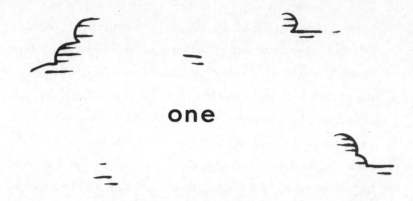

one

IN MY WESTERN CIV CLASS this year, I worked out a concept for a new superhero action figure. I call him Irony Man. He's a superhero who exists only to help others. Irony Man rescues those in distress—maidens on railroad tracks, cats up trees, victims of natural disasters, hostages—but then he always delivers them to a worse fate than if he just left them alone to begin with and let them figure their problems out themselves. Needless to say, Irony Man doesn't receive the kind of love he feels entitled to, and this makes him vengeful, and lonely. Sort of like Mr. C., my Western Civ teacher. Because I work on my superhero action figure during class and have to look like I'm paying attention, Mr. C. ends up being the model, and Irony Man comes out balding, with thick black glasses, earlobes that rest on his shoulders, and a big cross banging around his neck. Not the kind of guy you want to see coming at you in a cape and tights.

So on my final exam I sketch him in. Today, it's my grade that needs rescuing. I need a perfect score on this test to pull my grade out of the deep muck, pass the class, and turn into a senior in high school. Before I begin my quest for perfection, I stand up and look on my best and only friend Melody Grimshaw's final exam. To see how she's doing, I have to crane my head around the swollen neck and shoulders of Junior Davis, the alpha male of Colchis High. Junior has worn his football jersey to the final, so he can advertise his IQ in school colors. He has decorated the back of Grimshaw's head with lilac blossoms and is now keeping himself occupied by wrapping a lock of Grimshaw's hair around his pen. Aside from lounging in her chair and gazing out the window at a squirrel eating the end of a hot dog bun on a branch of this big pine tree, Grimshaw is hardly a bustle of academic activity. She has long brown hair, which spills down her back and over his desk, so the obvious thing for him to do is to wrap it around his pen.

Grimshaw is bored—by Junior, by the final exam, by history, by life. She wants to go somewhere, but she doesn't know where, and if she did know, she wouldn't be able to figure out how to get there. She wants to be a dancer, that's all she's ever wanted to be, but she doesn't know what that means she should do. There are no professional dancers in Colchis, not like the kind she wants to be, anyway, so she can't ask them what they did to get there. It's a dream for her, like a god she prays to. Nothing else matters to her. My family used to get her ballet lessons for her birthday down at Monique's Dance Academy, a Christian dance studio owned by one of my mother's church friends, on the condition that her family take her to them, but you can't really count on Grimshaws for anything. Her brothers are numerous, but when you need them they are always ending up in the emergency room, or jail, or needing her to babysit, or their cars have issues. Now my mom buys her subscriptions to dance magazines, which get delivered to our house, so it keeps the dream alive that way.

She doesn't have anything written on her paper. Mr. C. catches me looking.

"Miss Velasco," he enunciates.

"I'm not cheating." I sit back down. "But other people might be."

He stands up and scans the room, which interrupts these two vicious cheerleaders who are sitting in front of me and passing misinformation back and forth.

The cheerleaders give me dirty looks, and I smile at them. The football player who is playing with Grimshaw's hair belongs to one of them.

Mr. C.'s gaze comes back to rest on me. His eyes narrow. "Miss Velasco," he says again, with his usual complement of sarcasm. "I assume you've done the math."

"Yes."

"You need to hand in a perfect exam today if you expect to achieve one of your Ds and come back in the fall as a senior."

"I know."

Mr. C. stares out the same window as Grimshaw. "We know you know everything already," he says, "but what we don't know is if that's an asset or a liability."

I accomplish the short answer questions in less than ten minutes. Mr. C. is right: since my grade in Western Civ is currently a deep F, I do have to ace this test. Around me, my classmates are sighing while the grinding of the motor in the clock on the wall gets louder and louder. Grimshaw has picked up her exam and is staring at it with profound disinterest. Junior is still keeping busy with tying her hair into little bows. Junior's cheerleader girlfriend looks pretty upset about all the attention he's putting into Grimshaw's hair, but he ignores her.

Mr. C. paces the aisles a few more times, so I try to focus on the essay questions. The directions say to pick three out of five. The sixth, for extra credit, is actually fairly interesting.

"Is democracy a failed experiment? Pick another failed social experiment and compare."

This one is a soft pitch to me. I start by stating the obvious, which is that to determine whether or not an experiment has failed, you first have to define success. And then I introduce my favorite subject to talk about, which is communism, although I do point out that putting communism next to democracy like that often leads to sloppy thinking because one is an economic system and the other one is political, and they could go together, theoretically. And then I get into it. I drop the big names—Lenin, Marx, Mao—although strictly speaking, I don't know what they did or thought or said. I just know you're not supposed to like them, and that's good enough for me. I like how their names sound; they ring with this upsetting clang, like a pot dropped in the kitchen of an upscale restaurant, disturbing the dignity and repose of the capitalists at lunch. Or at least they should. My father was a radical political economics professor and had some theories about oppression and human liberation, which is all I know about him. By the time I'm two pages into my essay, though, it's not about my father. As I cover page after page, everything else disappears, the noise from the wall clock, the depressed sighs of the other students. One thought leads to the next thought until I'm scrawling down things I didn't even know I knew. It's like I'm learning something, maybe from myself.

"Miss Velasco." Mr. C. is standing next to my desk.

"What?" I look around. The classroom is empty. I'm the only one left. I slam the test down on his desk and run out of the room.

Outside, it's started to rain.

I thread my way down the stairs in front of the school, through groups of kids standing around in front of the buses on their last day of classes. Nobody says a word to me as I go by. Grimshaw and I are a pair of pariahs, like a virus in a lipid envelope. She's poor and I'm smart, so between the two of us we're practically an un-American activity. On the other side of the line of buses, Grimshaw is waiting for me on our bench.

When I sit down next to her, she puts two cigarettes in her mouth, lights both, and hands one to me. Every year at the end of the last day of school, it's our tradition to smoke a ceremonial cigarette on school property.

"A wet menthol," I comment. "Yum."

Today, Grimshaw has an enormous formerly pink suitcase next to her. The suitcase means she had a fight with her mother this morning and is running away to my house. The suitcase has a bumper sticker on it from Niagara Falls, which dates from her parents' honeymoon.

"We're free," I announce, taking my first pull.

"Freedom's just another word for nothing left to lose," she sings as she exhales her first drag. Grimshaw speaks mostly in lyrics

from prehistoric rock and roll, especially if the song is about getting free. She's obsessed with getting out of the Minnechaug Valley, which is our very small corner of New York State. She's never been anywhere else, so she's sure it's better there.

"Do you think you passed?" I ask her.

She shrugs. "I didn't really get the essay questions."

"Did you write anything?"

"I sure as hell didn't write a book."

"As long as you wrote something. It's not like he gave you much space to fill. I had to use extra paper."

"I know. You didn't even look up when I left. What did you write about? The usual?"

"Pretty much."

"You never learn."

"Neither do they."

Grimshaw grinds out her cigarette as she walks toward the bus. "I'm not coming back, anyway," she says. "I'll be eighteen. After that, what's the point?" I pick up her suitcase and follow her. I know what's in it—her toothbrush, toothpaste, and a set of rose-printed flannel sheets. My mother bought them for Christmas last year, a gesture that offended her mother. Mrs. Grimshaw doesn't drive, so one of her sons brought her over to our house to return them. As a matter of fact, Mrs. Grimshaw hardly ever leaves her house, and so coming over to my house and yelling at my mother was kind of a big outing for her. But of course, the next time Grimshaw spent the night at our house, she picked up the sheets again, so here they are. She walks ahead of me, still humming a tune. Her white T-shirt has fallen off one shoulder, revealing a shiny black bra strap. With her, it looks like an invitation. It's something about the way she moves. If her big ambition to be a dancer dies, plan B is to be a stripper.

"Slut," somebody says as we pass by a group of cheerleaders. I turn around. Of course—it was Junior Davis's girlfriend, no doubt pissed that her boyfriend spent the Western Civ exam playing with Grimshaw's hair and ignoring the death-looks of his girlfriend.

"Bitch," I say back, even though they weren't talking to me. "Cheaters."

"Like you don't," she says to me.

"At least we'll pass."

Grimshaw just keeps humming and gets on the bus.

Do you ever notice something, something that nobody else notices, you don't know why, something just makes you notice it, it catches your attention, it gets on your radar screen, and you pick out this little detail from far away? It doesn't even register as significant; you don't even know why you notice it. But you do. This gold Corvette struck me that way, like, why am I noticing that gold Corvette going so slowly down that street? It's too far away to see who's driving it, but it catches the afternoon sun and glints before it disappears, so I notice it and watch it move by.

"You coming on?" the bus driver calls down to me, and then I follow Grimshaw onto the bus.

"Hello, Prof," Grimshaw says cheerily, mounting the steps of the bus.

"Afternoon, darlin'," says the bus driver. "Miss Serena, how was history?"

"It's over," I tell him. "We passed."

"Remember what they say," he cautions with his finger in the air.

"What's that?"

"If you don't remember your history, you gotta repeat it." He laughs heartily at his own joke.

With the completion of our Western Civ exam, we are now seniors in high school, and strictly speaking, mature young ladies such as Grimshaw and I shouldn't be riding the school bus, which is really a rolling day care center. If I were more like my older sister, Allegra, I would be driving home with friends. But I'm not Allegra, and I don't have friends with cars. With all Grimshaw's brothers, we could have our choice of a whole rusty fleet of Blazers and pickup trucks, but she never took Driver's Ed, so she doesn't have her license, and I'm not old enough to drive.

I park the suitcase in the seat across the aisle and sit with her next to the window and get a book out of my backpack. I always keep a book in my backpack for the long ride home. I'm kind of a history nerd. I should really be in Honors classes, but Foundations is much livelier and funnier, so I make sure I keep my average at a D so I can be in there with Grimshaw. Today's book is called *The Gulag Archipelago* by Aleksandr Solzhenitsyn, which I took out of Mr. C.'s room. Reading a fat book guarantees that nobody will talk to me. Except for Prof, who usually has read it, too, and talks to me about what I'm reading. He's the kind of guy, if he sees you reading a book, he wants to know what it is. My mother told me that way back when, Prof got a PhD but had too many controversial opinions, and so here he is, an old black man driving white kids home every day on the school bus. Grimshaw sits down in the front seat and starts filing her nails.

"Fight with your mom?" Prof asks Grimshaw, looking at the seventh graders in the rearview mirror. Then he lets off the air brake and we lurch away from the high school behind the other buses. "What happened this time?"

"Well," she says. "First my brother gets busted."

"Dale?"

"Who else?"

Prof whistles. "That's too bad."

"So then Lisa gets mad and leaves."

Prof shakes his head. "She take the kids this time?"

"I wish." Grimshaw decides her nails are fine, and then gets up and flips through Prof's music collection, which he keeps in a cardboard shoe box under the dashboard. "Nope," she says. "Those kids always get left behind. With me. Because it's not like I have a life. So my mom wanted me to stay home and watch them today. But I told her I can't, I have these two big tests, first English and then Western Civ, like, hello, finals? Like pass the year and come back as a senior? So she gets mad and tells me it's time I get a job and help out with rent."

"School's important," Prof says philosophically. "You gotta finish school."

"So is Junior Davis after you now?" I ask her while Prof is exchanging good wishes for the summer. "You still have a lilac blossom in your hair."

"Be serious," she says, looking through the shoe box. "He's owned."

"His owner wasn't very happy with you just now. She had a bad word for you."

"It's the only word she knows. I would never go out with him. Junior Davis is poorer than I am. He doesn't even have a car." She holds up a CD and considers it. Prof rotates his CDs a lot, so there's always something new in the shoe box. "Is this one any good?" she asks Prof. "Marvin Gaye?"

"Put it on," Prof says. "You'll find out."

The school bus passes by the vacant mall in the middle of Colchis, the empty stores, and then under the shadow of the four smokestacks of Franklin Arms, where they made guns until they went bankrupt last year. Across the street from the entrance to the Arms is a bar called the Crossways Tavern, which has a neon martini glass with an olive that is already blinking on and off when the school bus passes it every day at three o'clock. Colchis is a special place to live. It's one of four small and grimy factory towns crammed together in the Minnechaug Valley. The others are Minnechaug, Bavaria, and Linerville. Although the towns appear uniformly depressing, each one is in fact unique, with its own history, extinct industry, and adjoining vacant mall.

Grimshaw is still telling Prof about her domestic woes. "So, anyway," she says as she puts the music on, "I'll be getting off at her house today."

"I have a name," I say to the window.

"Uh-oh," Prof says. "Your mom complains about that. She worries."

"Right." Grimshaw sits back down next to me. "Maybe I'll get kidnapped by the principal."

"Sst!" I throw an elbow into her ribs. "Careful with the state secrets, there."

"Will you relax," Grimshaw hisses back at me. "Nobody even cares."

Grimshaw's mom doesn't like me. There are a number of reasons for this. First is the issue of my mother's continuous faux pas. Second is that Grimshaws never graduate from high school. Around age fifteen and a half, they quit, and then let the clock run until the attendance specialist from the district gets tired of facing the Rottweiler mixes chained to the car wrecks in front of their house. Now, under my evil influence, the last Grimshaw is within a year of ruining her mother's perfect record.

After Prof disgorges half his passengers on the way out of town, we start climbing the highway into the country, past the dead farms and the double-wides. We pass the new church where my family worships. Well, except for me: I put a condom in the offering plate once, so they thought it would be better if I didn't go anymore. The farther we get from town, the smaller and shabbier the houses get. Eventually, we pass a driveway that you wouldn't notice if you didn't know it was there. It's the junkyard where Grimshaw lives. Her brothers make money by dragging old cars in there, fixing some, and selling parts out of the rest. The house used to be part of a dairy farm. There was a big barn there, and an old farmhouse, too, covered with graffiti and filled with broken glass, and as you drove by, you could look through the empty windows at the pastures growing over with thistles.

Grimshaw never gets off the bus there. She is embarrassed that she lives in a junkyard.

"The blackberries are blooming now," I remark as we pass by. She's listening to Prof's story of the time he saw Marvin Gaye play Cleveland, and how good he looked in his white suit.

"He sang real history, too," he is saying. "Not just entertainment. He was the real thing." As we pass by her house, I catch a glimpse of something in the rearview mirror. Is that that same gold Corvette again? I turn around and watch it slow down and signal to turn in her driveway.

"Some guy in a gold Corvette's about to go down your driveway."

"So?"

"I saw it down in town across from the school before we got on the bus."

"A 'Vette?" Prof asks. "I used to have one of those. Went like the devil, used to get me in trouble." He laughs.

"Do you know him, then," I demand, "that guy?"

Grimshaw looks at me and smiles. "Why, do you like him?"

"No, I'm just wondering who it is."

"He's too old for you. Leave him alone."

"That's not why I was asking."

"We'll find somebody for you," she says. "Don't worry."

"That's not why I was asking," I repeat. I go back behind my book.

"You listen to your friend, now," Prof says to me. "She's trying to take care of you. She's looking out for you."

"Who do you think would be good for Serena?" Grimshaw asks.

"When the heart is ready, the love will come," he says.

"Is that really how it works?" she asks. "I guess my heart's never been ready."

"There's no rush," says Prof. "No rush at all. That's what the rest of your life is for."

The story of Grimshaw and me started in sixth grade. I had skipped a grade, so everybody hated me, this little kid coming into their class who knew all the answers. At the same time, Grimshaw failed sixth grade, so nobody had any use for her, either, and we found each other at the bottom of the social food chain. In sixth grade, Grimshaw looked kind of like a dirty shoelace. She was skinny and grimy and had big mats in the back of her hair. One distinguishing characteristic of the Grimshaws is they all have olive skin and dark hair, but their eyelashes are white—long, stiff, and white. It's a genetic thing, she told me, from her father, who died. So at school, they started calling Grimshaw Pig-Eye, and made a game of it, like cooties. During lunch they would have to touch somebody else to get rid of it, and it would go all the way through the cafeteria—*Pig-Eye, Pig-Eye, pass it on.* It would go up one table and down the next, only it always skipped me, because I didn't exist. One day, while Grimshaw sat across from me, calmly chewing on her welfare lunch, and the day's game of Pig-Eye raged around us, I felt her eyes on me. I concentrated on my sandwich, but every time I looked up, there was her gaze—not friendly, not unfriendly, just steady and curious. Even though I was lonely, I didn't want any attention from her. It's a good thing I wasn't included in the Pig-Eye game, because I probably would have played along. If I had, we never would have been friends. People don't know this, but the Grimshaws have a lot of pride.

Even then, when she was little and dirty, boys were attracted to her. In seventh grade, my mother bought her some mascara, and that took care of the white eyelashes. Since then, she's always had a boyfriend, usually somebody else's, hence the hostility we have always enjoyed from every female in Colchis. Her relationships never last long: either they get serious and she gets bored with them, or they don't get serious and she gets bored with them, and then she throws them back like a used fish. By the time we started high school, she had this special Melody Grimshaw allure, this way of moving and looking at guys and smiling at them in a way that makes them think she is promising something, which might be why she thinks she could be a good stripper. This is a girl in search of an audience.

As for me, Serena Velasco, aside from being taller than average and hated for my brilliance by students and teachers alike, there's nothing all that special about me. I'm your basic middle-class American teenager, bored and disgusted by my surroundings. I'm a classic left-brained, linear learner, which means I can memorize long lists of unrelated and irrelevant facts and regurgitate them with ease but am challenged by tying my shoes, dancing, reading maps, telling time, and being nice to people. Since high school started, I have kept my hair dyed some patchy, hybrid-industrial color. I wear combat boots, and have a bad attitude but very good posture. Although some people say I would be pretty if I ever smiled, Grimshaw is my idea of beauty, and I don't look one little thing like Grimshaw. I never wear makeup. Most adults think I do drugs. If they'd rather think that than consider that my critique of the moronic society they've created might be based on hard evidence, that's fine with me.

I find that adults are very jaded these days. No combination of hair color, clothes, body piercing, or tattoos can shock them. About the only thing that can still guarantee a reaction in this factory town is communism. So I wear a Red Army cap every day, with the red star. I think it belonged to my father, who has been dead now a long time, at least I found it at his house in Maine, where I have to go every summer for an obligatory visit with my grandmother. I probably overdo it with the communist thing, but otherwise I'm not sure anyone would know I exist.

The development where my house is is at the very end of the bus route. As we turn onto our road, the bus shudders and clanks climbing the last hill. We're way up in the country now, and the air has cooled down and feels fresh, coming in through the open windows of the bus. As we approach the gates of the development where I live, what should be coming down the road but the same gold Corvette. The bus flashes its lights, and the Corvette slows down and stops, and waits.

"Look, there it is again."

"Like a bad penny," comments Prof. And it does look like a penny, a bright shiny new penny, even though it's an older model car, with curving lines. When the school bus stops to let us off, we walk in front of the Corvette. I have the impression of a really big guy squeezed into a space that's too small for him. Grimshaw walks in front of the car without looking at him. Something about the way she lifts her chin and ignores him makes me feel that she knows exactly who he is and why he's here. But I follow along behind her with her suitcase and we nod at each other briefly, this big guy in his low car. Out the window Prof wishes us a great summer and tells us it'll be September before we know it. I walk backward and wave at him, but Grimshaw just smiles to herself, like she knows the answer to questions the rest of us are too dumb to ask.

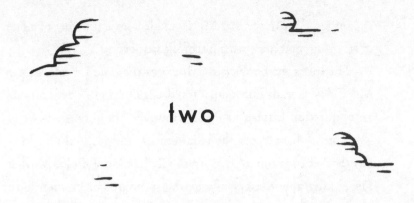

two

"**WE'LL NEVER KNOW IF COMMUNISM** is a good idea until we try it," the principal of Colchis High intones. Two days into my summer vacation, and I'm back at the high school listening to her read from my final exam essay. "The totalitarian state of the USSR was just a form of capitalism," she continues, "and government functionaries acted as owners." After that, she reads silently for a minute and then skips to my analysis of the failure of twentieth century communism, which is, objectively speaking, brilliant. "If you went to bake a chocolate cake," she reads, "and then you used no chocolate, no sugar, no butter, no flour, and no eggs, but cooked it and forced everyone to eat it anyway, and the sicker they got, the better they were supposed to say they felt, and you still insisted it was chocolate cake, you should not be surprised if your enemies outlaw chocolate cake and decree that from now on, anyone who tries to make or eat or know anything about chocolate cake will be summarily bombed." At that point, the principal sighs, shakes her head, and scans the next two pages. On the last page, next to a giant red F, I can see that Mr. C. made a little drawing of a pile of steaming manure with a pitchfork stuck in it.

She turns the booklet over and sees the note I wrote. "Dear Mr. C.," she reads out loud. "You'll notice I only wrote on one essay question instead of three. However, the total number of word-inches far exceeds the requirement, and it should be obvious that when it comes to Western Civilization, I do know what I'm talking about, especially by the standards of Foundations. Have a good summer. Sincerely, Serena Velasco."

Then she sees Irony Man. On the back of the last page of the exam, before I knew I would need the extra space for my essay, I drew a panel of him rescuing my Western Civ grade. I meant to erase him, but I ran out of time. He came out looking a little too much like Mr. C. in a cape and tights.

The principal looks up at me. She is deathly pale and gazing at me through slitted eyes, as if already planning the humiliation and dismemberment she will put me through as soon as it's legal, which will be soon.

The principal is my mother.

Nobody knows that yet, because she hasn't even been principal for two months. She was hired from a different district. We have different last names. She's Mrs. Pentz. Today, Mrs. Pentz is wearing a red linen pantsuit, which my sister Allegra picked out for her. Everyone who failed the Western Civ final is crammed in Mrs. Pentz's office—me, Grimshaw, and those two vicious cheerleaders, Angel Ciaramitaro and Claudette Mizerak, co-captains of next year's varsity squad. Angel and Claudette basically run the school. Of course, Mr. C. is there, too.

"So . . ." Mrs. Pentz begins. She turns to Mr. C. "Are you saying this essay was—"

"Plagiarized!" Mr. C. shouts. "That is not original thinking!"

"Okay," my mom says, tiptoeing through the minefield. "Can you . . . prove it?"

Boom. She hits the landmine.

Mr. C. stands up. "I have been teaching in this school for over three decades!" he yells. "I have read the essays of literally thousands of sixteen-year-olds. I know how they think!" He glares at me. "Even the so-called smart ones!"

My mom's face has gone very white, except for two red spots about the size of a quarter on each cheek. Her five children know those spots. They are warning signs. She's still breathing carefully. I'm not sure if she's angrier at me or Mr. C.

She opens her mouth to say something. But Mr. C. isn't done. "Why doesn't somebody call this girl's bluff?" he shouts. "She coasts along, acting like she's so much smarter than everybody else, no-o-o, she doesn't have to answer the essay question, she's too smart. She can write about whatever she wants! And I'm supposed to feel honored that *she* took the time to lecture *me* on everything *I* don't understand about history?" Mr. C.'s rant ends with a little shriek of indignation. His face has gotten bright red. He has to pause and gather himself so he doesn't have a stroke. "Why don't they put her in real classes? Let her take physics and calculus. Let her take AP, let's see if she's as smart as the kids who actually study."

"With Ds in Foundations," my mother points out, "we can't very well put her in Honors."

"She's playing a game, is all I'm saying," says Mr. C. "And she better make sure she doesn't lose."

"I think you make a good point," my mother says quietly. "How about the others?"

"Equally insulting!" Mr. C. snatches up Grimshaw's exam and skims it across my mother's desk. She picks it up and holds it at the end of her arm.

"The multiple choice looks okay," she says. Mr. C. snorts. The cheerleaders snicker together. My mother looks at them severely over the top of her glasses. She flips to the essays. She looks at them quickly, then looks at Grimshaw and takes off her glasses until the snickers subside. Grimshaw twists her fingers together in her lap and starts scratching the nail polish off one thumbnail. Grimshaw adores my mother.

"Oh, Melody," my mother says.

"Melody" looks mortified. "I never do good on essays," she mumbles. "I don't know how to begin."

"But to not even try . . ." my mother pleads. "To answer an essay question with—what are these, lyrics from rock and roll?"

"I'm sorry," Grimshaw whispers.

"This is just mockery," she continues. "This is the kind of thing Serena would do."

Grimshaw looks at me sideways. "I know," she whispers. "I just couldn't focus."

"They're willing to give you the benefit of the doubt here," Mrs. Pentz lectures her. "But you have to write something, any-thing at all, to prove . . . that you can do it! That you *want* to do it!" Grimshaw stops scratching at her nail polish and stares at the floor.

The principal sighs and shakes her head. "Okay. Next." She picks up the cheerleaders' exams.

Claudette Mizerak is really rich. She lives pretty close to Grimshaw and me, but she's never ridden the school bus in her life. Her father has the biggest dairy farm in the Valley, with a ten-thousand-dollar-a-month interest payment on his debt. Angel Ciaramitaro lives in a trailer park across the road from Claudette. Angel's dad was Mizerak's farm manager until he was automated out of a job. I know these details because my stepfather bought one of his cornfields to build the development we live in.

My mom looks down at their tests. "It looks like the two of you just plain failed."

"I'm ADD," says Claudette.

"Did you study?" my mom asks.

"Yes," Claudette says.

"No," Angel says.

"Did you study together?" she asks.

"No," Claudette says.

"Yes," Angel says.

"It looks," my mother says, tracing down each of their tests with a finger on each one, "as though your answers are both wrong *and* identical. That makes me wonder if—"

"Redundant!" interrupts Mr. C., holding up his hand. "They would have failed anyway. So spare us the paperwork."

"There is just so much else going *on*," Claudette explodes.

"We're very busy," says Angel.

"I can understand that," says my mother. "But—"

"We have so many responsibilities," Claudette continues. "We're co-captains for football *and* basketball spirit squads. *And* we're on student council *and* we single-handedly put the prom on this year because the junior class has negative school spirit." Here she stops to glare at me and Grimshaw. "Because some people never show up for anything."

"So?" I rise to the bait. "What's to show up for?"

"There is such a thing called pride," Angel says, studying her nails without looking at me.

"What's to be proud of?" I ask. "I don't see it."

"That reflects on *you*," says Claudette.

"Even so—" Mom interjects.

Claudette turns her attention back to my mother. "*And* we teach Sunday school," she finishes triumphantly.

"Except I don't teach Sunday school," Angel says, holding up her hand. "Just saying."

"Where's Junior Davis?" Mr. C. interrupts. "Wasn't he supposed to be here, too?"

"Well, he did fail the exam," says my mother. "But clearly other things are taking precedence for him today."

"He has a training schedule," Claudette says, using her indignant little head-wag. "He's going to a scouting camp, which is a pretty big deal, like, for his future?"

"He's the only chance Colchis has at winning any football games next year," Angel points out. "Like, at all."

"He can't play next year if he fails a class," I tell her. "It's policy. Read the handbook." The handbook is on my mother's desk, covered in gold and purple paper. "Here."

My mother stands up and takes the handbook away from me. "I will decide about Junior," she says. "The four of you can wait outside while Mr. C. and I talk this over."

We file out past Mrs. Kmiec, the principal's secretary. Mrs. Kmiec has been at Colchis High so long that nobody even sees her anymore. She just sits there at that big steel desk of hers, like lichen on a rock. Angel and Claudette repair immediately to the girls' room, while Grimshaw and I sit like bookends on the losers' bench outside the principal's office.

"Do you think we'll fail?" Grimshaw whispers.

"Not a chance," I tell her. "It's a pain in the ass for them to fail anyone. That's what Mr. C. meant when he talked about not wanting to do the paperwork. It's way easier to pass us. Also, they're worried about our self-esteem." I'm hoping Mr. C. hates me enough that he'll free me from Western Civ with a D. I'm a straight-D student, which keeps me in Foundations-level classes with Grimshaw. I used to take pride in that, like I was beating the system, like there was an art to achieving a D. I thought getting a D required the precision of a Swiss watchmaker—after all, there's only a five-point spread to aim for, as it hangs over the abyss, but then I look around at the other people who get Ds, and it seems that I got the metaphor wrong, that a D is actually a huge sack that has room for every loser in the school.

My mother is just the interim principal of Colchis High School. In April, Mr. Van Horton, the real principal, dropped dead of a brain aneurysm while repotting some African violets in this very office. Mr. Van was tall and bald, pink-cheeked and fairly fat, and wore gray suits and walked the halls all day, whistling tunelessly and jingling the change in his pockets. In the back hall of Colchis, there is a big picture window overlooking the football field, and you could find him there sometimes, not whistling, not jingling, just standing tipped back on the worn half-moons of his heels and gazing out at the white lines on the green. If he heard you coming, he'd frown and clear his throat and bark, "Where are you supposed to be?"

And then, bang, he died, which is how my mom got to be the principal for almost two months. She taught here once before, about seven years ago, but I was still in elementary school. Now that she's here again, she's trying to keep me a secret, too. I haven't exactly made her proud. In addition to the name difference, we don't look anything alike. Our voices are identical, though, when we answer the phone, a fact I took full advantage of until I got caught skipping school and grounded. She's going for the permanent job in the fall, but the school board is toying with her, pretending they have long lists of people clamoring to lead Colchis High School into the future. She's trying to prove her fitness for the job by instituting a regime of high academic standards.

From inside her office, we can hear Mr. C. yelling about how awful kids are today. There's no respect for rules, he says, no self-discipline, no manners. "She was right!" we can hear him yell. "There's no pride in this place anymore. None!"

Grimshaw leans over. "If they fail us," she whispers, "I'm not coming back."

"What are you talking about? What will you do?"

"I don't know," she says. "But I have to do something. I can't just wait around, like my life's gonna fall out of a tree and land on me. That's what I've been doing, just sitting on a rock and waiting. And it's not working."

"But you have to finish school."

"Why? Obviously, I'm not learning anything."

I wish I had an answer for this, a scheme for us, a vision, a plan, but I don't. We always talk about leaving Colchis and going to New York City, where she'll be a famous dancer and I'll be famous, too. She dances, and I—well, I don't know what I do, but I figure it out and do it and be famous, and we meet at sidewalk cafés and put our cold drinks on tiny tables. I feel like the future is coming at us too fast, though, and I wish I had known what to do to get ready for it. Claudette and Angel come out of the girls' room, and then Mrs. Kmiec comes out and signals us all back into Mr. Van's office.

"All of you have failed Western Civ for the year." The principal's voice is crisp. "If you plan to graduate next year, you do need that history credit."

Claudette's mouth hangs open. "You mean we have to repeat the whole *year*?"

"If you want to graduate, yes."

"What about summer school?" asks Angel.

"We're not offering Western Civ this summer."

"I'm talking to my father," Claudette storms.

"Good," my mother says. "I will be, too."

Mr. C. stands up. He rubs his hands triumphantly. "I'll see you in September, girls."

On the drive home, my mother seems more tired than mad. She informs me that of course she knows I didn't plagiarize, but I didn't deserve to pass Western Civ anyway, so yes, I do have to take it again next year, and so does Melody: she is not going to put her career in jeopardy defending my right to be an arrogant little smart-ass. Mr. C. plays golf with the chairman of the school board, and that's probably where her candidacy for principal will be decided. "Not that there shouldn't be further consequences—"

"Maybe you should get contact lenses," I suggest, trying to divert that one at the pass. "Your glasses make you look more liberal than you really are."

She lets out one long, irritated exhalation. "Serena," she starts.

"What? Allegra gives you career tips all the time."

She lets out another one of her tight sighs and grips the steering wheel. Then she remembers a recent commitment to take all her problems to the Lord, so she starts to pray. "Dear Lord," she starts, "please help this family and guide our thoughts toward You." When my mother prays, she has this creepy prayer voice she uses, which makes me feel like I have snails crawling up my back. "Lord," she continues, "we just thank You today, for Your blessings, and also for Your wisdom, Lord, and we know that if we trust in You as a family, You will bring us to the same place together." Then she gets to the point, which is to guide Serena's footsteps closer to the will of God. At this point, I sigh heavily. It's wrong to sigh in the middle of a prayer, but I can't help it. In addition to being the new principal of the high school and raising five kids, my mom is in church multiple times per week and maintains committed prayer relationships on the phone. When Mom started dating my stepfather, she joined his church, where the half of Colchis that isn't Catholic goes. That was seven years ago. Scot had been recently widowed and had a baby daughter, Nora, who is now my little sister. My mom got involved with him and then added religion later to smooth things out with his parents, who didn't trust this older woman, this highly educated single mother of three.

We—Aaron, Allegra, and I—thought her relationship with Scot was going to be short-lived—after all, we'd seen Mom through other guys before—but then she got pregnant.

Oops.

A prominent educator in a conservative county getting knocked up by a younger man, what a disaster. When Mom and Scot told us they were going to get married and have a baby, all I can remember is Allegra sobbing about overpopulation. My mom and the baby, Zack, were baptized on the same day.

Since the prayer's not likely to end soon, I take *The Communist Manifesto*, also from Mr. C.'s room, out of my backpack. When I open it up, it has that faint smell of burning paper that old books have.

"Put that away," my mother snaps.

I turn the page.

"I said put it away."

"Me? I can't read now?"

"I'm waiting."

"Fine." I put it back in my backpack. "I thought you were talking to someone else."

She resumes her prayer, still on the subject of Serena, which really irritates me. Even when talking to God, I think it's rude for people to refer to you in the third person when you are sitting right there. She's having a hard time maintaining her prayer voice, though, so she gives up and leaves God hanging.

"You're grounded," she says, "just on principle." She keeps going. I will have to babysit Nora and Zack every day until I leave for Maine. And, no, I won't get paid for it. Money is very tight right now, and Scot is moving his office to the bedroom over the garage, to save on rent.

"Does that mean Nanci Lee's gonna be at the house?" I ask.

Nanci Lee is Scot's secretary, so of course that's what it means, my mother says, and if her girls are with her, I can babysit for them, too. For free. She keeps thinking of more punishments. As a matter of fact, I won't even get to go to Maine. Nope, no Maine at all. I don't deserve it. The more she piles on, the angrier she gets. Oh yes, I will have to write an apology to Mr. C., and not with another one of my smart-ass screeds, either, she will read it first. And I have to start going to church again; she should never have let me get away with a stunt like I pulled with the condom. I owe an apology to Pastor Don for that one. I endure this onslaught of consequence without responding to it. Reason would just be wasted on her.

Eventually, we roll through stone pillars that spell out *Versailles* in wrought-iron lettering, and drive the quarter mile to the last and only house in the development. We're home.

When we pull up in front of the house, there is Scot, with his secretary and rumored mistress, Nanci Lee. Her nasty twins are with her, Madison and Taylor, looking like they drink ground glass out of their sippy cups. When we roll up in the car, everybody ignores us. Only our old dog seems happy that we're home by standing up and wagging his tail. Nanci Lee's glance flickers in our direction and dismisses us, like she's the one who owns the place and we are the uninvited guests. She is always entering Madison and Taylor into kiddie beauty pageants, and nobody cares that they bully my little sister, Nora.

We sit for a minute in the car without getting out.

"I don't understand this penchant for naming your baby daughters after early American presidents."

"Serena," my mother says with a tight jaw, "I've had just about enough of your—"

"If I had twin girls, I'd name them Hamilton and Burr and get it over with."

After a second of silence, my mother gets the joke. She lets out a yelp of laughter, which is loud enough for them to hear, and they look at us. Nanci Lee looks at me and narrows her eyes. I give her the peace sign, and she looks away. Some people just instantly recognize each other as enemies, and that is me and Nanci Lee. She's the cheerleading coach at the high school, and those two cheerleaders who failed Western Civ are her acolytes. My mother leans her head on the steering wheel, and her shoulders shake with laughter. Good. If you make your oppressors laugh, they can't keep punishing you, which is something anyone who has read *The Communist Manifesto* should know.

My mother gets out of the car and goes at Nanci Lee with a big, phony hug, which Nanci Lee returns with as little enthusiasm as she dares. Scot doesn't look up from his phone. I get out and slam the car door. I walk through the middle of them without saying anything to anybody and go inside and lock myself in my room with French poetry. I'm not taking French IV next year, which broke Mlle. O'Shea's heart. She gave me the poetry to keep my love of French alive "until college," an institution for which I have no use whatsoever. It seems like four more years of high school to me, four more years of people telling you what to read. But Mlle. O'Shea is right that I love how French sounds: sometimes I wonder what it would be like to live in a place where everything anyone says sounds like they're breathing love at each other. If my mother knew how much I like reading Baudelaire, she'd probably take that away, too, so I stay in my room all night, reading "Spleen" and listening to sounds of conviviality from the family dinner below, in honor of my sister Allegra's and brother Aaron's successful school year.

My punishment starts after Allegra and Aaron leave for Maine. On my first full day of babysitting, I take Nora and Zack and go to Grimshaw's. We ride bikes down the dirt road that comes out near the trailer park, and from there we cross the highway and coast about half a mile to the junkyard. It's almost noon. When we get there, two of Grimshaw's older brothers are staring into the engine of a blue Subaru station wagon.

"There she is," they say cheerily when they see me, like I'm the one who just got out of jail. "How you been?"

"Good." Nora and Zack shrink against me and say nothing.

"Hold this." Dale hands me a flashlight. "See right down there? That little pipe coming out of the engine wall? Shine it right on that spot. I can't trust these guys to do it right."

I hold the flashlight just so while Dale crawls under the car. "You should get a headlamp," I say down into the engine, which sets off a round of jokes about mining and joining the union and going on strike so you can get paid to do nothing. Under the car, Dale's laughter comes up through the engine as I watch him loosen the nut I'm pointing the flashlight at. Nora and Zack stare up at me with their mouths open, like they had no idea I had such impressive skills. Eventually, Dale gets the nut loose, and I help pull him out from under the car by his boots. Then we head toward the house.

None of Grimshaw's older brothers live at home, except for Gumby, who can't take care of himself and so will never leave, and Ruby, the closest to Grimshaw in age, who sleeps on the pool table in the basement. Ruby's boots are sticking out from underneath his pickup truck, a two-tone yellow and white antique, his pride and joy. I kick the sole of the left one as I go by. He grunts in his sleep. We find Grimshaw inside the house, already in her bathing suit. Her niece Whitney and her nephew Dallas are standing each with an arm inside a box of cereal, staring slack-jawed at a game show. I toss her the latest issue of her dance magazine. When she sees me, Mrs. Grimshaw greets me with her usual hospitality. She snaps off the TV, hauls herself to her feet, and shuffles massively away. She doesn't have her teeth in.

"Take those kids outside," she orders over her shoulder.

Grimshaw packs cookies and chips and soda, representing three of the four basic Grimshaw food groups—the other one being cigarettes—and we head outside into the June sunshine. The kids follow us in a line, like ducklings. At the edge of the woods behind her house is a field filled with old farm junk, plows and rakes and manure spreaders, as well as a wasp-infested wood-paneled Country Squire station wagon sitting on its axles. Grimshaw used to use the front hood as her stage, putting on dance performances for an audience of nobody. Between the field and the woods runs a stream where Grimshaw and I dammed a swimming hole a few summers back. Grimshaw sits down to read her magazine, and the rest of us slide down the shale and then pick our way upstream to a flat spot where the water pools. I start pulling rocks out of the swimming hole that have fallen in over the winter and spring. We build the dam back up so the water gets deep enough for the kids to dunk under. I catch a crawfish and show it to them. Then we make boats out of pieces of bark, decorate them with bottle caps and other trash, and race them down the stream.

I look up at Grimshaw, a nonparticipant in our fun. She's sitting cross-legged on the bank above us, with her face tilted up at the sun. Her chin makes a shadow that vees down between her breasts. Her eyes are closed. I climb up and sit next to her and throw grass at her face.

"Ruby says there's a big party in the gorge tonight," she says.

"That's cool. Except I'm grounded for failing history."

She's incredulous. "Just for that?"

"Yup. The only difference between me and a political prisoner is that I can lock my own door."

"Can't you sneak out tonight?" she asks.

"No problem. I'll sever the chain-link fence with my bolt cutters, crawl through the concertina wire on my elbows, and tunnel under the guards at the perimeter with a spoon."

Grimshaw sighs heavily. Her eyes remain shut. Sometimes my sarcasm wears her out.

"Is Ruby going?" I ask.

"Of course. He asked me if we wanted a ride." I don't exactly have a crush on Grimshaw's brother Ruby, but I do sort of think of him as mine. If Grimshaw has a boyfriend with a car, sometimes we go on double dates. Grimshaw and friend sit in the front and make out, and Ruby and I sit in the back, usually with Jake and Jaws, Ruby's two Rottweiler mixes. If Grimshaw and friend want to get serious, they get out and go somewhere else, and Ruby and I usually stop kissing and talk about cars.

"Are you going to meet up with Junior Davis?" I ask.

She opens her eyes. "Will you let go of Junior Davis? I told you, he doesn't have a car. Besides, he left for football camp yesterday."

"How do you know that?"

She shrugs. "I know things, too, you know."

"You better watch out for that cheerleader."

"I'm not worried about any cheerleader. So if you don't go tonight," she says, "I'm going with Mike Lyle."

"Not the one in the Corvette," I guess.

"Yes. That one."

"Figures. I knew you knew who it was."

"You're not allowed to be a snob, Serena. He has wheels."

"Yeah, but it'd probably go faster if he stuck his feet through the rust holes and ran." That gets a laugh out of her, the first one of the day.

"Don't give him any crap about it, okay? He paid a lot of money for that car. He's very sensitive about it."

"How old is it? How old is *he*?"

"I don't know. Old. Promise you won't give him any crap?"

"I won't give him any crap. It just looks like the car is about six sizes too small for him, that's all."

"He thinks you don't like him."

"I haven't even met him! He *is* sensitive. What does he want with you, anyway?"

"Nothing. He just comes by and we get to talking."

"Yeah. After he stalks you. What a loser."

"He's got a car," she says. "And he's not a loser, anyway, he's okay."

I remember how I noticed the car in the first place. There was something deliberate, something watchful about the way the car moved down the street. I would bet anything he was looking for her. And then he came here, which was weird. Not that she's not pretty, because of course she is. It's just that she comes from this long and proud line of Grimshaws, who are gun-shootin', chaw-chewin', school-quittin', weed-growin' rednecks, and if you take her on, you get the rest into the bargain. Not many guys come by here. Until Mike, I can't even think of one.

Grimshaw starts telling me not to be jealous, either, that there are guys out there for me, too, but I might have to wait for college to find them. They might not be here in the Valley, boys who walk around with their face in a book like I do.

"I'm not going to college," I remind her. "College is for people who can't figure it out on their own."

"Don't be a dumb-ass," she says.

It bothers me, this mention of the future. I don't like the Valley, either, but I've always gotten furloughed every summer, to Maine, while Grimshaw stays up here in the junkyard and can't even get down to town, which is not even much of a town to get to. At least I know a bigger world exists out there.

"Anyway," she concludes, "you shouldn't worry about Mike. I don't even like him. I mean, he's nice, but it's just that something needs to happen with me. I'll be eighteen, and if something doesn't happen soon, it won't ever, and then I'll be stuck here."

I try to think of something reassuring, like we can figure it out ourselves, but I can't really think of any specific ideas.

"Mike says he knows people who can help me."

"Help you do what?" I ask.

"I don't know," she says. "Dance? Make something happen?"

"You're sure he's not saying what he thinks you want to hear, just to make you happy?"

"What the hell's wrong with trying to make me happy? Who's ever wanted that?"

The four kids come clambering up the shale toward us for food. They're hungry.

"And try not to wear that stupid hat tonight, okay, just once?" she says. "Everyone thinks we're communists."

"I have to wear it. My roots are growing out."

She sighs. "Nobody even remembers what color your hair is. Or cares."

"That's the whole idea."

"I was buying cigarettes, and the guy behind the counter asked me how the revolution was going. Because of you."

"Dancers shouldn't smoke."

I pass out the food and the drinks. As far as asking my mom if I can go to the gorge tonight, I might as well ask her for permission to grow wings and flap them all the way to the moon. It would be one thing if I were Allegra, who gets away with murder because she's so trustworthy, but I'm not Allegra. If you're not trustworthy, you need a plan.

My plan starts after supper. I wash the dishes and wipe the counters and sweep the floor until the kitchen has never been so immaculate. After that I go upstairs and read for a while, from Mlle. O'Shea's anthology. I love Baudelaire, but now I'm getting into the twentieth century. My new favorite is by Jacques Prévert, called "Barbara."

Rapelle-toi Barbara
Il pleuvait sans cesse sur Brest ce jour-là.

It's about a woman he sees crossing the street in the rain. He hears her lover call her name, a man that has taken shelter under a porch, and Barbara runs into his arms. She's beautiful and happy with the rain on her face, but in between when that happens and when he remembers it in the poem, the war comes and takes everything away and changes what everything means, even rain. It really gets to me.

Eventually, I can hear my family assemble downstairs in the family room, and they've started a game of Uno. Usually at this juncture, I would lock myself in and read for the rest of the night, but step two of my plan is to take a deep breath, go downstairs, and watch them play cards. So that's what I do. They ignore me.

"Any objections if I sleep outside tonight?" I ask, casually, after a while. "Aaron said I could use his old sleeping bag."

My mother looks guarded. "Outside . . . where?"

"On the front lawn. You know how my bedroom heats up on these hot nights."

Mom looks at Scot, but Scot's face is a black hole. She looks at her watch. "It's kind of early for bed, isn't it?" she asks.

"Mom." Nora yanks on her sleeve. "It's your turn."

"I'm not going to bed now," I explain in a reasonable, even, and unexcited tone of voice. "I just mean for when I do go to bed." Scot doesn't say a word. He looks like he's going to have a problem no matter what happens.

"Well." My mother uses her Christian, sweet-but-firm voice. "In that case, why don't you sit down and join us?" I don't want to be here. Nobody else wants me here. But without commands coming down from the general, a mere lieutenant needs to cover her ass. Just because I failed Western Civ doesn't mean I didn't learn anything about history. As long as she's making me unhappy, she must be doing something right. So I sit down and join them. Scot deals. We look at our cards. Nobody talks. We play through a hand. I put down my first wild card, call it green, and then watch Scot have to pick up about twenty cards, getting angrier with each one. Three more cards, and I win the hand.

"Daddy," Nora says, "Serena made us a swimming pool today. I thought *we* were going to have a swimming pool at *our* house. When are you going to make *us* a swimming pool?"

Scot puts his cards down, gets up, and leaves the room without comment.

"Where's Daddy going?" asks Zack.

"It was a swimming *hole*, not a *pool*," I explain to my mother's furious face. "In the stream in back of Grimshaw's."

Scot turns around and comes back in the room. "She took our kids *where* today?" he shouts at my mother.

"I've taken them to the Grimshaws' before," I say. "It's no big deal."

"Do you know how they make their money?" Scot shouts at my mother.

"I don't think it's *so* bad," says my mother. "It's almost legal."

"Oh, that's great." Scot lifts both hands in the air. "Just great. Almost legal, the principal says. You heard it here." Scot turns in the doorway and points at me. "I don't want my kids hanging out at that place anymore. It's dangerous."

I start to laugh. "Dangerous?" I say to my mother. "That's really ridiculous."

"Serena fixed their car today!" Zack yells.

"Yeah!" chimes in Nora. "She fixed their car! Then we went swimming in their swimming pool!"

"I know those people," Scot says between clenched teeth.

"They don't have enough pride to bend over and pick up their own trash."

"You can't just say that about them!" I say to Scot.

"Melody's different," my mother pleads with Scot. "I really pray for that girl. And I'd like to think it's having some effect."

"I think," he says quietly, ignoring my mother, "in my own house, I can say whatever I want."

"No, you can't," I yell back. "You can't just talk trash about people."

Nora and then Zack start to cry. Scot sticks his chin out at me. "If it's true, I sure can."

"You want to know what people say about you, then?"

He is right in my face. "Okay," he says. "Tell me."

"Serena," says my mother, getting in between us. "Go upstairs to your room, right now."

"If we're being so free with what we've heard other people say," I tell him over her shoulder. "I hear things, too, you know, if we're passing rumors around. That's what you're doing. Talk about trash."

Scot rushes toward me with his fists clenched, and for a second I actually think he might punch me. "Go ahead, then," he says quietly. "Say it."

"Scot," my mother says behind him. "You are reasoning with a teenager. You won't win."

He spins toward her. Now he gets in her face. "Oh," he says, "I won't win, will I? And why is that? Because you're all so educated and I'm just a guy who works with his hands?" Now he's shouting at her, the dog is barking, and both kids are screaming in earnest. "Every day, I face my problems, even the ones I didn't create. I face another guy's problems who was too weak to hack it. I'm not as smart as him, I'm too dumb to kill myself. I just get up, every day, to keep a roof over his kids' heads. It's all on me."

Now my mother has started to cry, too. "Sweetheart," she says, holding out her hands in supplication. "Please don't do this. Please."

"No," he shouts. "Let's say it all. Let's get it all out." Scot keeps going. "She's so smart, and all we hear from her, all year long, is about how stupid everybody else is, her teachers, how stupid they are, how stupid the town is, my town—this is my town," he shouts again, jabbing his thumbnail into his chest, "and I have to listen to this, and now she's too smart to pass her dumb classes, and how does that make you look, Dr. Pentz, with your PhD? Like the laughingstock of the whole Valley, that's how! You think the school board is gonna hire you now?"

"Sweetheart, I really don't think—"

"You think they're gonna hire you now?" he repeats. "I wouldn't. You want to raise the standards for the whole town, but your own daughter—" He stops abruptly. "People are known by the company they keep, and that's all I'm gonna say." He leaves and slams the door. Zack and Nora run at my mother and cling to her leg and cry.

"It's okay," she says to them, with a hand on each of their heads. "Daddy's just having some feelings."

Then Scot comes back. "I don't want her watching my kids anymore," he yells. "Maybe you don't care about your kids, but I care about mine. From now on, hire a babysitter, and make sure it's somebody who's smart enough to keep them safe." Then he leaves again. We stand there, hear him slam the door again, start his BMW, and drive away, probably to meet Nanci Lee at the Crossways Tavern.

"That's ridiculous," I protest to my mother. "It's not dangerous at the Grimshaws'. And they're not trash, either. They're my friends."

"Serena," my mother says, rubbing her forehead, "do you think you can speak to Scot without a sneer in your voice?"

"Well, do you think it's right, what he said about them? It's the stupidest thing I've ever heard."

"Just go," she says. "Just go away."

"So can I sleep outside tonight?"

She gets up and starts to leave the room with Zack and Nora. "I don't care where you sleep."

"Fine," I mutter. "If you don't care where I sleep, maybe I'll sleep with the football team."

It comes out a little louder than I intend. She turns around and stares at me. "Get out," she says. "Get out of my sight right now."

So I get out. I take Aaron's sleeping bag outside and lurk by the gates of Versailles and watch the fireflies blink while I wait for Ruby to pick me up. As for the scene that just happened, it doesn't even bear thinking about. They need a babysitter, and they can't afford to pay anyone. I'll just tell Nora and Zack that instead of having a swimming hole, they now have a *secret* swimming hole. The fact that Scot now works from home complicates things, but I'll figure something out. It's not like the guy's a genius. My sister's analysis is that when the woman makes more money than the man, the man has to make up for it by swaggering around and threatening everybody and yelling a lot. Allegra says Scot's affair with Nanci Lee is his way of equalizing the difference in intelligence and power between him and Mom. As far as staying away from the Grimshaws', I can't say anything about it to Grimshaw. It will take her less than one second to guess why I've been forbidden to bring Zack and Nora over to play. She's very sensitive that way.

Eventually, Ruby's truck rolls up and stops. Only his parking lights are on.

"Melody's there already," he reports when I get in. "She went down with Dale and Lisa."

"Lisa's back?"

"Yeah. She just came back tonight. The kids were happier to see her than she was to see them."

We head down into the Valley, stopping to buy beer and pick up three of Ruby's friends, who all cram in front of the pickup with him. I stretch out in back with the Rottweilers and watch the stars go by over my head. I think about what Scot said about my father. He died when I was so young that I don't have any memory of him at all. If I ever ask anything about him, it's like it's none of my business and I should stop being so nosy and be grateful for what I have.

By the time we arrive, the party is raging. It's in a deep, ferny gorge above Colchis where tiny feathery waterfalls spill down steps of black shale into the same stream that winds in back of Grimshaw's house. A huge bonfire licks at the sky. A bunch of guys with their shirts tied around their heads are watching the fire. Some guys from the football team throw a car seat on the fire, and a column of sparks rises about thirty feet in the air, twisting around itself. Ruby puts a can of beer in my hands and then dissolves into the shadows. I crack it, take the first sip, and wander off in search of Grimshaw. The firelight makes people's faces strange and their shadows lurch against the trees. Cars keep pulling in, and their headlights illuminate more clumps of people leaning against cars and drinking. I thread through them. The gorge is the melting pot of Colchis. All the discrete, mildly antagonistic lifestyles—rednecks, jocks, stoners, even Christians— are like one-celled organisms whose membranes become permeable at parties to beer and drugs and sexually transmitted diseases. Nobody talks to me, though.

This year's valedictorian is standing on the roof of a pickup truck parked next to the fire. Allegra was salutatorian. He holds a bottle up and watches the fire through the glass. He tips it back, and as he starts to guzzle, a bunch of guys jump into the bed of the pickup and start rocking it. The crowd starts to clap in unison. "Chug, chug, chug," they chant as the guys in the bed keep rocking the truck. He empties the bottle, throws it into the flames, and holds both arms up in victory. I turn away to keep looking for my friend. If I don't find her, there is no point in my being here.

Headlights snap on, illuminating Claudette Mizerak and Angel Ciaramitaro, sitting right in front of me on the hood of a pickup truck. They're passing a bottle of wine back and forth. We freeze when we see each other, like we know we don't like each other but we can't really remember why. Then the headlights snap off and leave us in darkness again.

"Slut," one of them says.

"Bitch," I say back, and keep going.

It takes me a while to find Grimshaw, or rather, her shoes, because that's what I see first, placed neatly side by side next to the passenger door of the ugliest car on the planet, the ultimate in loser-mobiles, a metallic gold mid-'80s Corvette. A small knot of older guys, last year's football players, are standing in front of it. The passenger-side window is open about three inches. I knock on the side of the car.

"Bee-yootiful," I exclaim. "What an echo!" From the murky depths of the car, I hear her giggle. "It's Serena!" I hear her say. "She found us!" On the other side of the car, Mike Lyle gets out, slams the door, and lumbers off into the shadows. The window comes down, and a lit cigarette comes out in Grimshaw's hand. A menthol.

"No thanks." I give it back. "When I want more fiberglass in my diet, I'll chew on the insulation. Move over." I open the door and squeeze into the passenger seat with her. The car smells of sweat and cologne and cigarette smoke and beer.

"How old is that guy, anyway?" I whisper. "He's not very friendly."

"He says he knows your mom. He was in her English class back in the day. Schnapps?"

"Ew. Liquefied grasshopper guts."

"He likes it," she says. "Take off your shoes, too. He doesn't want to mess up the car."

"You better make sure he doesn't have a stroke. These old guys are kinda fragile, you know."

She blows a smoke ring and admires it as she turns up the radio. "He says he knows a lot of people where I can get a job."

The door opens. Mike Lyle is back, shoving the front of his shirt into his pants. He gets in on the other side of Grimshaw. It's impressive how quickly and easily such a big guy can fit into such a small space. He leans forward and stares at me.

"Corvettes don't rust," he announces.

I look at Grimshaw, and I can't help it, I burst out laughing. It just seems so silly to me, that a grown man would care what anyone says about his car. Then I realize he doesn't have a sense of humor about his car, or me, or maybe anything.

Grimshaw stares straight ahead of her. "Mike, Serena," she says. "Serena, Mike."

"Mike." I extend my hand to him. "Mike, I'm charmed."

He doesn't take my hand. "You think you're pretty funny, don't you?" he asks. In the darkness, all I can see are the dull reflections of his eyes. The glowing end of Grimshaw's cigarette flares up between our noses as she sucks down the last inch. Then headlights swing through the car and stop, and for a split second, Mike Lyle and I make eye contact. Although I wasn't expecting to see warm pools of affection, I'm taken aback by the paleness of his eyes. The blue of them is so light there's something empty-looking about them. I lean in closer to get a better look.

Then Mike says a bad word. He gets out and slams the door so hard it rocks the car. Mike walks into the light of the headlights. He's not that tall, but his shoulders are wide. Somebody holds a beer out for him. He drains it, and then he holds the can out and with a series of flexes, grunts, and grimaces, crushes it into a ball with one hand while the other two watch. Then he tosses it off into the dark distance.

I look at her and roll my eyes. "That was for your benefit." She doesn't answer. I watch her light a second cigarette off the first one. "What are you smoking so much for? Are you nervous or something?"

"Maybe."

"What do you see in that guy, anyway?"

"It's what he sees in me," she replies.

"And what's that?"

"A future."

I wait for her to explain, but she doesn't. "I don't get it."

"You wouldn't." She exhales a long blast of smoke. "You and Mike might get along if—I mean—can't you ever take a day off?"

"A day off what?"

"Isn't there ever a day when you get up and say, 'I'm not going to say anything sarcastic today until at least noon'?"

"Well, what did you go and tell him I thought his car was rusty for?" I demand.

"That was a mistake," she sighs. "I was telling him about you, trying to explain that most of the time you're not trying to be mean, you just want people to like you. Everything's an act with you, a show. Most people don't know that."

"Well, do me a favor and don't blow my cover."

"Let's just get out of here," she says. "I'm getting cold." I open the door and hand Grimshaw her shoes. I take off my sweater and give that to her, too.

"Take it," I tell her. "I'm too hot."

When we get to the bonfire, Grimshaw breaks into the circle surrounding it. She's still holding the bottle of schnapps, and she tips it up to take a sip.

"Nice swallow," a male voice says from far back. A smattering of female laughter breaks out. Grimshaw's face just twists up in a defiant smile, and she takes another sip from the bottle.

"Why don't you just get pregnant and stay home?" a female voice mutters near me. I don't know if it was loud enough for Grimshaw to hear. She could have anyone's boyfriend here, and often has, but she wouldn't like it if I heard that, so I leave the scene before it becomes an issue. And since Grimshaw's relationship with Mike Lyle seems destined to last at least a couple more hours, I should start exploring possibilities for a ride home. I still have to babysit tomorrow, so it would be good if I showed up for breakfast. I wander the outskirts of the party, through necking couples, heaps of beer cans, and people comatose in cars, but find nobody within six degrees of separation of either Grimshaw or me.

When my eyes adjust to the light, I pick my way down to the stream, take off my shoes, and find a flat rock that's big enough to sit cross-legged on. I mull over Grimshaw's comment about Mike Lyle. It's not what she sees in him, it's what he sees in her. So does she see anything in him? Does she look straight through him at his car? And what does he see in her, anyway? What other guys see, or something else? I don't know why I bother trying to solve her riddles, though. I always search for meaning in everything she says, until I find out she's just quoting old songs. Still, Mike Lyle is different from the others. She's gone out with other older guys, but this one's more determined, somehow. He's not bad-looking, I suppose, in an older-guy sort of way. He has a trim goatee, shiny black hair, the Corvette, of course, instead of a brain, and arms like the branches of an oak tree. If it'll really make her happy, I can try to be nice to him. But I don't have to like him.

I wish we could just go, just leave this town and this Valley, these people and their comments. If we just got on the bus and went to New York City, we could probably figure it out from there. We just have to make the first move. Every time Grimshaw starts a dance class, they tell her how much talent she has, and I'm smart enough to succeed at whatever I want, once I decide what that is, so I do have confidence that something is out there for us. I know what Grimshaw would say to that, though: confidence doesn't have wheels, and I'm not old enough to drive.

I stick my hand in the water and let it lap up to my elbow. The voice of the water slowly clears the beer out of my head. Somewhere on shaley cliffs above me, maidenhair ferns hang down, and every few minutes, a drop of water lands on my face. From here, the party is only a flickering orange glow against the trees and a few hoarse shouts.

I lie down on the rock and close my eyes. The moss is soft, and the occasional drops of water that reach my face remind me of the woman in the rain in the Jacques Prévert poem. If I pretend to be French, I might forget about where I live. I hear sirens, and blue lights flash over my head through the trees. I listen to the commotion that has started above me, shouts and the running of feet. The police coming to flush the underage drinkers home is a regularly scheduled feature of weekends in Colchis. After the excitement dies down, I make my way back up to the party. The fire has become a glowing orange mound of coals. People are quieter than they were before, but it's a warm night, and there's still a buzz in the air, like anything could still happen. I don't see Grimshaw anywhere, or Mike Lyle, or the Corvette. An old Blazer and a bashed-in pickup truck are parked on either side of the bonfire, close enough to blister the paint. Stretching over the fire from the top of one to the top of the other is a long board. I'm trying to figure out the point of this when somebody shouts, "Who's gonna walk the plank?"

"I'll walk it," somebody slurs. It's the valedictorian again. People cheer. He crawls on top of the pickup, and they help him up onto the roof. Of course, as soon as they let go of him, he staggers forward, twirls around, and then falls off, which everybody thinks is very funny. They beat him on the back, even though he falls clear of the fire, and he holds up his bottle like he has won a great victory. Then he gets dragged off by the armpits to retch into the poison ivy.

Heavy metal music comes buzzing and thumping out of the open windows of a truck. I while away some time thinking of the torture that awaits me at home as I watch the youth of the Minnechaug Valley fall one by one into the coals, which get grayer and dustier as they cool. The plank is kind of soft and spongy, and sags when they get to the middle of it. Nobody makes it to the other side. After a while, I notice a certain chill in the air and the sky getting a little darker. A yellow rind of moon climbs out of the trees. This night is ending, and I need to get home.

Then I see her, up on the roof of the Blazer. This might be what we were waiting for, it might be why we came to the party in the first place. For her it's not a party, it's an audience, but she has to be drunk enough, and so does the audience.

The bottle of schnapps is still with her. She takes a swig of it, makes it part of the dance, then lets the bottle lead her out to the middle of the plank. Everybody is quiet, watching her undulate into center stage. Grimshaw's dancer fantasy doesn't come out of nowhere. The girl really does know how to move. Even drunk and in heels, her balance is perfect, and she doesn't take a false step. She gets to the middle of the board and stops and sways with her eyes closed.

"Take it off!" somebody says, a male voice. Grimshaw smiles and closes her eyes and continues to sway. First she holds her hair up. Then she stretches her arms out and starts to unbutton her sweater—my sweater—with one hand.

Somebody turns the music up. Once her sweater is open, she starts peeling it slowly off her arms. I don't want it to end up in the fire, so I fight my way to the front of the crowd and grab it just before it lands in the coals.

Underneath the sweater is a lacy top, and under that is her bra. Liberated from the sweater, Grimshaw moves her arms more freely. The silence of the men around the fire has a particular focus to it, like they don't know Grimshaw is just dancing. They think she's promising them something. I seem to be the only other female present. With my eyes open, I say a silent prayer that the song will end and we'll go home with no more drama than that. The skin on the back of my neck starts to prickle. Behind me a stick cracks. Mike Lyle walks up behind me. I'm glad to see him. He'll defend our honor and drive us home in his Corvette. He's the answer to my prayer.

"Looks like all the good little girls have gone home," he says. "And you're still here."

"Could you take us home?" I ask him. "Like, right now?"

He focuses on me with those laser-vision eyes of his and pretends to be confused. "You want to go home with me, little girl? I thought you didn't like my car."

"I didn't say—"

He looks around. "Seems to me like the party's getting going again. All the little kids have gone home." He lets out a long, low belch. "Or almost all."

Suddenly, I feel like one of those little kids, and all I want to do is go home. We both look at Grimshaw. She's holding the bottle at the end of her arm and following it around in small circles.

"How much has she had to drink, anyway?" I ask.

"I don't know," he says. "I'm not her babysitter." He takes another swig of beer. "And neither are you."

The song stops, and I wait for her to get down. Mike and I stand there together and watch her twirling around on the plank in silence, smiling to herself while all these guys watch her from the shadows. But no, another song starts, and she moves to that. She could dance to anything, really.

"Somebody should stop her," I say. "It's not safe, what she's doing."

He takes a swig of his beer. "Life's not safe. You better get used to it, little girl. Or stay home." He leans in closer to me, without taking his eyes off Grimshaw. "You think you could do that?" he asks me softly. He doesn't look at me, just gestures with his chin toward Grimshaw.

"Do what?" I whisper. For some reason, my voice doesn't seem to work. I clear my throat. "Do what?" I ask again, louder.

I hear a low chuckle. "You know what I mean," he says. "Smart girl like you. I think you could," he says, still without taking his eyes off her. "I think you got it in you. You're still just a little . . ." Here he leans close to my ear. "Scared . . ." He breathes on my neck. "We're all just the same, underneath it all, we're just animals, you and me."

He clearly isn't going to help us, so I don't want to waste any more time on him, but there's something about the way he stares at you that you can't look away from.

Then he keeps going. "You and your mom," he says. "I know Scot. Put it this way—she ain't Mrs. Pentz because of their intellectual discussions." He laughs, like he's just told a joke. Then he winks at me.

Somebody throws something—a chunk of wood or a heavy rock—in the fire. I turn to look. A column of sparks swirls up around Grimshaw, who seems to enjoy it. Like she's been waiting for that cue, she holds the bottle over her head and twirls around. It's gotten light enough that I can see Ruby's pickup truck parked at a little distance. Why doesn't her own brother know what's going on? Ruby will do something about this if Mike won't. I run to the truck, and there is Ruby, asleep behind the steering wheel. I slug him in the arm as hard as I can, so he stirs, barely opens his eyes, sees me, and shuts them again.

"You better drive," he says. "I've had . . ." He doesn't finish the sentence.

"Move over, then."

I leave the driver's side door open, go back to the Blazer, walk out onto the plank, and reach for Grimshaw's hand. "Let's go," I tell her. "We have to go home."

She opens her eyes wide at me. "Come on." I snap my fingers. With drunken docility, she lets me lead her off the Blazer. I help her down, then I push her in front of me to Ruby's truck, and she gets in and slumps against the passenger-side window. Ruby is already stretched out in the back, sleeping next to Jake and Jaws. Before I get behind the wheel, though, I turn around. Mike is still standing in the same place, watching me.

"Remember what I said," he calls.

I rush up to him and get right in his face. "You leave us alone," I tell him. As I turn to go, his hand snakes out, he grabs me by the back of the shirt, and he pulls me in close to him.

"I'll give you some advice, little sister," he whispers into the back of my head. "Don't take me on."

He lets me go and I run to the truck. When I get to the door, I turn around and give him the finger. "You're too old," I shout at him. "We're still in high school."

He seems to think this is the funniest thing he's heard all night, and his laughter stays with me all the way up the hill.

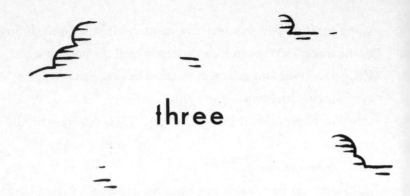

three

AFTER I SLEEP FOR MOST of the next day, I head out to an old cemetery, located halfway in between my house and Grimshaw's, going crosslots. It's on a little knob on the side of a hill, a swell in Mizerak's rising sea of corn. Ever since sixth grade, it's been our secret meeting place. There are about a dozen lichen-covered graves surrounded by cedar trees. There are only four families buried here—the Purdys, the Getmans, the Helmers, and the Spragues, all related. Nobody's been buried here since 1924. Grimshaw uses the Helmers as her stage.

I get there in the late afternoon and wait for about half an hour, when here comes Grimshaw, gliding up through June-high corn. She's wearing a sleeveless black Harley T-shirt that comes down almost to her knees. Maybe it's because it's a breezy day, with everything in motion—trees, clouds, corn, Grimshaw, all moving together in the same graceful rhythm—but she really looks like she's dancing. This is the last day I'll see her before our senior year begins. It turns out I'll be gone all summer after all. Tomorrow they're putting me on a bus to Maine.

"I like walking through corn," Grimshaw says as she reaches the graveyard. "I think it's my favorite crop to walk through."

"I'm leaving for Maine tomorrow," I tell her.

"Tomorrow?" Her eyes widen in surprise. "Did you get in trouble for last night?"

"No, but I'm banished anyway. Something very weird is going on at my house. Scot wasn't home, and my mom was on the phone, praying. Five o'clock in the morning. I just walked right by her and went to bed. There's no way Scot's not having an affair."

"With that secretary?"

"Yes. With the heinous, hideous, and hateful Nanci Lee." What I don't tell Grimshaw is that my mother interrupted her prayer to tell me that she already hired a babysitter and they're putting me on the bus for Maine tomorrow, and that if my attitude doesn't improve, I can do my senior year there in Maine and not bother coming home, which is ridiculous. They don't even like me in Maine.

Grimshaw reclines on the Helmers, and her hair spills over the edge. I sit on Mr. Sprague, who died in 1901, aged seventy-eight. She stares up at the sky.

"I don't have any cigarettes," she announces.

"Me neither."

"You never do."

"I don't smoke."

"You smoke mine."

"Dancers aren't supposed to smoke," I remind her. "It cuts down on their wind."

"It's too late for me, anyway. I read you're supposed to start training when you're eight."

"*Hold fast to dreams*," I quote Langston Hughes, with my finger in the air. "*For if dreams die—*"

"I'm not interested in dreams," she interrupts. "I'm interested in reality." She props her head up on her elbow, and we watch gusts of wind chase each other across the corn, making dark streaks against the brilliant green.

"Remember when we used to make a game of running through Mizerak's corn?" I ask. We'd start at opposite corners of the cornfield, pretend we were lost and had to find each other in the corn. The rules were that you had to keep running, and you couldn't break the stalks. You could only change rows if there was a break in the row or you had come to the end. It was really fun, running down the endless rows through the weeds, the blades whipping by your face, especially when you'd see the other person running by a couple of rows away, and then you'd start to laugh so hard you couldn't keep running. It was easy to miss each other. We'd play at the end of every summer, when the corn was way over our heads. By October it all gets cut to silage.

"If I had a car," she says, "I could get a job. I could get hired to teach down at Monique's. She knows I'm good with the kids. It takes money to get a car, and it takes a car to get money. And I don't have either one. Nice, huh? And I'm almost eighteen."

"You could come with me to Maine," I offer.

"But I need money." She stands up on the Helmers and starts swaying to her inner orchestra. "Some dancers make great money," she says. "They work at night. Mike says he knows people in the business."

"Mike," I say, investing the word with as much disgust as one syllable can contain. I shake my head and turn my back to her. While she stretches and lunges, Grimshaw keeps talking about the great outfits strippers get to wear.

"My brother Wayne's fiancée, Gloria, used to be an exotic dancer at this club in Florida," she rattles. "She doesn't do it anymore since she gained all that weight, but she kept the clothes." I roll my eyes and shake my head. Wayne and Gloria. Wayne has a part-time job unloading trucks at a grocery store. They live in the trailer park, and they're always trying to fall down the stairs so they can sue somebody. Grimshaw finishes warming up. She gets down from the Helmers and sits next to me. She's taken the Harley shirt off. She's wearing her bra and a pair of bike shorts.

"Do you ever have this . . . feeling?" she asks. "Like, you have this feeling you're going to die young?"

"Not exactly. I try to look into my future, but there's always a manhole cover in the way."

"It's just that—" She picks at the hem of her shorts. "I don't know—I can't see myself like Gloria, doing that."

"That's good."

"Or any of the others, either. Lisa or anybody, with kids and a job and stuff. But I can't see myself doing anything else, either, far away from here. That's why I always figure I'll be dead."

"I think there are other options than Colchis or death."

She executes a backbend on Mr. Sprague's bench. She is so flexible that her hands and feet almost touch. Then she runs through splits and then she wants me to spot her up on the Helmers again, while she jumps, so I stand up. Spotting her is just a formality: she lands every jump like a sparrow landing on a twig. Standing up on the Helmers, you can look down into the Valley and see the smokestacks and the steeples of Colchis.

"I think it's your fault, actually." She stops to catch her breath. "Not that I blame you."

"Go ahead. I'm getting used to having everything blamed on me."

"Because of you, I know that there's the big world out there, that people have dreams. If I didn't know you, I'd just think, *This is it*, and I'd probably be happy here." She lists the many blessings of being a Grimshaw—lots of family you can count on, and they all know how to fix a car. I say nothing. "But your big mouth and your big words," she continues. "It's like your words come from someplace else, so it makes me think I'm gonna go someplace else, too."

"We'll get there."

"How?"

"I don't know yet." We sit down again. "But just because we failed history, there's no reason for despair."

"But that's the point," she says. She gathers all her hair on top of her head and knots it into a bun. "It doesn't matter. We could pass history or fail it, and it wouldn't make any difference. So why are we doing it?"

I don't have an answer for that, so I'm quiet, feeling the despair come over us, like exhalations from the dead bodies underneath us.

"It's because I'm gonna be eighteen," she continues. "That's why I'm thinking about it. When you turn eighteen, you start thinking about death. You'll see."

"Also because you need a cigarette."

"Maybe. But seriously, Serena, what about all those bullshit classes we signed up for next year? Consumer Concepts? What the hell even is that?"

"We talked about it. We signed up for easy classes so we can have fun."

"Boring isn't fun," she says. "Mr. C. was right. You should be taking harder classes."

"Just be here when I get back, that's all I ask. And stay away from Junior Davis, too—I have a feeling those fascist cheerleaders are capable of violence."

Grimshaw pulls her shirt back over her head. "Anybody else you don't want me to see?"

"That goon in the rusty Corvette."

"He has ambition," she says. "He's getting a Dodge Viper."

"Right. And I'm getting a flying zeppelin. I know, I think I'll call it . . . the Hindenburg." Then I think of something. "Dammit," I say. "I forgot about my hair again. Can you do it tonight?"

"Leave it alone." She takes off my Red Army cap and pushes my hair around my head. "What would you do if you woke up one day and you were the prettiest girl in the room?"

I push her hand away and pull my hat back as low on my head as it will go. "That's your job."

"My job." She laughs. "That must be why I'm so rich."

I tell her how much my grandmother in Maine hates my hair, and then I imitate her, saying, "'I'd rather she were on drugs'—that's what she says every time she sees me. She takes one look at my hair and goes, 'I'd rather she were on drugs.'"

Grimshaw asks, "Are they rich?"

"Rich?" I repeat. "I don't think so. They stay in this old unpainted house every summer, and all their cars are old. No, they're not rich."

"Oh," she says. "When you imitated her, she sounded rich. She sounds like how rich people talk on TV."

"I don't know why she talks like that. But it's not because she's rich. Everything's old in that house. Old rugs, old furniture, old dishes. Old books." I imitate my grandmother again: "'*Don't* walk on that rug with your bare feet!' '*Don't* sit in that chair with your wet bathing suit!'"

It makes her laugh. "There," she says. "The way you just said that. Rich."

"No," I insist. "If they were rich, they'd buy new stuff."

"Right," she says. "Like these guys. They should buy new stuff." She makes a gesture that includes the Spragues, the Helmers, the Getmans, and the Purdys. She frowns at Mr. Sprague and affects an upper-class accent that actually sounds somewhat like my grandmother. "Don't lie *there*, Mr. Sprague," she says. "Your filthy bones are messing up our grass!"

I sigh about the shame of it all and shake my head. "I'd rather he were on drugs."

She lies down on the Helmers and stares up at the sky. "I'd rather *I* were on drugs," she sighs. "It's gonna be a long summer."

"Last night before I snuck out, Scot got really mad at me and said my father killed himself."

"Really?" She sits up. "I thought your father died in a car crash."

"That's what I always thought. But there's this unmentionable quality when his name comes up, like he did something so bad we cannot speak his name. Whenever I ask, my mother sighs and gets really sad and says she'll tell me when I'm older."

"Do you think he committed a crime?"

"Maybe. That's always the feeling I get about him."

"Wow. That's kind of sexy. I hope it was a good one. My father died when a car fell on his sternum and crushed him. How sexy is that?" She shakes her head, like you can't even trust a Grimshaw to die right. Then she thinks of something and snaps her fingers. "Hey! Your dad! Maybe he's alive! Maybe we pass by him all the time and don't even know it!"

We both think of it at the same time. "Mr. C.!" we say together.

"He's your dad!" she says, laughing. "That's why he failed us!"

"Because he cares!"

"Yes! So he can watch over us one more year!"

"Then his work is done!"

But when we're done laughing about that, Grimshaw gets very gloomy again. "I'm seventeen," she sighs. "Where's my life?"

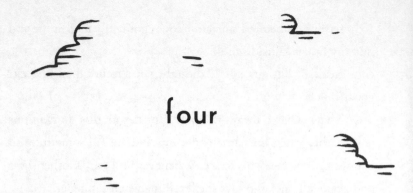

four

IN THE SUMMERS, MY DEAD father's family lives in a rambling, shingled place on a cliff overlooking a cove that opens to the ocean in Maine. It has a barn in back and a small beach down a steep walkway. No Internet, of course. We visit them there every year, although it's more like a summons than an invitation. We share their DNA, so they have to deal with us once a year. By the time I get there, Allegra has already found not just one job but two, at an ice cream store and a gift shop in town, and Aaron has been hired as a junior counselor in a youth soccer league. It's just me and my grandmother, so I try to make myself useful. I offer to paint the trim on the house, but no, I'd probably just drip paint on the shingles and make a mess. I offer to mow the lawn. No, I'd be taking bread out of the mouths of deserving local people. I offer to polish the—no, no no, my grandmother waves me away. After that, my choices are to either get a job and be a productive citizen or read, so I read. The house is full of books, and it takes me a week just to read all the titles, making sure I stay at least two rooms away from my grandmother.

Last summer I took sailing lessons, so when I find the book I want to read for the day, I go down to a little rocky beach on the cove and take out our sailboat, the *Signal*. I'm not a very courageous sailor, I just venture around and get to know the inlets and little islands. I always take a sandwich with me, too, and whole days can go by with nobody saying anything to me at all. This begins to feel like my real life, like there is this other Serena who lives with a family in a faraway place and has one friend, who occasionally laughs at her jokes. Sometimes I miss that Serena, and I can see that her life really isn't so bad, and I can't remember what she was always so angry about, and I can see that she could be nicer to people, even her stepfather, and follow more rules, maybe, and not act like it's her divine mission to point out the lapses in other people's logic.

Book by book, a month goes by, and on the first day of August, I turn sixteen. I wake up to another empty day. Nobody will remember it's my birthday. Nobody's even here to remember. Allegra isn't here, having found a bunch of very successful and attractive friends in town. Aaron is away at a soccer camp. My grandmother is out. The phone won't ring for me, and nothing will come in the mail. I go down to the beach and sit in the *Signal*. I can't face opening a book today. No matter what the book was, every page would say the same thing: *This is your fault. You have pushed everyone so far away that you don't even know where to find them again. You are so alone on your sixteenth birthday that nobody says anything at all, far less happy birthday.* I look out at the horizon and think that if I just went for it, just hopped in the *Signal* and got lost at sea, how long would it take for anyone to even notice I was gone? I imagine my own funeral and how sad and sorry everyone would be that they never realized I was really a nice person the whole time, and soon real tears are leaking down my face. But I don't have the courage to get lost at sea. Although I wouldn't mind being dead, I have no desire to be cold or wet or hungry, so there will be no funeral and no sorrow at my passing so young from this earth. So I just sit there in the boat on the beach with no book and feel more deserving of my own pity than anyone has ever felt.

When I see two people coming down the cliff toward me, I quickly dry my tears with the back of my hand. If I had a book, I could pretend I'm not as pathetic as I look, the abandoned birthday girl in a beached sailboat. It's a tallish, blondish man in sunglasses and white linen, which flutters in the breeze, and a woman, also in white, coming down behind him. They keep stopping on the path as they descend, and he points out different features of the landscape. It's a windy day, and they both sort of flutter together like they're walking through a painting. I have never seen anybody but me on this beach, and I wait for them to realize they're in the wrong place, turn around, and go away. They keep coming down, and when they reach the beach, I realize that it's my uncle, who is hardly ever here in the summer. His name is Hugh. People say he looks like my father. The woman he's with wears gold sandals and a white bathing suit and a sheer sarong knotted at the side of her waist. They smile gaily as they approach me and then greet me, then stoop down and kiss me on both cheeks, like we're in Europe.

"Hey, kid," Hugh says. "Remember me?"

I nod. "Hi," I whisper, my voice having atrophied over the last month.

"And this is Sabine." Sabine sort of squints up her face at me, which must be how people as glamorous as her smile at people as unglamorous as me.

"Nice to meet you," I whisper, and then feel even more stupid than before.

"That's a nice hat," Hugh says. "Where'd you get it?"

"Here, last summer," I tell him. "It was on the third floor of the house."

"What's your grandmother think of it?"

"Not too much."

That makes him laugh. "I bet she doesn't," he says. "She says you're quite the reader. Do you hole up on the third floor all day?"

"No," I answer. "I go sailing, too. A lot." I explain about the books and the boat and the cove, but the more I talk, the more inane I get, and I'm sure he thinks I'm a moron. Sometimes you meet a person who is as smart as you pretend to be, and then you realize your whole personality depends on the stupidity of your surroundings, and then once you realize that, you should stop talking.

Hugh smiles. "Reading and sailing," he says. "It must be genetic."

"Oh." I wonder if this is a reference to my father, but he just puts his hands in his pockets and looks out to sea.

"We should get back here more," Hugh says to Sabine. "I always forget how pretty it is in the summer."

"Beautiful," Sabine replies. "The colors. I feel like I'm in a watercolor painting."

They are including me in their conversation, expecting me to join them in their repartee, instead of sitting like a lump. I realize this might be the moment where I should stand up and get out of the boat, so I do, awkwardly.

"We watched your brother's game last night," Hugh says to me. "He's quite the athlete."

"And a handsome boy," adds Sabine.

"And then after that, your sister took us out for blackberry ice cream. We looked for you, but I guess you were out in the *Signal*."

"I've never had that flavor ice cream before," says Sabine. "It was fabulous."

"It's my birthday today," I blurt. "I'm sixteen."

Hugh looks at Sabine, then he looks at me, then he looks at Sabine. "Happy birthday," he says.

Sabine steps forward and once again kisses me on both cheeks. She wishes me happy birthday in French. Instead of coming up with something to say back, I just stand there staring at her with my mouth opening and closing like a guppy. And Hugh just keeps standing there with his hands in his pockets, looking out to sea.

"Do you know much about your father?" he asks me.

I shake my head. "No."

"Come on," he says. "I'll show you where he hung out." I follow them back up the steps of the cliff.

"Did he hang out in the barn?" I ask.

He stops and raises his hand. "Carriage house," he corrects me with his finger in the air. "A subtle but important distinction."

"Carriage house, then."

We walk past the house to the carriage house. The door slides open heavily but easily. "There used to be bats that would roost behind this door," Hugh says, "and they'd fly out every time you opened it. Bats were a big part of the excitement of summer." He tells me and Sabine a couple of bat stories, chasing bats that had got inside around the house with tennis rackets and fishing poles, leaping over couches, and crashing into furniture. While he talks, I look around at a big dusty space full of large, mysterious objects covered with sheets. Iron implements, horseshoes, bits of brass, leather harnesses hang on the walls. I see horse stalls with iron dividers, and you can detect a smell of leather and hay in the air. The afternoon light slanting through the windows catches the dust that hangs in the air and fills the place with a soft golden light. Against the far wall is a car-shaped lump.

"Is that an old MG?" I ask.

"No," Hugh says. "It's called a Sunbeam Alpine. Same idea, though. A little car that goes fast when it goes, which is rare."

I pick up a corner of the canvas that drapes it, and there is the cutest little red two-seater sports car you've ever seen, with a ripped convertible top. "You mean it doesn't work?"

He throws back his head and laughs. His laughter makes me laugh, too, like I just said something really funny. Sabine seems mostly concerned that her white clothes not brush up against anything dusty. "Follow me," Hugh says.

He goes up a set of narrow stairs at the back. The stairs are creaky and kind of spongy underfoot. The light gets clearer and brighter as we ascend. At the top of the stairs, he opens the door and we step into a high-ceilinged room with lots of dormers and roof angles, all paneled with beadboard painted white; a simple single bed with an iron bedstead; a table and a chair. And books, lots and lots of books. The light through the trees shifts around and throws shadows everywhere so the place looks alive.

"Let's get some windows open in here," he says.

"So we can breathe," says Sabine.

"Your father created this space," Hugh tells me. "It's where he came when he wanted to be left alone."

I start reading the spines along one shelf. "Are all the books in here about China?" I ask.

"Not necessarily," Hugh says. "Keep looking."

It's the most political library I've ever seen. Revolutions. Russia. Communism. The exact same books that Mr. C. has in his classroom, only more of them and just as dusty. I stand up and look around me. "I feel like I'm back in Western Civ. Mr. C. would absolutely love this place."

"Who is this?"

"He's the guy who failed me in history," I tell him, "and I have to take it over when I get back home. He has all these books, and I read them when things get a little slow."

"You failed history?" Hugh asks. "How could my brother's child possibly fail history?"

"It's complicated." While I leaf through books that feature Marx, Mao, Castro, and other people that would irritate my mother, I tell Hugh and Sabine about Mr. C. and why I'm in Foundations, and my friend Melody Grimshaw, and Irony Man, and how we failed the exam together, all of which Hugh seems to find amusing. He seems interested, though, so I keep talking, and as I tell them about my life, the Serena that is far away joins with the Serena that is here and makes me feel that I am still the Serena who can talk to people. I sort of talk the two Serenas together.

"Tell me more about Irony Man," Hugh says. "How does he fit in?"

"He's my new superhero action figure," I explain. "He rescues people in distress, but then he delivers them to a far worse situation than the one they escaped."

Hugh thinks this is a lot funnier than my mom did. "I like Irony Man," he says. "I relate to him." While we talk, Sabine stares out the window at the line of the sea, as if she is waiting for the ship that will rescue her from these books and this dust.

"Well." Hugh checks his watch. "It's time for cocktails. Your grandmother is hovering angrily near the bourbon at this very moment." He grimaces at Sabine. "Like a yellow jacket," he adds.

"She could come up here," I suggest.

"She could," Hugh agrees. "But she won't."

That night, my birthday is observed with lobsters on the beach, along with clams cooked in seaweed with potatoes and corn on the cob. Allegra is there with a new boyfriend, and Aaron makes an appearance, too, with some soccer players. Even my grandmother joins us. My mother has mailed me a birthday in a box: a cake, sixteen candles, cards from Nora and Zack, presents, money, and a long letter from her, which I read later. She says that she has officially been offered the principal's job, so it's going to be a challenging year for all of us, but that doesn't mean it can't be a good one.

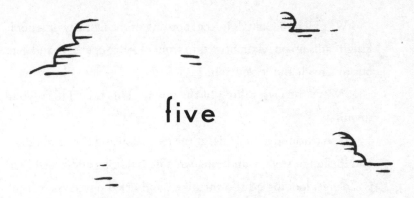

five

FOR THE MONTH OF AUGUST, I transfer reading from the beach to the carriage house. After Sabine leaves, it takes Hugh most of the month to fix the Sunbeam, working under the car, while I'm upstairs reading, or I bring a book down and read from it while he falls asleep under the car. He's not interested in ideas from the twentieth century. He doesn't have any answers about my father, either: they were very far apart in age, and his way of dealing with painful subjects is not to think about them. "Cauterize the wound and move on" is his philosophy. He is sorry he's been such a piss-poor uncle, though, and his plan is to fix the Sunbeam so he can drive me all the way to Colchis in it.

My mother agreed to the trip when she came to Maine two weeks ago, to take Allegra to college and get Aaron back for football practice. So on Labor Day, Hugh and I leave Maine for the Minnechaug Valley, keeping to the back roads in case the radiator overheats, stopping at antique stores and old barns and roadside stands, so what would normally be an eight-hour drive takes closer to eighteen. We take turns driving through the night with the top down.

We pull into Colchis in the morning of the first day of school. Hugh pulls up on Main Street, in front of Al's Superette, and gets out to stretch and look around.

"Wow," he says, taking in the town. "This is it? This is your town?"

I look around at Colchis, at the nail salon and the bridal shop and the liquor store, wondering what he is talking about. All I see is Colchis, looking a little shrunken and dried out at the end of the summer. About two thirds of the stores on Main Street are boarded up, and maybe if you'd never seen it before you might think it would be a good stage set for a zombie movie, but still, the sun is coming up and the day is fresh. I watch a line of school buses follow each other out of town.

"This is it," I tell him.

"I can't believe Harry's kids really grew up in a place like this," he says, as if he is talking to himself. "I should have been paying more attention. I'll be in touch this year, though, you'll see."

I get out of the car and stretch. "I can't believe I have to do the first day of school on no sleep."

"Wow," says Hugh again. "Here it is, the burned-over cinder of the American Dream." He looks across the car. I look around at the town. I don't really see what seems so dramatic to him. The town's two traffic lights are green. First one turns red, then the other one does. It's so quiet on Main Street, we can hear the clunk they make as they change colors.

"You didn't fail history," he tells me. "History failed you."

"I suppose I could just go to school," I tell him. "So you won't have to drive all the way up to my house just so I can catch the school bus back down."

"Right," he says. "But coffee first, school later. Not that I'm expecting to find anything drinkable around here."

We find some coffee, then we drive into the parking lot of Colchis High School just as the early bell is ringing on the first day of classes.

The new principal's opening speech at the assembly in the auditorium is rousing. The cure for all society's ills is in our hands. We have to start doing our homework, she scolds, and go to college. I look around, but I don't see Grimshaw anywhere. Mrs. Pentz launches into the importance of making good decisions, about trusting your thinking instead of your feelings. "Even at the height of passion," she says, "your brain is still working. Use it."

Then the bell rings and classes start. Still no sign of Grimshaw, and I start to wonder if she did quit school. My first period of the day is free, and I spend it on our bench, alone. It feels like it's going to be a long, quiet year. Sitting there, looking up at the school, I make the first decision of the rest of my life: I'm going to follow the principal's advice. I'll have myself my own future, a real one, complete with all the middle-class accoutrements. I go to the guidance counselor's office. I switch my classes around so that now I'm in physics, calculus, and French IV, as well as AP English.

The people in Guidance don't really want to let me change my schedule so drastically, since I have no prerequisites in place, and of course there is the small matter of my GPA. Guidance shows it to me, and we look at it together. There it is, the GPA of doom, the smallest number anyone has ever seen. But I bring up the fact of my near-perfect SAT scores and drop my-mother-the-new-principal's name casually into the conversation enough times, and how inspired I was by her speech, that obstacles to my ambition start to melt away like ice cream. Except for Western Civ, which I still have to repeat, they don't care who my mother is.

My French teacher, Mlle. O'Shea, is so happy to see me that she cries when I walk into her classroom. My other classes are full of middle-class strivers who look pretty sour to be sharing their station in life with the girl in the Red Army hat. They don't think I'm real competition. That's okay. Chiang Kai-shek thought the same thing about Mao. I eat lunch with a pile of textbooks for company. It's not so bad to be alone.

After lunch comes Western Civ, with Mr. C. as sarcastic as ever. Then who breezes in but Melody Grimshaw, chatting and laughing with Claudette Mizerak and Angel Ciaramitaro like they've always been best friends. When she sees me, she comes over and stands in front of my desk. She's wearing high heels and a skirt that's so tight it looks like it was duct-taped on.

"I thought you were going to be in Consumer Concepts with us," she says. "We signed up for it, remember?"

I shrug. "I switched all that up for physics and calculus."

"No way!" Grimshaw looks genuinely excited. "You know I always thought you should be taking that stuff."

I shrug again. "I'll probably fail them, anyway."

"No," she says. "You'll work hard. I'll make you do your

homework. Then you can go to a good college, and I'll come visit and scope out the cute college boys for you."

I shrug again. "Whatever." I yawn so hard my Red Army cap falls off my head.

"Wow." She reaches out and touches my hair. "Your hair really grew out. I forgot how blonde it is."

I pick my cap up off the floor and pull it down low. "I was out in the sun a lot this summer. I should take care of it."

"No. Leave it alone. It's beautiful."

Then this awkwardness opens up between us, like we have forgotten how to talk to each other. She drums long, crimson fingernails on my desk. The bell rings, and Mr. C. rises up from behind his desk.

"Sit," he greets us. There are no empty spaces around me, so Grimshaw leaves and sits near Claudette and Angel. Junior Davis doesn't seem to be in Western Civ. Mr. C. turns his back to us and writes on the board. He turns around. "Five-paragraph essay." People moan. "For a quiz grade. What is Western Civ, and how did it affect my summer vacation?"

At the end of the day, Grimshaw isn't waiting for me on our bench, so on the first day of my senior year, I ride the bus alone, an ill omen if there ever was one. Even Aaron has friends who drive now. It's just Serena Velasco, a senior, and a wild horde of brand-new seventh graders.

When I get home, I hop on my bike, and just for the heck of it, I ride the long way to the cemetery. Mizerak's corn has grown so high I can't see the gravestones from the road anymore. I swing

off my bike and push it up the weedy path. Up on the Helmers'
pedestal is my old friend Melody Grimshaw, practicing cheerleader jumps.

I sit on Mr. Sprague's bench and pick burrs off my socks. "I
knew I couldn't trust you."

"Serena, get over yourself," she pants.

I watch her execute a straddle jump. "What did you write on
your essay?" I ask. "About your summer vacation."

"It's private," she says when she lands. She does another jump.
"Did I point my toes?" I turn my back to her and face the wall of
corn.

"I think you picked up a virus from those cheerleaders. I hope
it's not contagious."

"We're going out for cheerleading," Grimshaw says primly.

"What? Who's *we*?"

"We is us. You and me. There are two spots open on the
varsity squad. The Decker twins moved away, and the alternate
quit. Angel and Rack are coming to coach us."

"Angel and who?"

"Rack. That's what everyone calls Claudette Mizerak."

"Oh." I squint up at Grimshaw and try to picture her bouncing around in school colors, a purple and gold phoenix rising up
out of the junkyard. I shake my head. Not a Grimshaw, not in
Colchis. I can't imagine the conditions under which that would
happen. But there are some things you don't say, even to your best
friend. "Why?" I ask. "I mean, what's the point?"

"Fun," she says.

"Fun," I repeat.

"We don't have enough fun," says Grimshaw. "It's our last year of high school. Why not have some fun?"

I'm trying to think of a delicate way to phrase to Grimshaw that being a cheerleader really doesn't signify much these days, and it's not worth risking the inevitable rejection. She's still poor, I'm still smart, this is still America, and we're not going to be cheerleaders.

"I just wonder if we're really cheerleader material," I say finally. She climbs down from the Helmers and sits next to me on Mr. Sprague.

"I know it's not dance," she says suddenly. "But it's movement, it's performance."

"Choreography," I provide helpfully, just to be sporting.

"Exactly!" she says. "It's a start, it's something. I mean, I have to work from where I am."

"Okay," I say slowly. So the notion might have some merits, at least for her. "But why does this need to involve me?" The instant that I say that, I remember earlier today, how the straight-D student signing up for Honors classes probably violated every notion Guidance had of people who deserve nice things, but the fact that my mother is now their boss made all those objections melt away, even though they were Mrs. Pentz's new standards I was violating. Privilege. The word just comes to me. I have it, and she wants to borrow it. I was just a tourist in Foundations.

"I'll think about it," I tell her. "You have to give me time to get used to the idea, though."

"I need an audience," she says. She starts telling me about her idea of starting a dance team at the high school, that she thought about it all summer, and that if she's a cheerleader, it'll be more likely to work, as she'll have more visibility and credibility. People will take her seriously. She worked at Monique's Dance Academy, she says, teaching the kids, so she had to get really good at technique.

"You taught at Monique's?" I repeat. "How did you get there?"

"It doesn't matter." She waves my question away. She was going to offer yoga, too, but Monique thought it was satanic, so that didn't go anywhere. But since my mother is the principal now, she might offer a class in yoga, too. I watch her as she talks and try to pin down the difference I see in her. She has definitely learned some things over the summer. She moves differently, with more intention, somehow. Maybe it's confidence. "It's not really about cheerleading," she says. "It's about the same thing it's always been."

"Dance."

"Yeah. I was ready to give up on it, but it was because of what you said, at the beginning of the summer."

"What did I say?"

"You said that if we wanted a future, we needed a plan. So— now—we have a plan."

"So you mean those two—"

"Yeah," she says. "I've been hanging out with them all summer, off and on, starting pretty much right after you left for Maine. They're not so bad."

"I thought they hated us. Because of Junior Davis."

"Serena, just let that whole Junior Davis thing go, okay? Rack and I worked it out. Anyway—" She looks around to make sure the deceased aren't eavesdropping. "He doesn't really love her"—she puts air quotes around the word *love*—"but he needs her. This is his fourth time taking algebra, and he needs to pass if he wants a football scholarship. She has organizational skills. And a car." She talks about all the pieces Junior needs to put together if he wants to go to college next year.

I narrow my eyes at her. "You didn't make any kind of a bargain, did you? Like, you'll leave Junior alone if she—"

She cuts me off. "It doesn't matter. They like us, those two. They think we're interesting."

"Do we get to decide if we think they're interesting?"

"Just go with it, okay, Serena? For once in your life? Angel and Rack get a kick out of you. They think you're funny. And the boys think you're kinda cute, so—"

"What boys?"

"See?" she says. "You're interested."

At that moment, an enormous pickup truck comes bumping up the cow path toward us, taking out a row of corn on either side. "Help us, Jesus!" I throw up my hands. "We're being invaded!" Claudette Mizerak is driving.

"That's her dad's truck," Grimshaw explains.

"It's her dad's corn, too."

They pull up and stop. Claudette Mizerak's head pops up through the sunroof and says, "Hi, cheerleaders!"

"Here's a quiz," says Angel, hanging out the window. "What's the most important ingredient in the making of a cheerleader?"

"I give up," I say.

"Beer!" the two of them cheer, tossing silver cans at us. Angel gets out of the truck and picks her way through the thistles in a miniskirt and high wedge heels, but Claudette just mows through them, talking a mile a minute. Claudette is big—well, big-boned, anyway, and Angel is tiny with glossy olive skin. Claudette has big ears and thin, bleached blonde hair and a loud honk of a laugh that you can hear all over the school. Angel has a curtain of dense black hair that hangs to her waist. Her eyebrows look like butterfly antennae. Her nails are two inches long. They seem to know their way around our dead and buried friends, so I take it they've been here before.

Talking at the same time, Angel and Rack report that Nanci Lee has empowered them to run the practice and to pick the replacements.

"She says she's giving us ownership of the team."

"She says it's all about leadership, that she wants us to pick girls who can represent the town."

"Like we're senators." Rack guffaws.

We discuss the plan of us becoming cheerleaders, and they are all for it. Nanci Lee is the only obstacle they can foresee. She won't like it if they let people walk in off the street and be cheerleaders, or at least not people like Grimshaw and me. Apparently, Grimshaw has filled them in on the details of my home life, and they know that Nanci Lee is not my staunchest ally.

"Nanci Lee is my aunt Teresa's friend," says Angel. "They went to high school together."

"Is she the one who has the bridal shop?" I ask.

"So is Nanci Lee hot for Serena's dad?" Rack asks her.

"*Step*dad," I correct them. "A subtle, but important, distinction."

That stops the cheerleading conversation dead for a minute. "You have to stop talking like that, Serena," says Rack. "It makes the boys think you're stuck-up."

"But what if I am stuck-up?" I ask.

"Just ignore her," says Grimshaw. "That's the only way to deal with it."

Rack laughs midswig and coughs up some beer. Angel and Grimshaw pound her on the back. "Oh my God," gasps Rack. "It's four o'clock. I forgot to take my pill." She runs down through the weeds and thistles to her truck.

"What pill is this?" asks Grimshaw.

Angel shakes her head. "The four o'clock one is so she can do her homework at night, even though she never does it." Angel sighs. "You wouldn't believe the pills that girl is on." Rack comes puffing back up and sits down heavily on Mr. Sprague. She puts a little pill in her mouth and washes it down with Lite beer. A burr sticks to her sweater and there are more on her socks and pant legs. Angel and Grimshaw start picking them off her.

"Ack," Angel says. "Now they're on me."

"It's not just ADD," Rack pants. "It's for depression, too. Then I'm on tetracycline for my skin, and don't tell anybody, but I just started birth control pills, too. I'm still technically a virgin, but I have a feeling I won't be for long. Junior is really, like, hot for me. All the time."

"Do you want to?" Grimshaw asks.

Rack shrugs. "It's inevitable when you're in love."

It seems to have been decided that we're all going to be pals, which I would prefer not to go along with, although even I find it challenging to hate people who laugh at my jokes. Besides, Grimshaw has this nonnegotiable look about her, which I know enough not to mess with, for the time being. But—our years as plankton in the social food chain of Colchis High are not going to be overcome by a few jokes in the cemetery, and I'm sure by tomorrow life will be back to normal.

"Anyway," Angel says, "I know Nanci Lee and your stepdad went out in high school. They were king and queen of homecoming back in the day."

"They say your first love is forever," Rack says dreamily. "I know it is for me and Junior. Don't you feel that way about Mike?"

"Mike?" I demand. "You mean Lyle? Is he still hanging around?"

"Why don't you like him?" Angel asks me. "He's always so nice to us."

"She doesn't like anyone," says Rack. "That's why she's so funny."

"You guys always look so happy together in that car," says Angel. They start to chatter about what a cute couple they are, about everything he's done for her and how much time they spend together. Mike and Melody, even their names sound good together. And it's so sweet, how he calls her Mel. Rack wishes Junior had a nickname like that for her. I have to admit, I had sort of forgotten about Mike Lyle over the summer. The sound of his name hits me in a surprising way, with a little shock.

"Riding around in a rusty Corvette, though, talking about a Viper—what a loser."

"He's getting the Viper," she says.

"He's not getting a Viper. Unless he's dealing something."

"He's not dealing anything, Serena," Grimshaw says tightly. Then she scrambles to her feet. "You guys, teach us some cheers."

"No, no," Rack says. "I think we should sit right here and work out our issues."

Grimshaw looks down at her. "Finish your beer, Rack," she says. "Then drive us home."

Rack drives me home in time for me to help make supper. Wednesday nights are our night to eat together as a family, and it's always been a pretty tense affair, a weekly cease-fire between me and Scot, usually brokered by Allegra. But Allegra is not here, and Scot and I have not seen each other since the blowup before I went to Maine.

"Do you know Mike Lyle, Mom?" I ask as I walk through the door. She's frying chicken legs. I seize a pot of boiling potatoes, stab them, and drain them.

"Wash your hands," she says. I wash my hands. She's impaling the chicken legs with a long-handled fork.

"I changed my classes around today," I tell her. "I added physics, calculus, and a fourth year of French." I watch little drops of grease hop out of the skillet and bounce across the stove. The one thing my mother cannot do is cook. Before she married Scot, she was a vegetarian.

"I know," she says. "Guidance wasn't very happy about your high-handed attitude."

"Well . . ." I mash the potatoes contemplatively. "I just wanted to see what it would feel like to do a little better, you know, to challenge myself."

"You're not used to that. Do you think you can handle it?"

"I can try."

"Well, I approved it."

"Thank you."

"As a new principal," she says, "I only have so much capital. I don't want to use it all up on you on the first day of school. Guidance thinks you'll fall flat on your face. In case that motivates you."

"I think I can come up with my own motivation," I tell her.

She actually smiles at me. "I'll look forward to that."

"So do you know Mike Lyle?" I ask her.

She sighs. "Unfortunately," she says. "Why?"

"What's he like?" I ask.

"Sullen. Rude. Lazy. Why?"

"Do you think he's potentially lethal, or just another harmless loser?"

She considers. "The latter. Basically." She collars Zack as he runs by and leads him to the sink. Then Scot comes in and takes over washing Zack. We don't make eye contact.

"Isn't Mike Lyle wanted in about twenty-five states?" he asks my mother. "That's what I heard."

"Wanted for what?" I ask.

"Fighting, I guess," Scot says. "Disturbing the peace. He played semipro ball for a while after he got out of the army. When he worked on the crew, he used to brag about all the people he messed up."

"I know his father was pretty rough," my mother says. "Mike senior."

Scot shrugs. "Those things get passed down."

Mom looks at me sharply. "Stay away from him. He's too old for you."

"Believe me, I know that. By the way, I'm going out for cheerleading."

My mother finishes turning the chicken. "Nora, call Aaron for supper and come wash your face." She takes away the mashed potatoes. "Set the table," she directs.

"Did you hear what she just said?" Scot asks. "About cheerleading?"

My mother looks at me and shakes her head. "She's not serious. She has nothing but contempt for cheerleaders."

"No, I'm not kidding," I insist. "There's an all-day clinic this Saturday in the gym. It costs twenty bucks."

"Twenty dollars just to try out? Well, I'd say that eliminates you."

"Ten for me and ten for Grimshaw."

"Why does it cost money just to try out? I'll have to check into that."

"Ten bucks apiece?" Then Scot smiles at me, too. This is getting weird. "That doesn't seem so bad," he says. "I'd cover it."

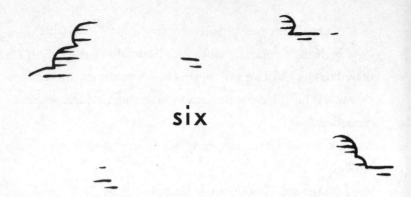

six

OUR ROAD TO CHEERLEADING NORMALNESS is supposed to be a carefully scripted event. Rack and Angel put out a fatwa on anyone who dares show up for the special tryout. Despite that, a few girls who don't know what's good for them come to the Saturday clinic, in addition to me and Grimshaw. Nanci Lee comes in wearing a warm-up suit with a Scottie terrier appliquéd all over it. She has a blonde pageboy and a row of diamond studs in one ear and a deep artificial tan. She looks around the sparsely populated gym, knows something is up, narrows her eyes at Rack and Angel, who maintain their innocence.

"We told everybody," they insist to Nanci Lee, which I suppose technically is true. So there is Nanci Lee, with her assistants and her clipboard and all the power in the world, about to be wasted on the two of us. There is a look on her face of pure determination, that we will never be cheerleaders, not if she has anything to do with it. Which is fine with me, I don't even want to be a cheerleader. Grimshaw, on the other hand, has clearly put the time in and knows every single cheer down cold. Which, if I know Nanci Lee, will make her even more determined to keep us off the squad.

The herd of hopefuls is separated into batches, and we are taught a cheer.

> *Strawberry shortcake*
>
> *Huckleberry pie*
>
> *V-I-C-T-O-R-Y*
>
> *Are we in it?*
>
> *No we're not!*
>
> *We're not in it,*
>
> *'Cause we're on top!*

Baudelaire it ain't. But this is what Grimshaw wants, so I snap my gum and smile until my face hurts, and the more cheerleading spirit I evince, the more suspicious Nanci Lee gets.

They put us through our paces, and Grimshaw if anything is overqualified—her toes are too pointed, her jumps are too high, her carriage is too . . . lofty, somehow. When she does anything, everyone stops to watch. She's very graceful and can do handsprings and aerials, and her jumps hang suspended about six feet in the air for a full minute, with her legs fully extended and her toes perfectly pointed. She has way, way too much technique. But the poor girl never opens her mouth or smiles. When Nanci Lee watches her, she shakes her head, turns aside, and visibly mouths, "No spirit," to the other two coaches. "This isn't ballet," she says. I, on the other hand, clap and shout peppy slogans without any display of rhythm or grace. I am not a bit ironic, either, not even during cheers like "Excellence, Perfection, Teamwork, Success," which make me feel like spitting on the ground. I go through the motions because I don't want this fiasco to be blamed on me. Between the two of us, we might make a whole cheerleader, but as individuals, I think we're safe from being selected for the squad.

At lunch, Rack and Angel stay very busy on their phones, so nobody comes back to the clinic after lunch except for me and Grimshaw. Nanci Lee has a speech prepared. Cheerleading is not just bouncing around with pompoms, she says, hoping you get a shot at being popular. It is a serious, highly competitive sport. If you don't make it as a freshman, your chances are basically nil. She stops. Nobody says anything. Her assistants stand behind her, looking nervous. You don't just wake up one day and decide you're going to be a cheerleader that day, she continues. You train, you condition, you follow the cheerleading code of conduct and sign a contract. She stops again. A silence opens up. There's only the cheerleaders getting her lecture, plus me and Grimshaw. Nobody says anything, or appears to be taking this too seriously. Nanci Lee throws her clipboard down on the ground and walks out of the gym.

Rack steps forward and picks up the clipboard. "So," she says. "They're gonna need sweaters." She looks at Grimshaw and points at her with the pen. "Size?"

"Medium."

Rack looks at me. "Medium?" she asks.

"Sure."

Upon becoming an official cheerleader, Grimshaw wastes no time in turning us into a dance team. She has better ways of doing everything. She wants to make us more dance-y, less jerky and stompy and stupid and old-fashioned. "It's not anything new," she insists. "Other schools started doing it this way a long time ago." The co-captains are okay with that idea. Who knows, it might even make cheerleading cool again.

Their only obstacle is what to do with me. Every morning, Rack and Angel meet me and Grimshaw in the cemetery before school. We all have the first period free, so depending on the time and the weather, we hang out there for a while, drinking coffee. Grimshaw teaches them how to blow smoke rings, and they teach her cheers. While I do my homework, they discuss my many shortcomings as a cheerleader.

"Maybe she can just stand there," Rack suggests, "and shake her pompoms."

"But she can't keep time," Angel says. "Or remember the words. She has no sense of rhythm."

I look up from solving a physics problem on acceleration. "I can lift," I offer.

No, they decide I should just be injured. If I hurt my knee, my back, or my shoulder, that'll keep me out of the way. They can pull me in if they need someone at the base of a pyramid.

"It's cool," says Grimshaw. "It's not like we're competing. We're just having fun."

Grimshaw's eyes glow, her cheeks are pink, she looks like she's in love, and all she's talking about is cheerleading.

In Scot's eyes, being a cheerleader is the first normal thing I've ever done. It's so normal that it threatens to make the whole family normal. The first time I wear my purple and gold cheerleading sweater home, they act like Jesus Christ just rode into Jerusalem on a donkey.

"Oh!" my mother gasps when I enter the kitchen. "Oh, Serena!" She's whipping up our weekly family dinner. "Sweetheart! Come and look!"

Scot rips himself away from the Sports Channel and appears in the doorway. "What is it?"

"Just look at Serena!" she warbles.

"Wow," he says, through a mouthful of chips. "That is really fantastic. It fits nice, too. Purple's your color."

My mother cocks her head and looks at me. "Not with silver earrings, though," she decides. She's holding a big wooden spoon and flings drops of dressing around the kitchen as she talks. "Go upstairs and get a gold pair off my dresser." Hypnotized by family approval, I go upstairs and do exactly as I'm told. I find the gold earrings and put them on. The cheerleader in the mirror waves at me. I wave back. She has blonde hair and blue eyes. No Red Army hat. I don't know what happened to it, but I suspect Grimshaw did something with it. The girl in the mirror tells me people in cheerleading sweaters and gold earrings are usually not communists. I tell her no, Mao said we could still swim among the fish in the sea. She tells me I'm doing this for my friend, so forget about Mao and just deal with it.

At dinner, football dominates the conversation. Aaron plays running back for the junior varsity football team, and in ancient times Scot was Colchis High's star quarterback. Even now, he makes sure he never misses a game. It used to take me about five minutes to turn these family dinners into a bloodbath, but not now, not in a Colchis Rockets cheerleading sweater with gold earrings. It's not so bad being neutralized, I find. You do get to eat.

"You're awfully quiet, Serena," my mother says when I finish.

"I don't have too much to say about football," I tell her, clearing my plate away. "So I'm just listening."

"Do you understand the game?" she asks.

"No, but it doesn't matter. Rack says she'll watch the game and tell us what cheers to do."

"Why don't you ask Scot?" Mom suggests.

I'm dubious. "Ask him . . . what?"

Scot brightens up. "Anything." He spreads his arms and looks around. "What do you want to know?"

I'd just as soon be upstairs starting my homework, since I now have about seven hours of it every night, but they seem to want me to know about football.

"Well," I tell him, "we could start with what the point is."

"First of all," he says, "you have four downs to advance ten yards in a hundred-yard field. If you don't get it in four downs, you lose possession of the ball."

Mom beams at us.

"Advance where?" I ask.

"Down the field," he says, like it's the most obvious thing.

"Oh."

"With the ball," he says.

Aaron gets into it. "The ball, Serena," he prompts, with his mouth full of food. "The football. It's that round brown thing that's pointy on both ends. Both teams want it, only one team can get it. Get it?" He is shouting at me, like I'm deaf.

"Yes . . ." I say doubtfully.

"Each team is trying to get the football, so they can put it into the other team's end zone," Aaron explains. "That's a touchdown."

"Right. For six points?"

"You didn't know that?" Scot asks. "Sit down. Football is complicated. It's not like other games. It's about relationships, and opportunities, and . . . dynamics. Sit down. Right there. Get her a piece of cake," he directs my mother. "Or she won't stay." He snaps his fingers at her. "The cake."

"I never paid attention to football," I tell them. "I didn't go to games, and I always got away with skipping out of pep rallies because Mom hates football."

"I don't hate football," Mom objects, cutting me a gigantic slice of cake. "I just think—"

Scot waves away what she thinks and repeats what he said about downs.

"Scot," Aaron says, "you can't start with downs when she doesn't even know what the basic object of the game is."

"Sweetheart," my mom interjects. "It's almost six thirty. Don't you think you should—"

"No!" Scot yells. "This is important. If she's a cheerleader, she's gotta understand the rules of the game. I can take one night off for that."

Scot talks about strategies, plays, and the importance of the quarterback. Scot's ideology is that in football, as in life, you can't just wait to see what happens, you can't just wait for the other guy to screw up. "It's like life," he says. "If you want to win the game, YOU have to make something happen. It's on you." As he describes the arc of the ball during the kickoff, he stands up and knocks his chair over backward. He ends up on one knee, looking heavenward with his arms crossed over his chest, which he says is the position a receiver is to assume who doesn't want to get mowed down while he waits for the ball to drop.

The less I say, the happier everybody is. That is how a tentative peace descends on the Velasco-Pentz household.

When the enemy advances, we retreat. When the enemy camps, we harass. When the enemy tires, we attack. That's what Chairman Mao said, and it's my strategy for surviving Western Civ.

But Mr. C. attacks first.

The second week of school has hardly begun when he asks me to come in to see him after school. I'm wary, but I show up. He makes me stand there waiting for about five minutes until he's quite through writing the year's first column of grades in his grade book.

"Serena." He caps his pen and stands up. "I'm afraid this year won't be much of a challenge for you. And I know how deadly boredom can be. I've been thinking about your essay. About Mao." He pauses as though I'm supposed to say something, but when I open my mouth, he doesn't give me a chance. "So—I'd like to offer you a yearlong independent study. Should you choose to accept, you'll still have to come to class and do the reading and the homework and participate fully, but instead of the regularly assigned papers and tests, you'll produce progress reports of your work. I've run it by your mother, and she said it sounded fine. What do you think?"

"No, I . . . I don't—"

"An independent study is a college-level challenge, requiring self-discipline and initiative. And it has to be local."

"Local?" I repeat stupidly.

"Of course. You should think of this as three to five times the normal workload." He gives me a week to come up with a topic and a syllabus. He tells me it'll be excellent preparation for college, puts on his hat, and walks out of the room while I'm still standing there with my mouth open. He might think he's outsmarted me, but there's no way I'm doing anything remotely like that independent study. Aside from French, Western Civ is my only easy class.

I leave the building and stand outside the back door by the faculty parking lot, but there is nobody there. Scot was supposed to pick me up here, but he must have forgotten. You used to be able to see the lit windows of the Arms from here, but now the factory is dark. I can see the neon martini glass shining over the Crossways

Tavern, though, by the main entrance to the Arms. I watch the olive blink on and off in the gathering dark before it occurs to me to walk down there and see if I can use someone's phone.

In the Crossways Tavern, the air has a smoky red glow, due to the red velvet wallpaper and fringed Chinese paper lanterns. A silent baseball game floats in a darkened corner, which a group of men watch. They're wearing dusty green work clothes, as if they still worked at the Arms. A woman at the end of the bar looks me over. She moves around behind the bar and stops in front of what would appear to be Scot and Nanci Lee, reading the real estate listings together. Nanci Lee's head is on Scot's shoulder. They're sharing earbuds. The Beatles are playing on the jukebox. The woman behind the bar picks up a cigarette that burns in an ashtray. She squints at me, then she squints at Scot. She takes a puff, then lifts her chin in my direction.

"That yours?" she asks.

"Oh, Jesus!" Scot hops off his bar stool, and Nanci Lee snaps to attention, clanking accessories and all.

"Serena!" She extends her hand for me to shake, and then withdraws it just enough for me to be hanging on to her fingernails. She crinkles her eyes at me, to approximate a smile. Scot tosses back the last swallow in his glass. He folds the newspaper, puts it under his arm, and slides a stack of papers off the bar. He turns to Nanci Lee.

"Just go," she mouths at him.

"Tomorrow," he tells her. "Later, Louise," he shouts over his shoulder as he pushes me out the door ahead of him. When we get outside, the Arms looms over us. "Serena," he calls. When I turn, he tosses me the keys to his BMW. "You drive." He gets in the passenger seat and puts the newspaper over his face. By the time we get home, he's actually asleep.

The next morning, by the time I get to the cemetery, Grimshaw has set up cream and sugar for coffee on the gravestones. I sit on Mr. Sprague and open my math book. Rack and Angel bring a box of donuts.

"Bad news," announces Rack. "Nanci Lee found out that you guys failed Western Civ."

Last night was the first heavy frost, and all the weeds are stiff and black and spiked with silver needles of ice. Angel sits next to me on Mr. Sprague. Rack's brought a blaze orange hunting cushion and settles in cross-legged on the ground with her back against a gravestone whose letters have been almost washed away by the weather. It's cold enough for her to be wearing Junior's football jacket, which she paid for, although we're not supposed to tell anyone that. Grimshaw's sitting cross-legged on the Helmers, slowly eating her daily breakfast of one tub of nonfat blueberry yogurt.

"So?" I look up from my mastery of functions. "So did you. So did Junior."

"Doesn't matter," says Rack.

"Why does it matter that we failed it and not you?"

"We're not saying we agree," Angel interjects. "We're just saying we have a situation is all."

They explain that Nanci Lee found the policy against kids on academic probation joining teams.

"It specifically says you can't *join* a team," explained Rack. "The implication is that if you're already playing, you're fine. It just says you can't join."

"She's already recruiting new girls," adds Angel. "She's on a mission."

I think of Nanci Lee, the way she kind of glittered with malice, even in a dark bar. She probably already had her plan in place for kicking me off the squad. Still, the news of our expulsion doesn't sound so bad to me. Even though expectations of me are very low, cheerleading still takes up too much of my time. If we're kicked out, so what? No more standing in the gym memorizing inanity, no more counting claps and stomps, no more getting yelled at for screwing up everyone else's rhythm. No more purple and gold sweater, no more normal. I could live with that. But I keep my face neutral and betray no emotion.

"What should we do?" Grimshaw asks me with a stricken look on her face. Then I think of my family, my cheerleading sweater casting its golden glow over our dinner table, creating harmonious discussions of football where before there was only strife. And I make the sacrifice.

"There might be a solution," I answer, "and if there is, it'll be the principal."

"What do you mean?" asks Grimshaw.

"Mrs. Pentz doesn't like Nanci Lee." I think about the way she and Scot sat together on the bar stool in the Crossways Tavern, sharing music. "And Nanci Lee doesn't like Mrs. Pentz."

"How does that work in our favor?" asks Grimshaw.

"My mom has had to swallow a lot on account of Nanci Lee," I tell her. "Even a Christian won't pass up a chance to kick Nanci Lee in the teeth. I think she will back us up."

"How?" Angel asks.

"It's worth a try," says Grimshaw. "What does that mean we should do?"

Rack and Angel are watching us. "Whatever you do, it's gotta happen fast," says Rack.

"Like, today," says Angel. "She already wants your sweaters back."

The plan we come up with is to take the legal approach: since we didn't know about any policy, and since we already joined the squad, we should qualify as cheerleaders already and therefore have immunity from obscure regulations that Nanci Lee digs up out of the back pages of the school handbook.

Grimshaw snaps her fingers. "So we should go in in our cheerleading sweaters."

Rack looks at her watch. "I don't think we have time."

"Wear mine," says Angel. "I've got two."

In town, we stop by the bridal shop to get Angel's two sweaters and put them on. Once we get to school, Grimshaw and I go directly to Mrs. Pentz's office. Grimshaw stops and looks through the window. Nanci Lee is already there.

"Shit," she says. "She beat us here."

"Looks like you have to get up early to get ahead of Nanci Lee."

My mother sees us and waves us in.

"Don't say anything when we get in there," Grimshaw says to me. "Don't argue. Let's just see how it plays out."

"Good morning, girls!" the principal says when we go in. "Thanks for coming in." She's holding a copy of the handbook. Grimshaw and I both say good morning, but Nanci Lee ignores us. The loudest thing in the room is my mother reading.

"First of all," she says, "I really want to thank Nanci Lee for bringing this policy to my attention." Another silence opens up. My mother frowns down at the policy.

"You're welcome," says Nanci Lee.

After another minute of careful study, Mrs. Pentz takes her glasses off, and with a look of deep concern on her face, clasps her hands in front of her. She starts talking about second chances and the importance of learning from one's mistakes. I honestly don't know which way this one is headed. But Grimshaw told me to keep my mouth shut. So I keep my mouth shut. "So," my mother concludes, "I think this one is really up to Mr. C."

"Excuse me?" Nanci Lee stands up. "What's he got to do with it?"

"I'm thinking that if the girls can get a signature of approval from the teacher whose class they failed—"

"I'm sorry," says Nanci Lee. "Can you show me in the handbook where it says anything about that, at all?"

"I think it's all in the interpretation, don't you?" my mother asks. She plays it straight. "Kids really need second chances, don't you think?"

Outside the office, I hold my hand up for a high five.

"Not yet," Grimshaw says. "We still have to get the signature. Just remember. He's your dad."

So at the end of the day, I prepare to broach the subject with Mr. C. Once again, he makes me stand there while he concentrates on his grade book. "Serena," he says finally.

"I've been thinking about that independent study you wanted me to do—"

"So I heard," he says. "Your mother told me." He sighs and shakes his head. "All right. The independent study is no longer optional, not if you want me to sign off on the cheerleading for you and Melody Grimshaw. May I remind you, I expect attendance, every day. Class discussion and participation, every day. And for the study, I'm thinking I want you to take some of your ideas in that essay on last year's final and use it on Colchis. An independent study on democracy's effect on upward mobility in your own town. Go ahead," he says, nodding to one of the desks. "Make me something I can sign for the principal."

He walks over to the window and looks out through the branches of the white pine. He has all the windows open, and a breeze blows papers off his desk, but he doesn't move. I sit down and start, and as I write the proposal, it occurs to me that I don't even like cheerleading—the clapping, the yelling, the tedium, my utter indifference to whatever is happening on the football field. Then I sign the paper on the bottom. When I hold it out to him, he draws a big slash across the bottom of it without even looking at what I have written and continues to look out over the yellowing leaves of the town of Colchis. I guess it's his signature.

"Thank you."

A few minutes later, I walk across the lobby with the signed piece of paper in my hand. I see Rack's pickup truck waiting for me in front of the school. I don't care about the class system, in Colchis or anywhere else, and I don't like cheerleading. It gives me this feeling in my gut, this heavy, anvil-shaped feeling. It's familiar. It's how I used to feel all the time. But I haven't felt this way a single time this year, not once. I go through the doors and then duck behind a pillar before they see me. How would I look if Mr. C. had turned us down? Resentful and sarcastic, how I always used to look. So I make sure I have my Serena-mask in place, but not too much, just kind of an average amount of Serena-tude. I go down the stairs, approach the truck, and knock on the window. They see my normal face and assume the worst.

In the passenger seat, Rack rolls down the window. "He turned us down?" she demands. "That son of a bitch."

"What?" Angel sits up in the back. "But I thought your mom said . . ."

Grimshaw sinks down behind the steering wheel. "That's it, then. I'm leaving for California," she says with her eyes closed. "Mike wants to go, so here we go. Good-bye, Colchis. Thanks for nothing."

I give Rack the paper. She sees Mr. C.'s signature. I smile at her and give her two thumbs up. She screams and leaps out of the truck and hugs me so tightly she almost breaks my neck.

"What happened?" Grimshaw looks dazed.

"You're officially a cheerleader, babe," says Rack. "Nobody can take it away now. So you better get used to it."

The next morning in the cemetery, I put the question to them: "Do you guys think there's a class system," I ask. "Where your family's economic situation defines you and determines your future?"

"It might influence you," Angel observes. "But I wouldn't say it defines you."

"Yeah," Rack says, brushing powdered sugar off the front of Junior's football jacket. "Because you can always change."

"That's called upward mobility," I tell them. "Mr. C.'s into it."

"So is that what you're doing for Mr. C.?" Angel asks. "Asking about the class system?"

"Aren't there more rich people than poor people?" asks Rack.

"Not in Colchis," says Angel. They both look at me.

"What are you looking at me for?" I ask. "I'm not rich."

"You talk rich," Angel says.

Grimshaw looks up and laughs. "She thinks her family hangs on to all their old rugs and furniture because they can't afford to buy new ones."

"Like, antiques and all?"

"Yes." Grimshaw laughs even harder. "She thinks it's because they can't afford to go to Walmart and buy new stuff."

"Serena," says Rack, "for someone who's so smart—"

"Don't say it," says Grimshaw.

Angel finishes Rack's sentence. "You sure are—"

"I said don't say it," Grimshaw says again.

"Well, I'm not rich," I say again. "The more land Scot buys, the poorer we get. Anyway, I always thought Rack was rich."

"Us, rich?" Rack hoots. "You know how my dad says grace every night? He thanks the bank for letting us eat one more meal."

"Here's how I figure it," says Grimshaw. "The class system is mostly about people pretending to be what they're not. Rich people pretend that they're normal, normal people pretend that they're rich, and poor people . . . just give up. They might be the only honest ones."

I stare at her. I never knew she had opinions about this stuff. "So what's the answer, then?" I ask her.

"There isn't one." She stands up on the Helmers and starts stretching. "We should go soon," she says. "Or we'll be late."

"Well," Rack proclaims, "my dad is definitely—what did you call it again?"

"Upwardly mobile."

"Right. In a big way." Rack knows all about it. "He grew up in a shack. He had ringworm, and nobody would talk to him. It makes your hair fall out in patches. They had a game they played, like cooties. Somebody would shove somebody against him, and then that kid would have to touch somebody else to get rid of it." He spent his childhood chasing other kids on the playground and having them scream and run away from him. She tells us her dad worked on their farm, married her mom, and inherited the farm when it was about a tenth the size it is now and mortgaged to the hilt.

"It's still mortgaged to the hilt," comments Angel.

"I know"—Rack laughs—"but now it's, like, mortgaged on a higher plane." She doesn't know anything about previous generations of her family and doesn't care. The future is what counts, not the past. Angel doesn't care, either. Ditto for Grimshaw. So that's a start.

Despite my obvious deficits in grace and skill and attitude, everybody thinks being a cheerleader is good for me. My purple and gold sweater and earrings attract this positive energy from all directions, which I find disorienting. But for my upward mobility project, I find that people are a lot more willing to talk to a cheerleader about what their parents do for work, or don't, than to a girl in a Red Army hat. I also get my calculus, French IV, AP English, and physics homework done every day. I get into the class discussions in Western Civ and even start to enjoy it. I get the best grade in AP English for a *Gatsby* essay. The teacher writes me a note on the bottom saying that it is one of the best high school papers she's ever read, but my statements about God are too extreme, and I need to back them up with quotes from the text. I stare at that A like I have a vitamin deficiency. It inspires me. It isn't throbbing and ugly and red, like one of my Fs. It's small and black and elegant.

Even though the class has moved on to Shakespeare, I go back to the book and look for quotes, and I do more research on Fitzgerald, about his life, his books, his booze, his early death. I reread the book as I rewrite the paper, fixing and fiddling with the words. The only sound in the room is the quiet scratch of my pen on paper.

Days later, it's two a.m. and I should be starting *Othello* when

I come to the sentence that Fitzgerald wrote almost a hundred years ago, which my teacher said described the eyes of God: *They look out of no face but, instead, from a pair of enormous yellow spectacles which pass over a nonexistent nose.* Suddenly, I feel a presence in the room, and I get a prickly sensation on the back of my neck, because I know who it is. I can even smell tobacco from his cigarette and a whiff of whiskey and hear the rustle of his white linen suit.

It's him. It's F. Scott Fitzgerald. He's in my room.

He's standing behind me, looking out the window at the Minnechaug Valley, just like Gatsby stood at the edge of his lawn and looked at the lights across Long Island Sound. When I turn around, he's gone. He was just checking in. I put the book away. I like knowing that he agrees with me about God being nearsighted and depressed and too old to take care of his creation. He doesn't think there's anything extreme about my statements.

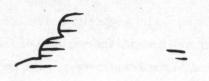

seven

Gold is our color

And purple is the other

So split the V

And dot the I

And roll the C-T-O-R-Y!

WITH THAT, OUR FIRST PEP rally is underway. For the *Y*, I lift Grimshaw, and she hits it like she was born to cheer, grabbing her ankle with one hand and extending her leg. She has the moves, all right. Everybody in the gym watches her. She is front and center on every cheer. She does a lot of flashy stunts because she's naturally acrobatic, basically fearless, and a glutton for attention. I stand on the side, because of my "sore elbow," rubbing it from time to time, in case anyone cares.

Then Junior Davis and the rest of the football team break through the paper decorated with their numbers in gold and purple paint, and the cheerleaders make a corridor for the boys to trot through while about ten percent of the gym claps. The football coach makes a speech about hope and promise and the crisp days of autumn. When everybody's numbed out by that, here comes the marching band, and the same ten percent of the gym sings first the national anthem and then our alma mater, a song featuring the noble iris—which, come to find out, is our school flower—growing tall by clear waters. Then the cheerleaders bounce to the middle of the gym again and do a cheer for which I have developed a sharp antipathy.

> *Hey, we're back*
>
> *The best is yet to come*
>
> *CHS! Look out for number one!*
>
> *Excellence, perfection, teamwork, success*
>
> *The Colchis Rockets*
>
> *A step above the rest*
>
> *Pride and spirit—need we say more?*
>
> *CHS! We rock the floor*
>
> *Rockets!*

The centerpiece of "Excellence, Perfection, Teamwork, Success" is Grimshaw's aerial handspring, which Nanci Lee told her not to do because of insurance reasons, and then the cheer ends. They do this dance that Grimshaw has choreographed, the audience gets into it, and for Colchis, it's pretty good. I stand to the side with my sore elbow and watch, until I feel a presence behind me, and I turn to see. It's Mike Lyle. We stare at each other for a long time, and, okay, physically I have to admit I do see what she sees in him. His hair is slightly longer than it was the last time I saw him, and it curls a little bit.

"Couldn't hack it out there, huh?" he says.

"I missed some practices." Then I remember about my injury. "And I hurt my back," I add, deciding on the spot that a sore elbow sounds kind of lame.

He laughs. "I bet you did." I don't know why everything he says seems like it insinuates something about me. We watch Grimshaw bouncing around and smiling like she's the happiest cheerleader in the world.

"What's your father do for work?" I ask without looking at him.

That gets his attention. "Why? Who wants to know?"

"Me." We stare at each other. "I'm doing research."

"He worked on a chicken farm." His voice is so soft I have to put my ear close to his mouth so I can hear him over the marching band.

"A chicken farm? That's really interesting. Does he still?"

He shakes his head. "He fell off a ladder and broke his back." He reaches out for a lock of my hair and pantomimes that I should cut the purple ends off. I shake my head. I like the purple ends.

The squad is signaling to me, so it's time for the pyramid. I get back in it, on the bottom.

As I'm bracing myself on my hands and knees, I look for Mike as he stands in the back of the crowd by the door. Even though it's not a cold day, he wears his leather jacket zipped up and keeps his arms folded across his chest. I feel bad about his dad, like maybe that explains why he's such a jerk. It occurs to me that if Grimshaw really likes him that much, maybe I should try harder to be friends with the guy.

The marching band comes out again, and the music director stops and makes a few remarks about freedom and patriotism and why it's more important than ever to sing our national anthem at football games. "Why do we put our hands on our hearts?" he asks rhetorically, and takes ten minutes to answer his own question. Then finally, it's the last cheer of the pep rally.

That night, we're at Angel's aunt Teresa's bridal shop, using the three-way mirrors in the back to get ready for a night game under the lights. While they're putting on their makeup, I'm stuck on an extra-credit physics problem, which I always do because of my secret ambition to make the high honor roll this term. But there is no answer to this one. They didn't give us enough information.

"Well, that pep rally was a blowout," Grimshaw remarks.

"It's always like that." Rack is covering up her complexion with some tan goop from a tube. "Colchis has no school spirit. It was better than last year, though."

"They liked your dances," Angel says to Grimshaw.

"Until now, we always skipped pep rallies," I chime in. I close my physics book and sweep it onto the floor, where it lands with a dull thump.

"Last year they booed and threw crumpled up Dixie cups at us. They planned it ahead of time." Angel sucks in her cheeks at herself and gives the mirror her best angle. "Mr. Van almost had a stroke. Did you take your pill, by the way? You wanted me to remind you."

"Yeah," Rack says, stroking the goop on under her chin. "Thanks."

"There is a solution, you know." I look around. Grimshaw is looking at me in the mirror. "If you don't give up on it," she says, "you'll figure it out."

"Are you talking to me?" I ask her.

"No," she says. "I'm talking to myself." She has her hair pushed away from her face with a hair band. Her forehead looks big and luminous, and the eyeliner she puts on makes her look like Cleopatra. I watch her paint an inverse parabola onto her eyelids. At that moment, it occurs to me that my physics teacher did talk a lot about quadratic equations in physics class today. I sigh heavily and pick up the book again. I apply the quadratic equation, and the last physics problem melts away and solves itself. Vertical motion. It's a parabola. It uses the quadratic equation. It comes so easily that I frown at the answer and scribble it out.

"It doesn't matter if you miss a day or two, though, does it?" Rack is saying. "The stuff is, like, in your system, right?"

"So long as you don't do it on that day," Grimshaw says.

"Oh." Rack thinks. "Well, I should be safe, then."

While they go at it with blow dryers and lipstick, speaking in code about the weighty issues of the day, I redo the vertical motion problem and come up with the same answer. Then I do every single extra-credit question with my new super-secret special power, the quadratic formula, and smile to myself. When I look up, the three of them are staring at me.

"So what are we going to do with her?" asks Rack.

"She won't let you," Grimshaw says. "I've tried."

"Oh, Grimshaw." I close my book. "You're just afraid I'm gonna steal Mike."

"Take him," she says. "I broke up with him."

"You broke up with him?" I repeat.

"You didn't know that?" Rack asks me.

"No." I cap my pen. "I was not informed. Why?"

"He kept pressuring me to go out to California." Grimshaw bats her eyes at herself. "He has this job opportunity out there, but he says he's not going without me. I used to really want to go, but now I don't. I changed my mind." She leans into the mirror and makes ducklips at herself. "He says he doesn't understand people who change their minds."

"Then what was he doing in the gym today, besides exuding his usual charm?" I ask.

"I don't know," she says. "Maybe he wants you now."

"Who can blame him?" I spread my arms wide. "Okay. Do me." So they do me. They put makeup all over my face and bark at me not to itch or wiggle or smile or move.

"I don't know," Angel muses as she wraps my eyelid halfway around my head and paints on some black trim. "Older guys are great. At least they have money. Will you hold still?"

"I can't help it," I squeak. "You're torturing me."

"Junior never has a dime," Rack says. "If we go anywhere, I always pay. Not that we ever go anywhere, or do anything. I bought our prom tickets last year, and my corsage, plus I paid for his tux. Don't tell anyone that, though."

"What's Junior's family do for work?" I ask.

"The Arms. Or did."

"His mom, too?"

"She cleans the church at night."

"How about his grandparents? Do you think they are moving up, economically, from generation to generation?"

"How should I know that?"

"Is he going to college?"

"If he passes algebra."

"What are you," Grimshaw says, "the FBI?"

"It's my independent study, remember? It's why we're cheerleaders. Jesus."

"He wants to go to the same college as my brothers," Rack explains. "They have a really good football team, and they've sent scouts to the games and seen his tapes and stuff. He has to pass algebra, though, or they won't give him a football scholarship. This is the fourth year he's taken it."

"How's he doing?" I ask.

"Terrible."

"I could help him," I offer. "I'm doing good in math."

"God, that would be great. I don't know if he'll have the time, though, until after the season's over. I'll ask him."

They talk about how romantic it is when someone loves you as much as Mike loves Grimshaw. "It's not that I don't love him," she says, "because I do."

"You're just not in love," clarifies Angel.

"Sometimes I am," says Grimshaw. "But—we're not going in

the same direction anymore, you know? He has this path out of Colchis, and I'm staying here until I graduate."

Angel gasps. "Did you give him back the laptop?"

"Yeah." She grimaces. "It sucks. It's where I kept all my ideas."

"You can use mine," both Rack and Angel chime at the same time. Then Rack remembers, no, she really needs hers on the farm, they keep records on there, so it's decided that Grimshaw can use Angel's. "Just stay here," says Angel. Even though it's too bad about the laptop, it's still romantic that he got one for her.

"Do you think Mike is really gonna go to California?" Angel asks.

"Yeah." Grimshaw says she started using Mike over the summer to get the hell off the hill and get down to Monique's, and how Mike was always available to run her back and forth. "Sometimes there was a class in the morning, and I wanted to show up, just be around in case Monique was tired or wanted to watch TV."

"You should have just come over here," says Angel.

"Are you going to take over the bridal shop someday?" I ask Angel, still thinking about upward mobility.

"No. Nursing," she says irritably, as though this was settled a long time ago. "I start night classes in January."

"So I felt bad," Grimshaw continues. "I felt that I owed him something."

"Didn't it create this pressure?" asks Angel.

"Yes!" says Grimshaw. "So I ended up, kind of initiating the relationship myself, because . . ."

"Because you had to," says Rack. "What the hell were you going to do?"

"Yeah, he was doing so much for me, and my life would have been nothing without his help, like, I'd be dead right now, from boredom, or I would have killed myself, and I'm not even kidding. Instead, he showed up every day and drove me down to the Valley and then back up. And then Monique started a dance camp, which was my idea, which I ran, and then you know the rest."

"That's kind of romantic," sighs Rack. "I mean, in my relationship, I'm like, the Mike. I bring him everywhere and kind of pay attention to what he has to do. I'm kind of like his mom."

"Or his wife," says Angel.

"Right. It's not that romantic, trust me."

"Ta-da," Angel sings to me. "You're done." I put my hands up to my cheeks.

"Don't touch!" Rack slaps my hands down. My face feels chalky, like if I smile, it'll fall off. They spin me around in front of the mirror. I look at a plaster replica of myself. She looks surprised to see me looking back at her.

"Oh my God," Rack murmurs. "Tim is gonna go nuts."

"Who?" I ask.

"You haven't noticed the way Tim Marhaver stares at you all the time?"

"Tim Marhaver! What have I ever done to him?"

"She doesn't notice things like that," puts in Grimshaw. "She has no idea."

"Don't worry about it," says Angel. "We'll draw you a map." The three of them burst out laughing.

"How far have you gone, anyway?" asks Rack.

"Not that far," I admit. Better not tell them about the time Ruby Grimshaw grabbed my breast and gave it a painful squeeze and I responded by slugging him in the stomach.

"Well," says Rack, "it's something to look forward to."

"Hey, Rack," Angel says tentatively, "do you, like, you know, with Junior?"

"Of course I do," she snaps. "What do you think I take pills for?"

"I know *that*, I just meant when . . ."

"Oh. That. I don't know. I don't think so. Junior doesn't—I mean, I'm his first one. Before me, there was only football."

"That's what older guys are good for," says Grimshaw. "You don't have to draw them a map."

The blonde girl in the mirror stares at me with bright eager eyes and soft pink lips. She is pretty, but she's nobody I know.

After the Colchis Rockets win their first game, the Colchis Rockets win their next game. The Colchis Rockets have been losing football games for so many years that even winning two in a row makes headlines in the *Valley Vision-Standard*, and a front page story featuring Junior Davis. Their third game is away, against Bavaria. Colchis and Bavaria have a common Main Street, and going from east to west, one town blurs into the other. Once you're in them, though, they look completely different. Whereas

Colchis's factory looms gothically over us, Bavaria's factory, a tool-and-die plant, sprawls quietly along the river, never getting more than one and a half stories tall. The school colors of Bavaria are orange and black.

The weather on game day is bright and sunny. Early in the fourth quarter, the game is tied, twelve to twelve, when Junior Davis comes pumping down the field, looks behind him, leaps, pulls a football out of the sky, trips, stumbles, and keeps running, while Bavaria screams that the ball is down. Junior gets tackled about ten yards from the enemy end zone under a pile of orange and black uniforms. For the longest time, the two teams stay right where they are, as Colchis tries to score a touchdown. Then Colchis tries for a field goal, which Bavaria blocks. Their star player gets injured and carried off the field on a stretcher, while both teams go down on one knee. Rack tells us to get our bleachers to stand and applaud him as he leaves the field, but then he sits up and gives the Colchis bleachers the finger, and our fans boo and throw empty soda cans onto the field. Coach Ellis screams for a penalty, and the referee screams that he didn't see a thing. People in the bleachers on both sides are screaming nonstop. The cheerleaders are hopping up and down, and that includes me, but I am also trying to remember what Scot explained about downs, because I don't understand why we still have the ball after all this time. I stick to my job as a cheerleader, though, which is to scream and keep screaming until we either lose the ball or score, and I will know when that happens by watching Rack. So the guys on the field heap on top of each other in piles, and the crowd screams, and whistles blow. Then the ball pops up, and an orange and black amoeba with many arms enfolds it, and then a bunch of gold and purple swarms on top of the orange and black. The ball squirts out to the orange and black, and they start heading down the field. Everybody screams except the members of the marching band, who sit in their section of the bleachers and read comic books. Coach Ellis starts screaming in the referee's face again, who screams back that he'll throw him out of the game. There's a timeout. Bavaria tries to pass, but Lars Madsen intercepts and then the whole mass of bodies and colors and helmets and cleats ends up back in the enemy end zone. Then the whistle blows, Junior dances backward, jumps up to avoid a tackle, spins in midair, and fires the football into the end zone. It hits Brian MacAlery, a sophomore, in the chest and knocks the wind out of him. He bobbles it for a moment before he gets both arms around the ball and clings to it, looking terrified. Gradually, it occurs to people that it's a touchdown and Colchis has won the game. The fans spill out of the bleachers, a couple of fights break out, the cops intervene, and everybody goes home on the school buses, screaming insults out the windows as we roll through Bavaria.

After the win against Bavaria, a virus starts, then Colchis wins another one and it's a fever. Even people who dropped out of school start coming to the football games. Then Junior Davis wins a big game against last year's champion with a touchdown—a real one, this time—in overtime, and Coach Ellis breaks down in sobs. Self-esteem in Colchis soars to dangerous levels. Cars honk. Stores hang out banners. Anonymous nerds high-five each other in the halls. The school board chairman announces he's running for state office. Rack parades around the halls like a queen, daring her teachers to expect any homework out of her. Scot decides the reason he's not making any money in real estate is he's not taking enough risks. He plans another spec house. My mother slides into a grim depression. She comes home from her prayer sessions more irritable than ever. One night, she asks me if I want to drive to Maine with her the last weekend of October to visit Allegra in college.

"But, Mom! That's homecoming weekend!"

"I know," she says quietly. "That's the point." She sighs. "That's all right. I'll take a couple days off and drive out with Nora and Zack."

One Sunday, I practically collide with Mike Lyle coming out of the front door of Al's Superette.

"Oh! Hi, Mike," I say, very surprised and friendly.

He grunts at me and walks away.

"Hey, Mike." I hurry after him back to the parking lot. "You must be off to California soon." He stops. "Are you?"

"When the time is right," he says. "Timing is everything." He's been working on his image. His hair is shorter, shinier, and a shade blacker than it used to be.

"What do you do out there, anyway?" I ask. "For work?" Mike and I stand very close, face-to-face. We're about the same height. In addition to being very light blue, his eyes have an interesting crystalline pattern to them.

"Entertainment."

"Entertainment?" I parrot.

"Adult entertainment," he says. "Not for kids. Video production."

"Oh! That's really impressive," I babble.

He opens the car door. "I'm glad you're impressed. I didn't think it was going to be so easy." He's lost weight, and the features of his face have gotten chiseled-looking. But he's still massive, which gives him an eerie gravitational pull that makes you feel like you're falling into him. There's a stillness about those light eyes, too, like he's not really looking at you, but just using them to sense heat and motion. I've never stood this close to a man who would just as soon crush my head like an empty beer can.

"What does your dad do now?" I ask him.

This takes him by surprise. I don't explain, though. I wait for the answer.

"You know," he says, "here's why I don't like your mother: when I had her for English way back when, she made us read fairy tales. One time she asked us, why do all the little girls in the fairy tales have golden hair? I said, because gold is the color of money." He laughs, then he takes a lock of my hair and tucks it behind my ear. "I'll never forget the look of shock on your mother's face. She thought I was pretty dumb."

He points at me and winks. "But I might be smarter than you think. So don't underestimate me."

I meet his gaze and challenge. "I don't estimate you at all," I tell him, "one way or the other."

He puts the key in the ignition and starts the car. "Maybe you should. Maybe I'm giving you fair warning not to start what you can't finish."

"Is your father on disability?" I ask. "With the back injury?"

"Not him. He's got too much pride to coast on the government."

"So what's he do now?" I ask again.

"You really want to know?" he asks. I nod.

"I'll give you a hint," he says. "Then you can think about it in your little blonde head. You walk all over his work, every day. But you don't see it."

"A farmer?"

"You see him every day," he says again. "But you look right through him."

Then he backs up and drives away.

At the next practice, there's another problem we have to deal with: Nanci Lee has an issue with Grimshaw's dance innovations to the squad. She wants to know where the "cheer" came from at the pep rally, which had nothing to do with the football team, or Colchis. She doesn't care if the crowd liked it. It's not up to the crowd what teams do.

"We've kind of made her a tri-captain," Rack explains to Nanci Lee.

"Yeah," chimes in Angel. "She knows a lot more about it than we do."

"Ummm . . ." Nanci Lee smiles. "That's not really your choice, is it?"

"But you said at the beginning that this was our team, not yours."

"Yeah, that we needed to take ownership of it, remember? That we 'needed to put our big-girl pants on'?"

"It is your team"—Nanci Lee concedes—"but we have two cheerleaders that aren't even qualified to be on the squad, and you're making them captains now? That might be owning something, but it's not the team."

So instead of letting us get more dance-y and choreographed, Nanci Lee, out of spite, is going super traditional, humiliating us with the dumbest cheers ever.

Ricker-racker, ricker-racker, sis-boom-bah
Bugs Bunny, Bugs Bunny, rah-rah-rah.

We talk about it the next morning at the graveyard.

"If we do those cheers," says Grimshaw, "they'll throw a lot more than Dixie cups at us."

"So just do what you want to do," Angel advises Grimshaw, "but we'll do it as a separate team."

"Like start our own dance team?"

"Yeah. For next semester. That'll be better, anyway. Then we don't have to deal with their stupid rules. We don't have to deal with them at all."

"And we can pick the girls we want anyway. I mean, ask them."

"And can we still be cheerleaders, too?"

Rack shrugs. "Sure. The cheers are so old and so stupid anyway, and we know them all, so there's nothing to practice."

"And then we do halftime shows as the dance team."

"Not her, though," Grimshaw says, nodding in my direction. "She won't have time."

"You have to do your homework," Angel tells me.

"I'm doing it."

"You have to keep pulling down those big fat sexy As," says Rack.

"I'm pulling them."

"So make us proud."

Grimshaw looks at me. "Do you think your mom would let us do it? Set up a separate dance squad and just get away from Nanci Lee?"

"Why wouldn't she? She's been pretty useful so far."

Grimshaw gets even more excited about her idea for a new dance team than she was about reupholstering the dead old Colchis cheerleading. She also starts talking about how founding a high school dance team might be her shot at getting to New York City next year. Knowing she'd have to convince my mother the principal, Grimshaw outlines how exactly we could be both cheerleaders and start the dance team, and how it might help her get into a real dance school.

"Upward mobility," I say.

Angel reaches back her hand, and Grimshaw slaps her high five.

After lunch, Grimshaw and I meet in my mother's office to talk it over.

"Melody," the principal starts. "I'm really liking this new Melody we're seeing this year. Active, engaged, really participating." Without her glasses, her eyes seem very round and bright. "For right now, though," she says, "I'm thinking we should stick to cheerleading, and really focus on getting those grades up."

"My grades are up," Grimshaw says.

"And I think that's great," my mother says. "Good for you, really. So our next step should be let's see if we can really sustain that. Let's get those good grades locked right in, at least past midterms, and then we'll see—"

"When?" I ask. "When will we see?"

"January, end of January." My mother snaps her fingers. "Coming right up. And those good midterm grades will be on your transcript, which is so important for . . ." She searches the air above Grimshaw's head for what it might be important for. "For the future, for your future."

"So . . . we can't start a dance team, then?"

"No!" My mother holds both hands in the air as if warding off attack. "I didn't say that. What I'm saying, what I'm talking about right now, is prioritizing." She launches into it, she talks about Grimshaw's transcript, as one's permanent record, how it communicates to the future. "Who you are, what you're capable of, it really sends a message." It's like if she talks enough, she'll arrive at some actual logic, if Grimshaw ever wants to . . . "I don't know, get a certificate, perhaps, or look into community college." She keeps talking, as if she can talk her way to reality, when actually we have floated farther and farther away from it, until reality is a distant shore and we're so far out to sea we don't even know what direction we'd row in to get back there. And still the principal keeps talking, about how dance should be thought of not as a career, but an avocation, part of a balanced life. She, for instance, although very busy in her profession, loves to sing, "just loves it," how singing helps her keep her perspective, just let it all go, while

I try to think of a single time I have heard this woman sing and can't come up with one. Grimshaw has long since gone numb. Her face is stone, and her eyes don't move. Eventually, Mrs. Pentz stops talking, rubs a spot on the desk she just noticed, and asks if there are any questions.

I raise my hand. "Are you on crack?"

After we get thrown out of the principal's office, there is still more school left in the day, but we go to our bench in front of the school to wait for Rack and Angel. I feel like crying. I'm so ashamed of my mother I can't take the cigarette when Grimshaw offers one to me. Ankle-deep in dead leaves, I keep my head in my hands.

"I'm really sorry."

"It's not your fault." She lights up. "I'm the stupid one. I should have left town last summer while I had the chance. Now it's too late."

"Is Mike gone?"

"Yup."

I look at the street where I saw the gold Corvette on the last day of school, as if it will always be there, some ghost of it lurking behind those bushes. It occurs to me that I just saw Mike, but she broke up with him, so it doesn't seem relevant enough to mention. So much is different now, anyway, not just that it was lush and green then and gray and cold now.

"I feel like we've just been checkmated," I say.

"Why does Nanci Lee hate you so much, anyway?" she asks. "She's so committed to it."

"I don't know. I think she might be like Iago, she just likes evil for its own sake. It's fun for her, messing with people and destroying their dreams."

But when I look up, Grimshaw is smiling broadly at me.

"What?" I ask.

"That question that you asked your mom at the end almost made it all worth it," she said. "That was classic Serena." She throws back her head and laughs. "Promise me that your grades will never get so good that you stop being yourself, okay?" She's looking at the bank of windows right above the front doors of the high school. For the longest time, it was Mr. Van's office. Now it's hers. Grimshaw shakes her head. "I will always love your mom, but . . . wow."

"I'm really sorry," I say. "I don't think she used to be like that."

"Yeah," Grimshaw says. "We definitely should have started playing this game earlier."

"Well, we didn't know we were going to be good at it."

"Time to find a new game," she says.

"Maybe we should just do it anyway. The dance team. Just go ahead and do it. Do it out of Monique's. What can they say?"

"No," she says. "What killed me was how nice she was." Rack pulls up in front of us. "Once they're nice to you like that, you're dead."

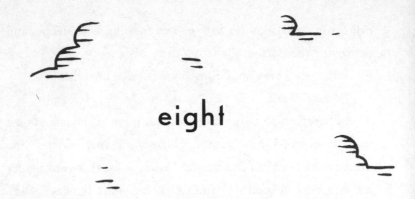

eight

NO MIKE, NO DANCE TEAM, now we're just high school girls with no future but plenty to think about in the present. When tomorrow dies, you still have today. Be a cheerleader, have friends, laugh, drink, be normal. It's not so bad. I'd do it, too, if I were her.

For homecoming, the Rockets are playing the Minnechaug Cougars, the only other undefeated team in the conference. Minnechaug is just like Colchis and Linerville and Bavaria, only smaller and grimier. For the first time in eighteen years, there's going to be a homecoming parade through the middle of Colchis, and each class has to build a float. Somebody will be king and somebody queen. None of this will happen democratically. When the football team started to win, Rack basically assumed command of the high school. When Rack and Angel pick us up at the cemetery every morning, it's getting cold enough that I have to do my homework wearing gloves. Rack decides to build the senior float down in Scot's hot-rod shop, which he never rented out. Rack wants to dub Scot the Official Realtor of Homecoming, but Scot says no thanks. It'll look bad, him being married to the principal. We can use the garage he owns, about two blocks from the high school. Grimshaw's brothers offer us the use of their flatbed.

At our first meeting, the interested members of the senior class meet at the shop to go through the motions of consensus, even though Rack has already decided what the float is going to be. Her vision is to make a rocket with the slogan *Colchis Shoots for the Stars*, and she doesn't expect any dissent. A healthy fraction of the senior class is there. Scot's shop is a big empty space with the iron arch for lifting motors still in place. Old license plates are nailed to the wall, along with calendars using semiclad females to sell fan belts and car wax and oil filters. There are old automobile seats around the edge to sit on. The pool table is pushed against the back wall with plywood panels and a tarp over it. On it, a foam board model of Versailles is laid out, complete with the missing manor homes.

"What a great place," Junior Davis says, walking around the shop. "This should definitely be a bar. Colchis needs a bar with a pool table, because I don't drink."

Rack takes center stage. "Okay, let's get started," she says. She whips out her poster. Her rocket is quite impressive-looking, with purple and gold lettering down the side and a lot of stars and planets dancing around on springs.

"The rocket needs to be about twelve feet high," she says.

"That's not big enough," says Junior. This, for some reason, strikes all the guys as profoundly funny.

"It's not violent enough, either," says Tony Beech. Tony smokes pot and captains the badminton team, usually on the same day.

"How about something like *Hunt the Cougars to Extinction and Then Skin Them and Mount Their Heads on Spikes*?" This suggestion proves popular.

"It's not very sustainable, though," I put in. "Aren't cougars an endangered species?"

"It's not real, Serena." Junior claps his hand on my shoulder. "It's only a game. Just a bunch of guys with a football."

"Can we stop wasting time, please?" Rack cuts in. "Can we have a vote on *Colchis Shoots for the Stars*?"

"How about *Bomb the Cougars*?" Lars Madsen asks Junior.

"No," Tony says. "Not *Bomb*. *Bomb* sucks." Dozens of dissenting opinions are fielded.

"How about *Crush*?"

"How about *Kill*?"

"What do you think their floats will say?"

"Lick the Rockets!"

"Lick my rocket!"

"Is Junior going to be the model for the missile?"

"It's not a missile!" shouts Rack over all the voices. "It's a rocket!"

"I can't be the model," says Junior. "The trailer's too small." Again, all the boys double over laughing.

"How about *Castrate*?" asks Angel, lighting two cigarettes and giving one to Grimshaw.

Junior howls and covers his crotch.

"How about *Excellence, Perfection, Teamwork, Success*?" My idea gets booed. "Sorry. Just a thought."

"Hey—how about *Trap*?" says a voice that has not been heard yet. Everybody looks around to see who's talking. It's Martin Gerard. Martin Gerard is one of those people you never notice unless you're forced to be his lab partner. But that never seems to bother him. He makes bad puns and always seems to have a drip of toothpaste lather on his shirt.

"How about *what*?" Rack asks with as much scorn as she can muster.

"Trap!" says Martin, all happy. "As in—*Trap the Cougars!* My grandfather was a trapper, up in Canada. Those traps are wicked-looking. Big steel teeth." He bares his teeth at us and bugs his eyes out behind his glasses.

Junior laughs and claps him on the shoulder. "I like it," he says.

"And the float—" Marty keeps going. "The float could be this giant trap with big teeth, and we could have someone dressed in a cougar suit—"

"Like their mascot—" Lars gets excited. "Let's kidnap Minnechaug's mascot!"

"They don't have a mascot," Rack sneers. "Nobody has mascots, you dumb-ass." But it's too late—Martin's idea is taking off. Everyone crowds around him, suddenly excited.

"Isn't there a football play called the trap, too?"

"And then put the slogan *Trap the Cougars* over the top of the trap!"

Everybody except Rack goes home happy from that meeting, but one thing's still on my mind. It's a delicate matter. I call Rack about it. But when I tell her that I think Grimshaw should be homecoming queen this year, she's offended.

"Serena, queens are *elected*," she says. "Everybody *votes*. What planet do you live on?"

So a couple of nights later, we get together in Scot's shop again, to start building a giant trap for the Minnechaug Cougars. Martin has drawn the plans. The boys get out the two-by-fours and start hammering. The girls have collected half-gallon juice containers for the teeth. Then we dip sheets of newspaper in flour paste and drape them around the chicken wire and blow-dry them so that we can spray paint them primer black. Then the boys make a trip to McDonald's before it closes, and the girls glue the teeth on. The senior float starts to look like a huge pair of dentures.

When Martin comes back from McDonald's, he has a fit. "That doesn't look like a bear trap!" he shouts. "It looks like a mouth of a whale! The teeth are supposed to be serrated, you idiots!"

Rack looks at him like he's so far out of line she can't even take him personally. "Martin," she says. "Do you even exist?"

Junior laughs hysterically. Overnight, he seems to have adopted Martin Gerard as his personal mascot.

"How about *Hey Cougars, Bite My Missile*?" This is my idea. Martin glares at me. It was only a joke, and not a very good one, but I watch incredulously as the idea takes flight. They take out Rack's drawing of the missile again and talk about building it and putting it in the mouth.

"I *hate* it!" storms Rack. "And anyway, we're not the Colchis Missiles, we're the Rockets!"

"How about *Hey Cougars, Eat My Rocket*? And the rocket can

be upside down in the mouth, and we can build a cougar head around the teeth." It's Lars. When everybody turns to look at him, his face turns bright red. Everyone starts talking at once.

"That is so stupid."

"It doesn't even make any sense."

"If we build the head around the teeth, we won't be able to get it out of here."

"Do we even have a trailer?"

"We're using the Grimshaws' flatbed."

"Do we even know how we're going to get it on the flatbed?"

"What time is it?"

"One thirty a.m."

Everybody groans. "I have practice tomorrow morning," Junior says. "Hey Marty, give me a ride home." In ten minutes, everyone's cleared out except for me and Rack. Grimshaw's gone home with Angel to her aunt's apartment over the bridal shop.

"I have a physics test tomorrow," I remember. Rack sits down on one of the car seats, reaches in her purse, and gets out a bottle of beer. I'm sitting up on an oil drum. She offers me the first sip.

"It's still cold," she says.

"Thanks." The beer leaves a clear, cold track down my center. "Wow." I exhale slowly. "That was really good." I hand it back to her. She's studying her purse.

"You keep that one." She takes another one from her purse. "I was going to save this one till later, but what the hell, right?"

"Later when? It's almost two o'clock in the morning."

"I know. But I always keep an extra beer around. I like to have something to look forward to. Cheers." I lean over, and we touch bottles. She pours half of hers down her throat and slowly exhales. "Can you believe I've been dumped for that dork Marty Gerard?" she asks.

"You've been dumped?" I parrot.

"Basically. You didn't notice how Junior treated me all night?"

"No."

"It's been going on all fall, off and on. He pretends I don't exist. He's playing the game of treating me like dog shit so *I* break up with *him* and *he* doesn't have to take any responsibility for it."

"Oh." I've never heard of that game. Grimshaw never got dumped. The more I know about other people, the less I know about Grimshaw.

Rack sighs. "It sucks." She holds her beer bottle up to her lips and blows a long, sad note. "Never have sex, Serena," she says. "It's kind of . . . this lie."

She concentrates on picking fuzz balls off her socks.

I clear my throat. "What do you mean, it's a lie?"

"Oh, it's not that big of a deal." She checks her watch. "It's just another stupid promise that stupid people believe in until they learn. You know what I mean?"

I don't, but I nod. Grimshaw's been with a lot of guys. But I don't know if she took any of it as a promise *or* a lie. She seems happiest now, actually, staying with Angel on Main Street without any boyfriend at all. If she gets out of the junkyard and off the hill, maybe that's as big as her dream needs to get.

"Well, shit," Rack sighs again. "What *are* we going to do with this damn thing?"

We look at the dentures, each take our last big swig of beer, and then look back at each other. We start laughing at the same time. Suds come out of my nose and Rack's nose, and we sit there laughing, holding the rest of the beer in our mouths until it foams out between our fingers. I manage to swallow mine and keep laughing. Then I realize she isn't laughing anymore. She's crying. She's sobbing into her hands with her elbows on her knees. I don't really know what to do, so I get off the drum and sit on the bucket seat next to her. I touch her knee.

"I'm really sorry," I tell her. "About Junior and everything."

"Oh my God, Serena," she wails. "I am so stupid. I am such a jerk. I wish someone would hit me on the head with this beer bottle." She starts hitting her forehead with the butt of the beer bottle. Drops of foam fly out. "I am the stupidest cow alive." I watch her bang herself on the head until it occurs to me to hold her hand and take the bottle away. She lets me do it and then collapses with her forehead on her knees, crying and crying.

"You're not stupid." At first I sound sort of doubtful, like I'm not really sure it's true. I'm the one who sounds stupid.

"Yes, I am stupid," she insists angrily. "I am just a dumb cow. You're the smart one." She stops crying and just sits there miserably, waiting for me to say something.

"I *know* you're not stupid." I try a little more conviction this time. She looks at me doubtfully and sniffles. She rummages through her bag again, just in case there's more beer in there. There isn't. She studies me for a minute, picks a last flake of red polish off her thumbnail, and looks up at me again. Her eyes are cinnamon brown, and soft and bright.

"My period's late," she announces.

"Oh."

"Two weeks."

It takes me a minute to get it. "Oh. Oh my God."

She doesn't take her eyes off me. While I gaze back at her, her eyes get dull and old, like she's suddenly on the other side of the big divide and she will never get back to where I am.

"But do you *know*, have you gotten—"

"Tested? It would be the only test I ever took where I actually knew the answer."

I reach for her hand again. *We can handle this*, I want to say. The four of us—we can handle anything as long as we stick together. We can't let anything drive us apart—nothing. Just as I'm trying to figure out how to tell her all this, she takes her hand back and turns away from me.

"So what *are* we going to do with those teeth?" she asks. She stares at the bear trap. "Let's do something really nasty to it."

"Like what?" I ask.

"Like, I wish we had some better—paint, or something."

"Rack."

"What?"

"We're in a hot-rod shop."

"So?"

"So what color paint do you want, Candy Red or Maui Blue?" She screams, literally screams with joy, twirls around, picks me up, and hugs me.

We work silently until Rack's phone alarm goes off at seven o'clock. Twenty minutes later, the early bell rings at the high school, and we stand back to admire our creation. The senior float has become a pair of red plush lips. While we were looking for paint, we found a roll of deep crimson polyester fur and covered the bear trap with that. With two-by-fours and some chicken wire, we've made a long cigarette held up by two fingers. We made a pink smoke ring using fiberglass insulation, which we pulled out of the wall. The fingernails are long and shiny, painted with Metal Flake Candy Red.

Our slogan? *Smoke the Cougars.*

Homecoming is a perfect football day—raw and cold and windy, with the year's first hint of snow. The sky is the color of concrete and hangs about ten feet over our heads. At the parade, our float is disqualified as sending the wrong message. The sophomores win it with—guess what—a purple and gold rocket. The smoking lips are banned from the game. But we take it anyway and park it outside. Everyone loves it.

It's another tense game, lots of points scored, and at halftime, the Rockets are trailing the Cougars by a field goal, with the crowd on the verge of violent hysteria. After the marching band manages to screw up "Rock Around the Clock," Rack gets on the winning float, takes the microphone, and presents me to the fans as the queen of homecoming. It happened yesterday at the pep rally. They pulled me off the sidelines, where I was sitting with my "sore knee" cramming Shakespeare into my head, and suddenly I was in the middle of the gym with a crown on, and everyone was laughing like it was the funniest joke in the world. My king is Tim Marhaver—how he got elected I'll never know, because nobody likes him either, but I strongly suspect authoritarian practices, stuffed ballot boxes, and underhanded deals late at night in smoke-filled rooms. Suddenly we all hear honks, and here comes the Grimshaw brothers' flatbed tearing across the football field, with the smoking lips on the back. Ruby's driving. I hold my crown on my head and jump off the purple and gold rocket. My attendants run after me, and my king trails them. As I hike up my velveteen cape and get on the flatbed, Rack passes out the cigarettes and we sit on the bear trap and blow smoke rings at the crowd. They love it. The band tries "Rock Around the Clock" again, and gets it right this time, and the crowd gets very rowdy. I put the crown on Grimshaw. Tim reclines on the bear trap in the middle of his four queens.

"Hey, buddy, can ya handle it?" someone yells.

He gives them a thumbs-up, and the crowd goes wild.

Toward the end of the third quarter, Rack insists we leave a tie game to go up to the farm and get her house ready for a party after the homecoming dance tonight. Rack's parents have gone away for the weekend, which means she has to do the evening milking, which means we have to help.

"The cows come first," she says. "Even before football."

We all clamber into her truck. "Doesn't anybody want to listen to the radio to hear who wins the end of the game?" Grimshaw asks.

"I don't," says Rack.

"Don't you care who wins?" Angel asks her.

"No. Do you?"

Angel shrugs. "I guess we'll find out sooner or later."

"Anyway, I just broke up with him," Rack announces.

"You did?" Angel and Grimshaw gasp together.

"Yeah. In the first quarter. I told him I was sick of his shit and tired of looking at his ugly-ass face."

"Why?" Grimshaw asks.

"Because I am. I told him he didn't know how to play football, either. Among other things."

"Wow."

"Hey, Grimshaw." I turn around. She looks particularly pretty and happy today. "Did Mike ever get that Viper?"

She looks blank. "Mike?"

"Mike Lyle. That Viper he was always going to get."

"Maybe," she says slowly. "But I think he's in California."

"I saw him last Sunday."

"She practically lives at Angel's aunt's these days," explains Rack. "So she wouldn't know."

"Do you know what his father does for work?" I ask.

"I don't know," Grimshaw says stonily. "I don't think about him."

"Doesn't Mike's father work at the high school?" asks Angel. "Isn't he one of the janitors or something? That's what my dad told me one time."

"Never tell Mike you know that, okay, Serena?" says Grimshaw. "He doesn't want anybody to know. If he knew you knew, my God . . ."

"I won't. Who cares, anyway?" I ask. "Do you want someone else to drive, Rack? You haven't had much sleep lately."

"I'm fine," she says. "Never been better." Rack exhales the first drag of her cigarette and speeds down Main Street. Colchis is eerily empty for a Saturday afternoon. She runs both red lights. The whole town is at the game.

"Jesus. That's probably why his game was off today," Angel says from the back.

Rack shrugs. "Not my problem." For the rest of the way up the hill, nobody speaks. When we get to the farm, we pull in next to her parents' car.

"Oh my God," Angel says. "Are they home?"

"No, that's Allen's now. I wonder what he's doing here."

As we get out of the car, Allen Mizerak walks out of the house. He has a dimple in his chin, electric green eyes, a small diamond in one ear, and curly brown hair still damp from the shower. I know who he is because he always handled the details of Scot's real estate deals with Mr. Mizerak. Allegra always had an insane crush on him. He plays soccer and the jazz guitar. He's one of those guys who's sure everyone will find him as charming as he does, and in his case, there's something to it. Even I find him disturbingly handsome. He's dressed in a tuxedo.

"Oh, good," he says, walking toward us. "Here's somebody to do my cuff links."

"Look at you." Rack folds her arms and leans against the car. "La-di-da."

"Wedding," he says. "My soccer coach. I'm an usher. Don't worry about the girls. They're all milked, fed, and tucked into bed. Dad asked me to come by."

"I was going to do it," Rack says. "You were supposed to drain the pool, and I was supposed to milk."

Allen shrugs. "I didn't mind. You can milk tomorrow." We

all stare at him. You can't help staring at him, and he expects it, and so we all stare. All except Grimshaw, who is climbing out of Rack's truck.

"Look," she says. "Snow." She strikes a pose like a ballet dancer, arms out, palms up, to a pewter-gray sky.

"I don't see any snow," Rack says. We search the air over our heads, and sure enough, there are a million little gray specks swimming around against the whiteness. Grimshaw makes a sweeping gesture, as if she zipped open the sky, and suddenly, there is snow floating around us. She steps up on the running board of the pickup, arches her back, and leans out, hanging on with one hand. Snowflakes are everywhere swirling around us, fat and soft. Angel nudges me. Allen's noticed Grimshaw. Her cheeks are pink from the wind and the cold. The wind is blowing her hair around her face. She turns her face up to the snow and sticks her tongue out. One feather lands on her tongue and melts. Then she sees Allen staring at her. Her eyes open wide. She jumps down from the running board and brushes snow off her sweater.

"Do you make other kinds of weather happen as well?" he asks. "Or mostly just snow?"

"Just snow," she says.

"For the wedding," Rack adds. Allen backs up a step and puts his hands in his pockets.

"Really," he says finally. "Do you think the bride wanted snow?"

"Maybe," Grimshaw says. "If I had a wedding at this time of year, I'd want snow, instead of all the gray."

"It's a weird time to get married, though," Rack remarks. "Halloween weekend."

Allen pantomimes cocking a shotgun.

"Ka-pow," he says.

"I see," Rack says.

"She's a freshman." Allen's talking to his sister, but he can't keep his eyes off Grimshaw. "It was love at first sight. That's what Coach wants us to say. So they don't cancel his contract." He looks at Grimshaw. "How about you? Do you believe in love at first sight?"

"I don't believe in love at all." Rack keeps her arms folded over her chest. "But the bride'll probably need snow for the baby shower, too, then, if it's that soon." She turns to Grimshaw. "So it's a good thing you didn't go to California."

"California?" asks Allen, moving in. "Pretty ambitious for a girl from Minnechaug Valley."

"She's starting a dance team," says Angel. "She's very talented."

"Do you do cuff links, too, among your talents?" Allen asks Grimshaw. I don't think she's met Allen before. He graduated three years ago and mostly comes back to sell cornfields to Scot. I watch her take him all in—the tux, the cuff links, the dimple, the diamond.

"Sure," she says carelessly. With a clink, he drops the gold cuff links into her hand. She pushes up his tuxedo sleeve, folds the cuff over like a pro, and begins wrestling the cuff link through the layers of cloth.

"Great game," Allen tells her. "I listened to the radio during milking."

Grimshaw looks up at him. "Who won?" she asks. Her voice is slightly husky from shouting all day.

"You don't know?"

"We left early."

"We have better things to do," Rack puts in.

Grimshaw finishes the cuff link.

"Well done," Allen says. "It feels right." She starts on the second one while we watch him watch her.

When she finishes, she takes a step back from him and straightens his bow tie. She squints at him, brushes a few snowflakes off his lapels, and then nods. "You're all set."

"You got a dress?" he asks her.

"Sure. Why?"

"I need a date."

"My house is closer," offers Angel. "You can get one of mine."

"God, Allen!" Rack explodes. "You're so forward! Do you even know her name?"

"I will when you introduce us." Allen winks at Grimshaw. "They're your friends."

"Allen," Rack exaggerates, gesturing at me. "This is Serena Velasco."

"Serena," Allen says, smiling at Grimshaw. "That's a beautiful name." He takes her hand and lifts it to his lips. Grimshaw blushes.

"That's Serena." She giggles, pointing at me. "I'm Melody."

"Melody," he says. He draws her to him and puts his other hand around her waist. "I'll sing harmony." He twirls her suddenly under his arm and then snaps her back to him. "We'll dance."

Rack rolls her eyes. "And this is Melody Grimshaw."

"Oh!" Allen's smile freezes. "So you're a Grimshaw! Who knew?" He lets go of her and backs away. "Well, I gotta go, girls," he says. He points at Rack. "Don't wreck the house." In a minute, he's gone. Grimshaw's hands stay in the air where he left them, still dancing, no partner. Then she sees me watching her and pretends she was just brushing the snow off her sweater.

Angel comes forward. "I like that idea, actually, getting dressed up for the dance. In the back of the bridal shop are all these dresses left over from people who, you know, changed their minds? Let's get dressed up."

"He shouldn't be done milking this early." Rack frowns a little as she stares after Allen's car. "My father always says he cuts corners. Anyway, I don't like how he treats the cows."

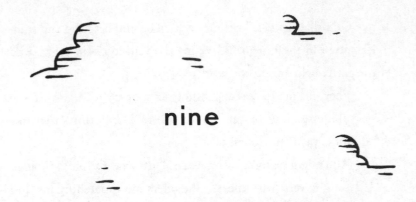

nine

WE GO BY TERESA'S BRIDAL Shoppe before the dance. The back room is stuffed with the unused gowns of rejected brides and unemployed bridesmaids. Angel says that most of them get sold eventually, but there are some leftovers that have hung around for a long time, and we can have our pick of those. Grimshaw, who has her own little flask of whiskey underway, picks out a wedding gown with lace that looks like it will dissolve if you touch it. It takes the three of us to get her into it. The stark white against her light olive skin is dramatic.

"You should get married," Rack tells her. "Just because you look so damn good in white. Don't do it for any other reason."

"Remember when we were in middle school, that girl who died of brain cancer right before her wedding?" Angel picks up the hem and starts shaking the dust out of the folds. "This was going to be hers. It's still here." She chokes out the last words. The ensuing dust cloud is so thick we have to open all the windows.

Grimshaw gathers her hair back up behind her head and studies herself in the mirror. "Give me the veil, too," she says. "And the garter belt. I want the works."

They put me in tea-length hot pink, or try to. I go through several dresses, but they are all too short. "I don't think they like tall bridesmaids in Colchis."

"You might be right," Angel says. "Just wear the pink, though. At least it covers your knees." She offers me a matching hat and then kneels down next to me and rips both seams up to the thigh. She gets out a pair of scissors and makes several other strategic rips. "There," she says. "That's sexier. Now you can go have your big night with Tim."

I stand in front of a full-length mirror and do some voguing. "Pink is too springy, though, don't you think, for an October dance?"

I am eclipsed by Grimshaw, a glowing vision in white. She tips up the flask and wipes her mouth with the back of her hand. She points at herself. "Nice swallow," she says. At this, Grimshaw lets out a long peal of laughter and takes another swig of whiskey. "Why don't you just get pregnant and stay home?" She sees me over her shoulder, looking at her reflection in the mirror. I look away.

Behind us, Angel is squirming into a strapless sapphire gown that lets out its own cloud of dust. "Help me with the zipper," she says. We stuff her into the bodice, find the hooks and eyes, and fasten them.

Near the window, Rack watches snow falling into the street.

Her outfit is her barn jeans and a gray sweatshirt. "No dress for me," she says.

At the dance in the gym, the best I can do is sit on the bleachers near my friend while she gets drunk on whiskey. I've done it before, but this time she's trying to get caught, and if that happens, she's automatically off the squad. She takes nips from the flask tucked into her garter belt, while I stand between her and the chaperones. Fortunately, Colchis won the football game, which packs the dance and gives the chaperones plenty of other people to worry about.

Like a heat-seeking slug, Tim Marhaver finds me on the bleachers and comes up to me with his hand out. "My queen," he says. "I require this dance."

"Um, no thanks, Tim," I mumble.

Rack comes over. "Will you go dance?" she hisses. "What's wrong with you?" I glance at Grimshaw.

"Go ahead," Grimshaw says without looking at me. "Dance."

So I dance. Tim takes my hand, and I follow him doubtfully into the middle of the mass of bodies. Just as I get the hang of faking it, a slow dance starts. Again, I watch what other people do, and we start to slowly revolve around each other, me with my hands on his shoulders, Tim with his hands on my back, telling me how hot I look in my pink dress.

"The band's really wasted," he shouts in my ear. "I got them high before they went on. Out in the parking lot." He looks around the gym, very pleased with himself. "I made bank, too. Everyone's really wasted."

I try to position myself so as to keep an eye on Grimshaw. She's not even bothering to hide her flask.

"What is it with you two?" Tim asks me.

"Nothing. I'm just a little worried about her, that's all."

"She looks fine to me."

"You don't know her."

"I'd like to get to know you better," he says in a smoky voice. He moves his hands from my back to my hips and draws me in closer. "Relax," he whispers in my ear. "Just go with it." I have never much liked anyone's hot breath on my neck. But there is so much else going on that I really don't need to precipitate a scene with the king of homecoming, who seems to feel that it's his prerogative to put his hands wherever he wants and grind any part of his body against any part of mine. And it might be, for all I know. Everyone else is doing it.

Halfway through the night, a ceremony takes place. Everybody gets down on one knee, and Rack puts the crowns on our respective heads again. I'm not into it, though, especially when Tim grabs me, bends me over backward, and practically drowns me in his salivary juices, while the crowd cheers. For the rest of the night, Tim monopolizes me. We dance every single dance.

At one point, Rack comes up to me and gushes, "Oh my God, you and Tim look *so* good together."

Angel's right behind her, iridescent in sapphire. "You're both so tall," she says.

"And smart," Rack says. "You probably have a lot to talk about." I smile weakly at them. As far as I can tell, the only things Tim and I have in common are everyone else's assumptions.

Besides, he has soft hands. I've always had a prejudice against guys with soft hands.

I manage to escape Tim long enough to help Rack pay the band. The four of us are the last to leave the gym. When we get up to the Mizeraks' farm, the party is already in full force. Two pickup trucks with MY SON IS AN HONOR STUDENT AT MIN-NECHAUG REGIONAL HS bumper stickers are there. A fight between Junior Davis and the other team's quarterback has broken out in the driveway. A bonfire is blazing where I think Mrs. Mizerak's rhododendrons used to be. The band is there ahead of us. There are even some trick-or-treaters, guys with panty hose pulled over their heads, sticking people up for beers. It's still snowing, soft and wet, melting as soon as it touches the ground.

My heart sinks when Tim emerges from the crowd, opens my door, and lays claim to me. He takes me away into his truck, but then starts talking about his early decision application to college and how he can't wait to get away from a depressing redneck pit like Colchis before his brain atrophies. It's warm in the cab of the truck, and I haven't slept much lately. He talks about the rock-climbing camp he goes to every summer and how everyone there is from private school, which would totally rule, and he never really knew what good drugs were until he went camping at Mesa Verde. As I doze off, he is making the case that I am definitely college material, and I should consider distancing myself from some people who will just drag me down.

"Jesus, look at that old Corvette," Tim says suddenly. "Who owns a cool car like that in this town?"

"Oh my God, is it gold—where?" I'm half out of the door

147

before I'm even awake. By the time I fight my way through the bodies to the Corvette, Mike Lyle is just getting out. A small crowd of admirers flocks around.

"Nice car," a voice says.

Mike turns around. "Anyone touches this car, they're dead." He shoulders his way through the crowd. He looks like he's been lifting weights. He hasn't seen me.

With great authority, I step forward. Just because it's after midnight doesn't mean I'm not still the queen. Everyone's staring at me. I point at Martin.

"Not so close to the car," I bark at him. "You heard what the guy said."

"Yeah?" Martin challenges me. "What if I piss all over it?"

I draw a line across my throat. "He'll kill you," I whisper.

"Go for it, Martin," a guy behind him whispers.

Martin snaps his fingers. "Somebody get me another beer," he orders.

I thread my way into Rack's kitchen. The place is mobbed with people I've never seen before. It's loud and dark and smoky, and the walls are throbbing with the music. Everybody looks like they're having the best time they've ever had in their lives. I keep looking for Mike. I see a head rising above the crowd. It's Grimshaw, still in the wedding dress. If she weren't so drunk, she'd be half frozen. She's walking in extremely high platform shoes—Angel's, of course—stepping from chair to chair, picking her way across the room. She stands up on the kitchen table, which is covered with beer bottles and pitchers of melting ice and plates of cigarette butts and half-empty bags of chips. She bends down to pick up a jug of vodka and continues across the table. I still don't see Mike. I see Angel nuzzling with some anonymous underclassman—it's Brian, whose stock has risen since he accidentally won the game against Bavaria—feeding off the dazzled look in his eyes. I haven't seen Rack since we got here.

The sliding plate glass door to the patio opens, and Junior and the Cougars' quarterback step into the kitchen with their arms around each other's shoulders. Everybody cheers. They've been wrestling outside in the snow, and they're smeared with mud. As a committed athlete, Junior doesn't drink, but it looks like the enemy quarterback does, and lost the fight.

"Somebody get this man some alcohol!" Junior yells.

"I have some!" Grimshaw holds out her bottle of vodka, and Junior holds up his hands, like he's going to catch the football. Grimshaw cocks her arm behind her head and extends her other arm, like she's going to throw the bottle in a Hail Mary pass into the end zone. But instead of letting go of it, she holds on to it, and Junior keeps his hands next to his face ready to catch it, and their eyes lock on to each other, and they just stare at each other, smiling across the room like they share a secret, private moment of open mutual admiration. All in the same split second, I remember the lilac blossoms Junior put in her hair during the Western Civ exam and I remember the bargain she struck with Rack over the summer and where that stands now that the cheerleading dream has come to nothing, and I wonder if Rack really is pregnant, and I worry because Mike Lyle is here right now, and I wish

I had appreciated how uncomplicated life was when Grimshaw and I had only had one friend apiece. Then she gets an idea, and her eyes open wide.

"I know!" she calls to him. "We should go swimming!" For a minute, everyone is quiet. We all look out at the swimming pool. The Mizeraks have it lit from beneath, and it is a thin rectangle of turquoise wavering in the night.

"Yeah!" Junior bawls, holding his arms up for a touchdown. "Everybody into the pool!" The throng pushes out through the sliding doors, and I am carried with it.

Outside, the snow quiets everybody down as it touches our faces and disappears into the pool with a soft hiss. The impulse to jump in the water has just about died when Junior comes out of the house naked, gets up on the diving board, and poses like a statue of a Greek god.

"No clothes in the pool!" he announces.

"You're full of shit," says Lars Madsen.

"Hey—" Junior points at him. "Anyone wearing clothes in the pool is a loser." He turns, moons everyone, and then does a backflip into the water. Everybody screams as he splashes them. More drunk football players start pulling off their clothes, from both Minnechaug and Colchis. They get up on the diving board, pose, and dive. Bodies start to fall. The pool fills up with naked guys, and they start playing water polo, using a pair of balled-up blue jeans.

Then Grimshaw breaks out of the crowd, in her wedding dress, still holding the bottle of vodka upside down. She approaches the water and stands there on her toes. All action stops.

"No clothes," Junior orders from the shallow end of the pool. "If the boys do it, you have to do it."

"I don't care," Grimshaw says. "I'll do it."

"Well, come on in, then," he says. "Do it. The water's fine."

She walks down the perimeter of the pool to the deep end. Junior follows her with his eyes. She gets up on the diving board, picks through the piles of clothes, kicks some into the water, and waits there for a minute. Her shoes are off, and she stands on her toes, holding the hem of her dress up with her left hand while using the vodka bottle in her right for balance. The music stops. From the other end of the farm, we can hear the Mizeraks' dogs barking. A cow moos.

"Well, are you gonna take it off, or aren't you?" the Minnechaug quarterback calls.

"Don't rush her," says Junior. "She'll do it. Then all the girls are gonna do it."

"I'll do it," says Grimshaw. "But we need some music."

"Mu-SIC!" bellows Junior at the house.

"You don't own this place." Angel appears at the edge of the pool, wagging a talon in his face. "You want some music, get your ass out of the pool and get it yourself."

"OW!" Junior yells. He covers his crotch underwater with both hands.

At that moment, Mike Lyle appears on the patio behind Grimshaw.

"What are you doing here?" Junior Davis might not own the place, but he won the football game today, and his challenge to Mike is full of authority. Everybody turns to see who he's talking about. For a split second, Mike doesn't have an answer to that question. He looks out of place, a leftover, like everybody but him is in high school, everybody belongs here, everybody knows who they are and what they're doing, except for him. Grimshaw hasn't seen him yet. She is dancing on the diving board, moving her arms in a kind of drunken flamenco. She doesn't need music.

Mike snaps his fingers at her. "Come on, Mel."

Grimshaw stops dancing and turns slowly and blinks at him. She tilts her head at him like he looks familiar, but she can't remember who he is.

"Let's go," he says again, more forcefully this time. He goes to the edge of the pool and reaches for her. She leans away from him, and he stretches forward. She loses her balance and starts flailing her arms. Mike lunges forward to grab her by the wrist.

"Let's go," he repeats. "I'm taking you home." She manages to break his grip.

I step out. As he reaches for her, I pull her away. He leans out over the water, gets his feet caught in the clothes piled by the end of the diving board, and trips forward. As he falls, he puts his hands out for Grimshaw to catch him, but at that moment I step up onto the diving board and grab her. Just as I get her off the diving board, I hear a massive splash behind me. But I don't turn around to see what happened. I push her in front of me through the house, past all the people, and out into the front yard. We find Tim asleep in his truck, with his head tipped back and his mouth wide open. I get in first and pull Grimshaw in after me.

"Tim." I shake him awake. "We need you to drive us home, like, now."

"Ah, sure," he says. He sits there for a minute, staring straight ahead of him. "Where are we, again?"

"Mizerak's. Now go."

By now, Grimshaw is crying. "I didn't know he was here. I thought he went to California." She's trying to get out of the truck. "But he stayed. For me! Because he loves me."

"So what?" I snap at her. I turn to Tim. "Will you start your truck now?"

"I can't remember where I put my keys," he says slowly.

"In the ignition."

"Everyone else thinks I'm trash," she cries. "Did you see that today, with Allen Mizerak?"

"Allen Mizerak—Tim, can you please turn on your headlights?—has no class at all." At that moment, Mike Lyle staggers out, sopping wet and coughing and held up by a crowd of naked football players from all the towns of the Minnechaug Valley, who are doubled over, laughing and yelling. Grimshaw doesn't see any of this. Her eyes are closed.

"Yeah," she says. "Who does he think he is, anyway?" She starts to cry into her hands. "Why do people have to be so mean? I don't understand."

"Melody!" Mike bellows.

She picks her head up and sees him. "Mike!" she screams, and throws herself at the door.

I reach across Grimshaw and hit the door lock. I turn my attention to Tim, who has forgotten how to drive his truck. "Reverse," I coach him. "Turn to the right. Watch the van there. That's good. Now shift into first. Watch the maple tree. Brake,

brake! Turn left, out the driveway. Now second . . ." and so on, down Robinson Road, up Kingdom Road, while Grimshaw sobs out her guilt for how bad she's treated the only one who loves her, until we roll underneath the gates of Versailles. We're on private property now. I look behind us—no Corvette in sight. By this time, Grimshaw has bawled herself into semiconsciousness.

As we pull up to the front of the house, it occurs to me that my mother is in Maine, so I brace myself for dealing with Scot. The front door is locked, so I have to ring the doorbell. Tim and I are holding Grimshaw up by the armpits. I put my coat over her. As deadweight, she's surprisingly heavy. When Scot comes to the door, he stares at us for a minute, nods, and lets us in. Grimshaw throws up in the hallway on the way to the bathroom. For about half an hour, she stays in the bathroom, half conscious, clinging to the toilet, still in her wedding gown and crying about how bad she's treated Mike Lyle.

"He loves me," she sobs. "He really loves me. Nobody else loves me. To them I'm a Grimshaw. Just trash by the side of the road. Like I fell off a truck."

Scot and I get Grimshaw's face washed. We ply her with vitamins, aspirin, and water, and then get her down the hall, up the stairs, and into my bedroom. I cover her up and smooth the sheets. She lies there, barely breathing.

"Poor kid." Scot looks down at her and shakes his head. "It's not like anybody chooses their family." He pauses. "It's just the luck of the draw. It's not like my family's any great shakes. She's not . . . like them, is she?"

His question takes me aback. What are they like, the

Grimshaws? Fierce. Loyal. Funny. Is she like them? But that's not what he means. "No," I tell him. "She's not like them."

"Who was she crying about?" he asks. "Some creep?"

"Yeah." Actually, I wouldn't mind getting some advice on the Mike Lyle situation. As of tonight, I think we're in over our heads. Scot looks from the crumpled wedding dress on the floor to me, still in ripped tea-length pink.

He gestures at her with his chin. "I think she's out now," he says.

But she opens her eyes. She stares at the ceiling. "I'm a Grimshaw," she announces, and then passes out.

"Poor kid," he says again. "She wasn't really getting married, was she?"

"No. It was sort of a joke."

"Like a homecoming prank?"

"Sort of."

"Good." He nods. "It was a good game. That Junior Davis is a talented son of a gun. I hope he's got some colleges looking at him." Scot pantomimes throwing a football. "You'll be glad for these memories, later on, so make as many as you can." He nods again and puts a hand on my shoulder. "You've always been a good friend to her," he says. "You get credit for that."

Our landline ringing about twenty times into an empty house wakes me up. It's Angel.

"Oh my God," she says when I pick up. "Serena. I'm with Claudette. You have to come immediately. No joke. Do you have the car?" I look out the window. About three inches of snow have accumulated on the ground. From the fresh tire tracks on the driveway, I know Scot's gone. He must have gone to church.

"No."

"Well, you have to run, then. Melody, too. We need both of you."

"What ha—"

"Just RUN!" she says, and hangs up.

I look at the clock. It's almost ten. I shake Grimshaw, but she doesn't move. "Grimshaw—"

"Leave me alone." She sounds awake and stone cold sober. I keep shaking her.

"Grimshaw—it's—"

She sits up and looks around her in disgust. "How did I get *here*?" she asks, like she's never seen my bedroom before in her life.

"It's some emergency at Mizerak's," I tell her. "Angel called."

"Were you the one who pushed him in the pool last night?"

"What? No! He tripped and fell in." But my voice is very high, the way it gets when I'm guilty of something. *Was* I the one who pushed him in? What do I care, anyway—if she wants that clumsy idiot and his loser car, that's not my problem.

"I'm going to Mizerak's," I hiss at her. "And you better come, too, or you are *shit* for a friend. Not to me. To her." I grab my coat and run out into a gray morning. It's not that cold, and I run with my jacket open. Crosslots, the Mizeraks' barns are only two pastures and a cornfield away from Versailles, but they're big fields. The snow is wet and slushy and splashes with every step. I run across corn stubble, climb a fence, dodge semifrozen cow flops, and climb another fence. When I can see the tops of the big blue Harvestore silos, I start to hear the Mizeraks' cows. I stop and listen. I'm not a farmer, but even I can hear an urgency to their mooing, like they know something's wrong.

"Serena!" Angel is waving to me from the barn doorway. "We have to milk the cows!" she shouts. "The bulk tank comes at two o'clock!"

The shrubbery in front of Rack's house is completely wrecked. Beer bottles are everywhere. "This is a disaster."

"No, it's not," she says. "It's a mess, not a disaster. Not getting the cows milked, *that's* a disaster."

"Where's—"

"She won't get up. I don't know what's wrong with her. She can't stop crying. She tries to walk and then she collapses, crying."

"Junior."

"Well, yeah. Obviously."

"Was she drunk?"

"No. She went to bed last night." I follow her into the barn. "What about Melody?" she asks over her shoulder. "I thought she went to your house. We need her."

I look up at the hill. No Grimshaw. I follow Angel into the milking parlor, where she puts a rubber apron over my head and shows me what to do. We're down in the pit, and the cows are on a concrete platform raised about three feet. All I have to do is go from cow to cow, she tells me, and swab off the udders with this rag, like so. Then I take this apparatus off a hook and flip a lever on a black rubber tube which starts the suction going in these cups. I'm supposed to reach between the back legs of this very big cow and put the cups on the teats, like so. I'm to go down a line of twelve cows, doing that to each of them, then go back to the first cow, snap off the suction, and take the cups off with one hand and give the teats a squirt of iodine with the other, from a squirt bottle that hooks on the front pocket of my apron. Then those twelve cows will file out, Angel says, and twelve more will come into the parlor, and I do it all over again. She tells me all this in about ten seconds while she does the first cow, and then rushes back out of the milking parlor, leaving me to face the back end of the second cow alone. I do just what Angel told me to do with the lever and hose and when I reach between the legs with the cups for the teats, it seems to be exactly what the cow expects me to do. It doesn't help that my hands are shaking, on account of my conversation with Grimshaw. Apparently, I am such a terrible person that I do terrible things without even knowing what they are. I'm just glad to have something to do. Cow by cow, I slowly get over my fear that I will be kicked in the face. Sometimes they try to lash me with their tails, which are wet and caked with burrs and manure. When you're right up close to them, doing obnoxious things to their private parts, they seem like very big, very dangerous animals. But they just stick their noses in the grain, and don't seem to notice.

After I get through two cycles of cows, Grimshaw shows up. Her job is to work with me, do what I do, and also give the cows grain as they come into the parlor. Angel keeps bustling in and out of the milking parlor, correcting what we're doing, or telling Grimshaw to wash something. After half an hour, my back is about to break. My feet are cold and wet. My hands are numb, and I have a drip permanently established on the end of my nose that I can't get rid of because my hands are covered with cow shit. I go out into the main barn to straighten up for a minute, and Angel rides into view on a little Ford tractor. It's gray with red trim and a bucket on the front.

"I'm feeding out silage," she explains. "With the new tractor you can feed out in, like, two scoops. This one takes about twenty. We're not allowed to use the new one. Rack's dad hides the keys." She pats the fender. "I like this one, though. It's so cute."

"How many cows are there on this farm, again?" I ask her.

"I don't know. Five hundred?"

"Did she really break up with Junior yesterday?"

Angel just looks at me and shakes her head, like there is so much I don't know, why bother starting to explain.

I go back into the milking parlor. I get an udder folded in half in one of the suction cups and the cow does try to kick me. So I stop thinking about my feet and my back and my hands and the drip on the end of my nose. The rest of the world goes away. I am left with steam rising off the black and white backs, their sweet, grassy breath, the humming of the generator, the rhythmic *thunk, thunk, thunk* of the machines, the milk pulsing through the clear plastic tubing on its way to the bulk tank, the aluminum clang of the gates, and the swish of Grimshaw feeding out grain. I'm unhooking a cow when she lifts her tail and lets loose with a prodigious stream of liquid manure. It hits the cement floor and splashes up all over me. I've just wiped off my face when the one next to her lifts her tail and does the same thing. I look up at

Grimshaw, and she's laughing at me. She doesn't have a speck on her. And then another one does it. She jumps back, but I'm too slow and I get covered. We both double over laughing. I wipe off my face with my sleeve. Then those cows leave and twelve more cows file in.

We get the milking done, and the tank truck comes. We watch the guy hook up, and then Angel and Grimshaw and I go up to the haymow to throw down hay for the heifers. When that's done, we lie on bales and look at the cobwebs up in the rafters.

"Wow," I sigh. "I can't believe her dad does that every day."

"Twice a day," says Angel. She takes off her leather work gloves and studies the damage to her fingernails. "We have to do it again later on."

At that moment, the big sliding doors to the outside open. Rack creeps into view and sits carefully on a bale of hay next to us. I've never seen anyone look so bad. Her face is gray and creased. Her eyes are puffy, and it looks like she burst a blood vessel in one of them. She's carrying a big bag of pretzels. She tries to open the bag, but it's like she's too weak. She gives up, and she hands it to me.

"I do it, too, you know," she says. "Out here at a quarter to five in the morning."

I open the bag and hand her back the pretzels. "Even on school days?"

"Yup, before I come to get you guys. But my brothers really want my dad to sell."

"They don't want to come back and farm?"

"Hell, no. Allen wants to make a million bucks by the time

he's twenty-five so he can retire and focus on his guitar. You don't do that farming."

We crunch pretzels in silence. The haymow is peaceful. Above us, the pigeons flutter and coo. It doesn't take us long to eat the whole bag. Angel leaves and comes back with a big jug of warm Coke, which we pass around and drink out of the bottle. We hear a car pull up outside. The Mizeraks' collie dog starts barking. A car door slams.

"Oh, please God." Rack stands up and puts her hand over her mouth. "Tell me it's not my parents. This place is *so* trashed."

"You should see it inside," Angel whispers to us. "It looks like a bomb went off. There's frozen clothes outside stuck to the patio." Then more vehicles pull up and we hear more car doors slamming, and voices. Angel and Grimshaw clamber up a wall of hay bales and rub a clear spot in the glass of a small, dusty window.

"It's the football team!" they call down.

Rack looks happy. "Junior probably told them to come and clean up."

Is he there? Eagerness is all over her face, but she doesn't ask the question. And they don't tell her.

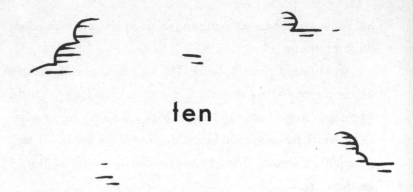

ten

AFTER HOMECOMING, EVERYTHING CHANGES.

The picture of Mike Lyle hitting the water was well documented, and everybody has seen it and has an opinion about how it happened. Mike can't swim, so it took both football teams to get him out of the deep end of the pool without anyone else getting drowned. The event went viral, and every shot seems to have a picture of me in it, too, still in hot pink, leaving the scene of the crime. So Rack and Angel have once again decided I'm a rich snob, poor Mike being my victim, and they've spread it all over town that I think I can get away with anything because my mother's the principal. Apparently, he caught a sniffle that night, like it's my fault he can't swim. He should have watched where he was going. No matter how I logic it out, I still can't figure out how anybody thinks I even could have pushed him in, but it doesn't matter. Everybody is mad at me anyway, and reason would just be wasted on them. Rack tells everybody that Grimshaw told her that Mike said if he sees me, he'll kill me, even though it wasn't my fault he fell in her swimming pool. Maybe everybody just got tired of me, since all I do is study, anyway. Grimshaw takes no position one way or the other. She now has a full-time job named Mike, and he hardly lets her out of his sight. The gold Corvette is in front of the high school in the morning and again in the afternoon. I have fewer friends than ever, and a lot more enemies, but it's not like I have time for them anyway. It turns out the beginning of the year was just a joke academically, and now in order to stay abreast of my schoolwork, I have to learn everything I was too smart to learn during my first three years of high school. After homecoming, I turn in my cheerleading sweater, and so weekends come and go, bringing with them only deadlines for more tests and more papers, which rise up and get beaten back like the tide.

After the football season ends, Scot finds himself without anything to talk about at our weekly dinners, so he makes himself the expert on cell phones and colleges, but I'm too busy to think about college, and I don't need a phone to remind me that I am the worst person in the school and that I will never have any friends again. But I humor him. Since Mom is busy with her career, Scot takes on the job of finding a college that will accept a bad bet like me. He never had a chance to go, he says, so he doesn't mind. I say I'm willing to go to the same college as Allegra, but Guidance thinks that someone with my GPA should aim low, prove myself, and then consider applying to a place like that. So Scot takes a couple of weekends to drive me deep into the puckerbrush to tour campuses that are very far from civilization and still too close to Colchis. I try to be nice about it. One morning at breakfast, he's looking through a catalog, sees the tuition, and almost chokes on a donut. I pound him on the back and ask him if he needs me to perform the Heimlich maneuver.

"No, I'm all set," he says. "I just—I had no idea."

"Allegra got a scholarship," I said.

"It's okay, we'll figure it out." But that's the last college visit we go on.

Weeks are going by, and I still have no friends. I get used to it. Winter starts and the snow comes and stays this time, and Allegra comes home for Thanksgiving and then Christmas, and I work my way straight through both vacations. On a cold day in January, I'm sitting on our bench in front of the high school, just like the old days, waiting for the bus. Suddenly there is Grimshaw walking toward me, and guess what she's dragging along behind her.

"That damn suitcase," I comment.

"Yeah," she says. "I haven't used it in a while."

She sits down, lights two cigarettes, and hands me one. We haven't talked to each other since the day after homecoming.

"Mike's picking me up here," she says. "He has a job for me."

"Is he going to kill me?"

"Not today," she says.

"Nobody was in Western Civ today but me."

"Rack had a doctor's appointment," she says.

"Angel wasn't there, either."

"She's switching to evening classes, remember, because she's starting that program for a nursing certificate."

"Oh, yeah, I forgot about that."

"I saw your name on the honor roll," she says.

"The *high* honor roll," I correct her.

She laughs. "I know. I just said that so you'd correct me. Otherwise, you'd pretend you didn't care."

I shrug. "Foundations was more fun."

"The job is in Los Angeles," she says. "California," she adds.

"Scot says Mike is wanted in about twenty-five states. Did you know that?"

"He hasn't even *been* in twenty-five states."

"He acts like he's been everywhere."

"I'll be a dancer there. You know I can dance."

"Believe me, I know you can dance. That's not the point."

"What do you want me to do, Serena, stay in the Valley and be a Grimshaw for the rest of my life?"

"What are you going to be if you don't even graduate from high school?"

"What am I going to be if I do?" she counters. "It's not like you graduate from high school and suddenly all these opportunities start flying at you. At least not for me. Be serious. Anyway, he's going to pick me up here. I told him I wasn't going to go without saying good-bye to you."

I just sit there and smoke like I hardly even hear what she's saying. "You're headed in the wrong direction," I inform her. "I thought you wanted New York."

"I do, but . . . everyone's gotta start somewhere—" She keeps talking, but at that moment all the buses let out their air brakes and the noise drowns out what she says. All I get is the last part.

"—and you'll be going to college," is all I hear.

165

I don't wait for the Corvette. He won. I grind out my cigarette and get on the bus.

With Grimshaw gone for real, my life shrinks still further, which is fine: without Grimshaw, I have even less in common with Rack or Angel, or anyone else, except maybe for Mr. C. He's not letting me give up on my upward mobility project, he says. He assigns me people to talk to, and I get good at listening and asking questions and writing down what they say. I even get a tour of the Arms, which is vast and silent and amazing and depressing at the same time. Kids have already started to break the windows. I go in after school and tell Mr. C. the stories, and he gets excited, and we have arguments about upward mobility and capitalism and if there's any hope for the Valley now that there's no industry.

About midway through the winter, my mother notices that I'm getting too isolated, so she brings me to the pastor of her church, who must have a certificate in talking to teenagers, because he thinks he's really good at it. I come in at the appointed time and see that Pastor Don has set up a chessboard. I float a problem or two just to nip this therapy thing in the bud. I don't tell him about the sucking sinkhole in my chest that, despite being empty, weighs more than I do. I don't tell him that my best and only friend has gone to start her future without me and this winter has felt like ten years in solitary confinement, which I probably deserve, although I have no idea what I'm guilty of. Instead, I lie to him about panic attacks I get before math tests, and then I move some pawns around the board and listen earnestly while he tells me about relaxation techniques and the health benefits of a daily meditation practice.

When my mother comes to pick me up, he's ready with a diagnosis. "I recommend a strong dose of college," he says, smiling broadly at me.

"Yes!" she says. "Good advice."

The winter stretches into spring. As predicted, Scot stops talking about college, and they forget about the cell phone. I get ahead of the learning curve, and school gets easier. I get my driver's license. Junior Davis wins the wrestling championship for his weight class and has started to drink alcohol. He's still failing math. Everybody knows that Rack is pregnant and that Junior is having nothing to do with it. One day, Rack calls me up and asks me if I want to go shopping for baby clothes with her. She says she's finishing high school online. We spend an awkward Saturday afternoon in Walmart, looking at pink onesies and talking about names. It's going to be a girl. She shows me an app for baby names. She can't decide between Olivia Hope and Hannah Rose. And Penelope. "I know it's weird," she says about Penelope, "but it's coming back." The real reason she wants to see me is for news about Junior. She knows he won All-State, and she heard he started to drink, but she doesn't know if that's a good sign or not. Who is he seeing? What are people saying about her? Who's flirting with him? What have I heard? Angel's not talking to her, she says. I tell her she probably knows more about what happens at the high school than I do. She says I'm probably right. After that, she doesn't call me again.

In Western Civ on the last day before spring vacation starts, Mr. C. walks to the back of the classroom and hands me a postcard.

"It came to the school," he says. "Addressed to you. Your mother asked me to give it to you."

The postcard isn't really a postcard. It is a photograph of a bar at sunset. In neon letters, the sign on the roof says OVER EASY. On either side of the sign there's a neon silhouette of a naked woman, in red lines against a purple sky. The bar is a plain, flat-roofed one-story building made out of cinder block painted green. No windows. A single palm tree sticks up over the roof. I look at it for a long time before I turn it over. On the back, in Grimshaw's handwriting, is a single line. *Freedom's just another word for nothing left to lose.* She's written her address along the bottom. That's it.

Mr. C. has launched the day's lecture. We're leaving the nineteenth century now, with its labor wars and socialist unrest in the middle of the country. He talks about Marx, Engels, and the crude theory they concocted called communism, and how it came over from Europe with ships of immigrants, along with smallpox and Norway rats, while I try to figure out what the line on her postcard means.

How can she have "nothing left," when nothing is what she left Colchis with—her parents' old suitcase from their honeymoon and a set of flannel sheets are pretty close to nothing. Everything else she left with was Mike's—Mike's car, Mike's money, Mike's plans, connections, and schemes. She did have her dreams, but if she's turned them over to him for management, no doubt she's lost those, too. But maybe they were gone before she left Colchis.

Mr. C. keeps sending me easy pitches, wanting me to engage, claiming how wrong Marx got everything, including his own phone number. I stare out the same window at the same pine tree I've been staring at for almost two years. It's mid-April now, the world is still brown, but you can feel the green coming. Grimshaw is out there with nothing left to lose, while I'm still in here, breathing the stale air of childhood. Suddenly, I feel so restless it's all I can do not to leave, just stand up and go, just like she did, and not come back.

So what has she lost, then? The only thing she had that she didn't take with her was me. Maybe she thinks she's lost me.

Mr. C. stops talking.

Nobody says anything. Everybody's just waiting for the vacation to start. Mr. C. looks up. Minutes tick by. The only sound is the motor in the wall clock, which seems to get louder and louder with every second. Mr. C. notices the piece of chalk in his hand and walks over and drops it in the trash can by his desk. Then he picks up all the chalk in the chalk tray and drops that in the trash, too. Then he picks up the erasers and dumps them in. Then he puts the Western Civ textbook in the trash. Then he folds up his plan book, where he keeps everybody's grades. That goes in the trash. He walks to his closet, puts on his coat, and places his hat on his head. He leaves the room, closing the door quietly behind him. More seconds tick by. Ten minutes. Fifteen minutes. Nobody talks. Nobody moves. After twenty minutes, the bell rings. We get up and file toward the door.

Outside the classroom, the halls are noisy with prevacation euphoria. I make my way down to my mom's office to see if she's going to go straight home after school. I can't face the school bus today. Mrs. Pentz is not there. She must be close by, though, because her purse is open on the chair next to her desk. I take Grimshaw's postcard out of my upward mobility notebook. *Freedom's just another word for nothing left to lose.* I find my mother's wallet, open it, and take out a wad of twenties. I leave school, walk to the bank, and empty out my pitiful savings account.

There's no bus station in Colchis, just a window at the Off-Track Betting counter in Al's Superette. I learn that there's a daily bus to Buffalo, which will connect me to buses going to Chicago and points west. Without taking his eyes off a racing form, the guy behind the counter sells me a one-way ticket to LA.

"Bus leaves in forty-five," he says.

"How long does it take to get there?"

"Depends on your ticket."

I study the ticket I just bought. Buffalo, Chicago, St. Louis, Amarillo, Los Angeles. It sounds like the world to me, or at least a good start. A smile spreads across my face, I can't help it. There are two doors out. One says EASTBOUND and one says WESTBOUND.

"LA is . . . west, right?" I joke.

"Don't worry about it," he says. "There's only one bus."

He lets me use his phone. I ask Mrs. Kmiec to patch me through to my mother's voice mail. I tell Mrs. Pentz that I've gone to visit a friend in California, and I'll be in touch when I get there. I borrowed some money, but I'll pay her back. There. Now I'm not a teenage runaway.

I sit in the parking lot of the Superette and look through my backpack. I will certainly not lack for reading. My independent study notebook for Western Civ is in there, my calculus textbook, with homework for over the vacation, a couple of disorganized binders, and a copy of *Moby-Dick*, which I told my AP English teacher I would look at over the break.

Before long, the bus pulls in, its headlights shining.

Although I've gone down Main Street many times on a bus, this bus is higher than the school bus, and the windows are bigger. I look down on the brief bit of town—Al's Superette, the Arms, the used furniture store, the discount liquors, Teresa's Bridal Shoppe, the Crossways Tavern.

When we get to the on-ramp of the highway, one sign says EAST, and the other says WEST. The bus swings to the left instead of to the right, and I'm going down a road I've never been on before.

I get to Buffalo, wait, and change buses. It isn't until I cross the first state line that I get it. It hits me so hard that I actually start to cry. I get out my upward mobility notebook and write it down. *I get it, Grimshaw,* I write. *You had to go. I get it now.*

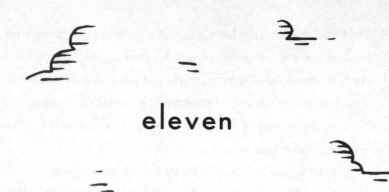

eleven

IT'S A GOOD THING I HAD no idea how big the country was going to be. By Chicago, the bus driver's told us not to smoke, drink, or cross the yellow line enough times in Spanish that I have the announcement memorized. By St. Louis, she forgets to say it in English a couple of times. In Tulsa, and somewhere in Arizona, I borrow phones and leave messages at home, but I don't get anyone in person.

Four days later, LA is huge and hot and dirty. In front of the bus station, I show Grimshaw's address to a cab driver, who asks me how much money I have. He takes all of it and brings me to a little white bungalow with an orange-tiled roof and closed green shutters and a chain-link fence drawn tight around a narrow collar of asphalt. The door is on the right-hand side of the house, with a stoop and a walkway that leads to the gate where I'm standing. The gold Corvette sits next to it in the driveway. It now has a California vanity plate that reads VIPER. I'm here. There's a buzzer on the gate. I push the button and hear it ring inside.

Nothing happens, so I ring again. After a minute, the door opens and my friend Melody Grimshaw comes out and stands, shielding her eyes against the strong sunlight. She's in a white T-shirt that comes down almost to her knees. She closes the door behind her and drifts down the little concrete walkway and stops on the other side of the gate. She hasn't put her makeup on yet, so there are those white eyelashes, which nobody has seen since sixth grade. She touches my hand on the metal post, like she's making sure it's real. I hold my hand up, and our fingers lace together. We stand there together on either side of the gate, not saying anything. When you haven't seen someone in a long time that you used to see every day, it's a lot like seeing the ghost of the person you used to know. You act like it's nothing, like you see ghosts all the time, like all you see are ghosts. We stand there like that and watch a kid across the street bouncing a basketball off the side of his building. Chained to a stop sign there's a bicycle with no tires or handlebars that looks like it's been there for a while.

"It's funny to see palm trees, isn't it?" she says.

"It is. It must make you feel like you're in a movie."

"It kinda does." We fill up the awkwardness with small talk. "How long did it take you to get here?" she asks.

"About four months."

"Shut up."

"I was in Missouri for three weeks. I thought I died and went to hell."

"Missouri is nothing. You should see Nebraska."

"Missouri is literally ten times the size of Nebraska."

"No, it's not!"

"In Texas, this guy fell asleep on me and the brim of his cowboy hat rubbed a hole in my neck. Look."

"That's the worst cover story for a hickey I ever heard. I bet Tim Marhaver gave it to you."

I burst out laughing, and she looks pleased that she made me laugh first. At the sound of my laughter, the kid with the basketball turns around and tucks it under his arm and watches us.

The front door of the house opens again. Mike Lyle stands on top of the stoop. When she hears the door open, Grimshaw stiffens a little in front of me and doesn't look up. But I'm taller than her, and I look over her head directly into those snake eyes. She puts her arms around my waist. I put my arms around Grimshaw and rest my chin on her head.

"Is it him?" she asks.

"Mm-hm."

Mike folds his arms across his chest.

"Well, well, well," he says. "Look what the cat dragged across. Somebody just couldn't stay away, could they?" He's still tinkering with his image. The black hair now has streaks of blond in it, and he's grown a beard, very trim and shiny. A diamond stud in one ear flashes in the sun. He gazes down at me through slitted eyes, like he thinks I'm in his territory now and all the rules are different. A thin thread of fear slices lengthwise through my body. But I don't know why I should be afraid: he's still Mike Lyle, from Colchis, who doesn't know how to swim.

Grimshaw steps aside and opens the gate for me. "Be prepared," she says in a low voice.

"Hey, Grimshaw," I whisper. "You don't have an extra toothbrush, by any chance. I forgot mine."

She stops. "For four days?" she demands.

We stop halfway up the walkway, and I tell her about the worst chicken salad sandwich in the world, which I bought out of a vending machine. "It was so bad, I can still taste it. I only had one bite."

She tips back her head and laughs, this clear flutelike sound I've never heard from her before. While Mike watches, she kisses me. She looks like she did when I first met her. With her pale eyelashes, she looks innocent, more like a little girl than she did when she was one. She smiles, and we link arms and walk together toward Mike. She lifts her chin up in the way that you do when you're letting somebody know that you don't care what they think. So I do it, too.

She leads me into what must be the hottest kitchen in California, and that's where we stay, chain-smoking Grimshaw's menthols and going through three pots of lousy coffee. The house is tiny— just the kitchen, a bedroom, and a bathroom. Mike doesn't want us to talk because he has a bunch of really important phone calls to make, which have to happen in the kitchen, so I lower my voice to a whisper and tell her about my trip, which makes it come out like an adventure, instead of what it really was, four days of bleakness and depression and dirty windows, and a little girl in Texas teaching me words in Spanish, and the guy in the advanced stages of alcoholism falling asleep on me with his cowboy hat rubbing against my neck all the way from Albuquerque to Phoenix. She listens for a while, then she wants to know how my classes are going.

"I had this really big book I read all the way across, *Moby-Dick*. People thought it was the Bible, and I got blessed a bunch of times in Spanish."

I get out *Moby-Dick*, and she sees all the books in my backpack. "Tell me you applied to college," she says.

"I didn't have time!"

She shakes her head and sighs. "How's—" And then she coughs. I know who she's talking about. Junior Davis. A cough is code for someone whose name we aren't supposed to say out loud. Mike is standing over us, with one foot up on a chair, frowning into his phone. I make her stand up, then I get her on the floor in a headlock, while she laughs, then I stand up and hold her arm up in victory.

"All-State."

Her eyes open wide. "The championship?"

"Yup." We sit back down. And then I crack a can of beer, lift it to my mouth, and chug it.

"No!" she says.

I nod my head. "Afraid so."

She looks stricken. "But"—cough—"is the only person in the whole Valley who doesn't drink!" she says.

I shrug. "He's failing math. For the fourth time. And also—"

But before I get a chance to update her on Rack's baby, Mike swears and brings his fist down on the table and makes all the coffee cups jump and the spoons rattle. A glass falls off the table. Something on his phone made him mad, but Grimshaw doesn't ask what happened. This hard look of irritation shoots through her eyes. She's not afraid of him, I can see that. In fact, she's sick of him. I make the mistake of looking from her to Mike and then back to her right then, and he sees that I see it. I wonder if she even knows about Rack's baby. An idea occurs to me. I wonder if she would come back with me.

"Also they broke up," I finish.

She shrugs. "No surprises. Can't you do something, though?" she asks. "You're good at math."

Leaning close together so we don't bother Mike, we go through all the people we know in Colchis—who's dating, who doesn't come to school anymore, who the new cheerleaders are. When we get to Rack, Grimshaw doesn't seem to know about the pregnancy, and I don't tell her.

From the one side of the conversations on the phone, I have no idea what he does except pretend to be a big Hollywood producer. He shouts into the phone about "talent" and "product." The one time the phone rings for him, though, it's all "yes, sir," and "no, sir," and "I understand how you feel, sir."

"So what's the book about?" Grimshaw asks when Mike looks over at us.

"A whale." We both explode laughing, put our foreheads on the table and our shoulders shake, just like the laughing attacks we'd have when she came to church with us.

When Mike goes to the bathroom, he leaves the door open and positions himself so that he can watch us in the mirror while he takes a piss. When he comes out, he tells Grimshaw to get ready for work. They have to go in early today, he says.

Grimshaw disagrees. "We have a whole hour before we have to go in. Anyway, it's Monday. We can go in late if we want to."

"I got things I gotta do," he says.

"Well, fine, then. I need time to put my makeup on, though."

"Do it at work," he says, staring at me. "We gotta go."

She opens her eyes wide at me. "Fine," she says. She doubles over laughing again and has a hard time walking across the kitchen.

While she's in the bedroom changing, Mike stays where he is, still on his phone, posted by the door. He doesn't take his eyes off me.

He's trying to intimidate me, but I'm not afraid of him. I understand why I came out here. His girlfriend doesn't need him anymore, and he knows it, and now I know it, too. I'm not sure she knows it yet. I pick up *Moby-Dick*. "Can I use your washing machine?" I call to Grimshaw.

"It's in the bathroom," she calls back. "But the big dryer doesn't blow very hot." For some reason, we both crack up at the same time. I can hear her in the bedroom. She's still laughing when she comes out and picks up my upward mobility notebook. She leafs through it, remarks on how much I've written in it, then on the first blank page, she draws me a map of how to get to the Over Easy and then she draws a diagram of the place where she will be. Mike is the manager there. She says it's a long walk, but close enough for me to meet her there tonight, when she takes her break.

"Stick to the main streets," she says. "Follow the map."

After they leave, I sit there for a while, looking at Grimshaw's handwriting, which hasn't changed since sixth grade. At this point, my only plan is to ask my mother for a plane ticket home, so now I'll ask her for two plane tickets. But then what would Grimshaw do back in Colchis, where would she go? Back to the junkyard? Help out with the bridal shop? Anywhere but here, I suppose, being ruled by Mike Lyle. I'll just give her the option, that's all. I noticed the way that little fork of irritation appears next to her eyebrow whenever he says anything. A best friend picks up on things like that. When I get there tonight, we'll talk it over. Then I remember my next step in life: the washing machine, which is in the bathroom. My clothes are so glad to be off my body after four days in a row that they dive into the washer.

In the mirror, I inspect my hair, which has never gone four days without being washed. It's so greasy it's not even blonde anymore. Usually, I hate mirrors. Grimshaw is my idea of beauty, and I don't look one little thing like Grimshaw. I look into my own blue eyes and smile at my friend in the mirror. I remember the guy on the bus in Albuquerque who told me that my eyes reminded him of the sky. "Very far away." If we have this much courage to do things like this, imagine how much more we'll have for things that actually make sense. It occurs to me what a brave thing it was I just did, just as brave as what she did.

After I get out of the shower, I realize I didn't plan things out very well. I don't have anything to wear while I wait for my clothes.

I walk over to a clothes rack in the corner. Grimshaw seems to have invested heavily in underwear, which are arranged on a drying rack in the corner of the bathroom. They have straps and rivets, with fringe and lace and sequins, the kind that look like they'd be itchy and uncomfortable to wear. I pick up a pair of black lace stockings, trying to figure out how they work. I get my legs in, and then I discover there are arms, too, and pull on a body stocking. It's so tight on me it's hard to breathe in it, but that might be because my heart has started to beat really fast. I stare at myself in it in the mirror. It's crotchless. I see a girl who looks a little scared, who just figured out that she's a long way from home. I remember what Mike said to me the first night I met him, that underneath our clothes, we're no different than animals. The body stocking is itchy on my skin and kind of greasy-feeling, like I need to take another shower. I peel it off and fling it away from me. I look over the things on the drying rack—for someone who's so smart, I sure am a slow learner. I had to come a long way to find out what everybody but me knew from the beginning, even Mike—that if Grimshaw wanted to be a stripper, she was always going to be a stripper. All that drama, all that strategy about having a dream just led to this. This is the plan she always had, and now she's living it, but it doesn't seem glamorous. It seems depressing, like the body stocking now coiled in the corner like something that just crawled out of the drain.

The washing machine makes its loud buzz. I throw my clothes in the dryer, and I put on Grimshaw's silky little bathrobe that I find on the back of the bathroom door and go back out into the kitchen. I am aware of the quiet, the cars passing by. Suddenly it feels really creepy and kind of exposed to be here all by myself in Mike's house. The minute my clothes are dry, I'll start walking to Grimshaw's work. I wonder if I should just put my clothes on wet and go now. No, that's stupid. I get out my upward mobility notebook and reread her directions to the Over Easy. I wish I'd asked to use her phone before she left. The last call I made was from Bakersfield. Then I open up *Moby-Dick* and as I look for my place, I become aware of the rest of the sounds of the neighborhood, that kid still bouncing a basketball the way he's been doing all day, somebody's small dog barking, car horns and diesel engines, music out open car windows, people talking nearby, maybe on television, and I start to relax and be a little curious about where I am. I start to wish that Grimshaw had her own place here where I could actually visit her instead of being watched and silenced by Mike.

A car door slams next to the house, and then there he is, coming in the screen door. He stops in the doorway and looks at me and all the noises of the neighborhood go away. Everything in my mind goes blank. I wait to see if Grimshaw is coming up behind him, but he just stands there, like he doesn't know what to do next.

"Where's Melody?" I ask, knowing the answer as soon as I hear myself ask the question.

He laughs. "The first time I met you, you were asking me that. 'Where's Melody?'" he mimics. "'Where's Melody?'" He kicks something across the kitchen floor. It's the cup that fell when he pounded the table that nobody picked up. It gets to a point on the linoleum and then spins by itself.

"I needed to get some stuff," he says when it stops.

"It's okay," I reply.

"I guess it's okay," he says. "It's my house." But he doesn't move, he just stands there. I am barely breathing, just a thread of air coming in and out of my lungs. The moment extends, and still he doesn't move.

I look down at the book in my lap. There are no words on the page anymore, not even when I put my finger underneath the line so I can focus. He walks across the kitchen, and I watch his feet go by. He goes into their bedroom, and I can hear him moving around, opening and shutting drawers, banging things. There's no reason to be afraid of Mike Lyle, I tell myself, just because he's in California, he's the same guy he's ever been, just a loser in a shiny car. It occurs to me that I should go into the bathroom and just put my clothes on wet, and then leave. I don't need to say another word to him. I close the book, but then he comes out of the bedroom, goes in the bathroom himself, and shuts the door. I listen to the sound of my clothes scraping around in the dryer. I wish I'd never washed them. It seems like the worst idea I ever had.

When the door opens again, he stands there without moving, but I don't look up. "Hey," he says softly. "You tried on her things." He's smiling.

"No."

He holds out the body stocking. It lies across his hands like a long black rope. "You stretched it out," he says. "These things aren't cheap." While I watch, he wraps it around each hand and pulls it tight so it looks like a cord, and his smile disappears. Then he laughs. "I'm just kiddin' around, you know that. We're old friends, you and me." He walks over to me with the body stocking coiled around one hand. I tighten my grip on *Moby-Dick*. He drops it into my lap, kind of wrapping it on the book. He chuckles. "I'm just playing with you," he says. "Just like you do when you're home, you play with people. But you're not home now." He moves a strand of damp hair from front to back, and as he does so, drags a fingernail across the side of my neck. He stands very close, breathing down on me. He works his fingers into my hair on the back of my head. Everything goes white for a second, and I hear wind rushing in my ears.

"I like your hair long," he whispers. "Rich girl." His leg is against my arm. "Your long blonde hair. Rich girl," he says again.

"I'm not rich."

I move my arm. He steps even closer so that I am aware of his penis pushing out the front of his pants and I can feel the heat of it against the side of my arm. I move my arm away, but he steps in closer, and this time he starts rubbing against it. "You think you're better than we are, don't you?" He waits for me to answer.

"No," I whisper.

"Yes, you do. You think your blood is better, your bones are better." As he talks he moves my wet hair off my neck. "You're just a better cut of meat, I guess. Some people are born that way, nothing you can do about it. But you know what?" His fingers feel like worms on my neck, dry worms running up and down. He tightens his grip, leans down, and whispers in my ear. "I said, you know what?"

"What?" I whisper to the wall.

"Here's something we know about in LA: meat is meat."

He has me wedged against the wall, his fingers tangled in my hair, his hips grinding against my shoulder as he presses me harder and harder. I know he's waiting for me to push him away. That will be his moment to strike. For some reason, Scot's words about football flash into my mind, so clear it's like he's in the room with me, about how quarterbacks read movement on the field, how they look for patterns instead of at individual players, how they see danger and opportunity in masses of moving bodies. Just do something. Make a move. I can hear Scot's voice in my head: *Call the play.*

So I put the book down. I put my hands on the kitchen table, and I stand up. Mike Lyle is not tall, and that gives me one second's advantage. Right into those light eyes of his, I smile at him, like everything is going according to plan and he's gotten everything all wrong, as usual. That surprises him, and for a split second, he looks uncertain. There are about six inches of space between us. I lean into it. He steps back. I step forward.

"I'll bet you don't know why I came," I whisper at him. He waits for me to tell him. I don't tell him anything. He folds his arms over his chest.

"I sure as shit know you didn't come for me." But he's not so sure he couldn't be persuaded. I keep smiling. He hasn't fumbled anything yet, but his grip on the football is not firm. But, like Scot said, you can't wait for the other guy to lose.

"Are you sure about that?" I ask. "Would you bet the farm on it?" Then I wait, and watch. I hear Scot's voice in my head like I'm a quarterback with a wired helmet. The other team has the ball, but eventually they'll fumble, and when I intercept it, I'm going to run like hell. Wait, says the voice in the helmet. Wait. Waiting is action, Scot says. Let him make the move now. My question still hangs in the air.

Slowly, as I wait, I watch ego start to fight with reality, all over Mike's face. I don't let myself think about anything but football. That keeps the fear away. I release my tight hold on Grimshaw's bathrobe, and it falls open, and I let him search for what's underneath. Never taking my eyes off him, I slowly reach out and pick up Grimshaw's menthols, which she left on the table. I brush past him and walk to the sink. When I get there, I pivot, just like a stripper. I put the cigarette in my mouth.

"Have a light?"

"Ah . . ." He starts patting all his pockets and then he sees Grimshaw's lighter on the table. "Here we go." He picks it up and holds it out for me. I inhale and hold the smoke in my lungs for a minute. My mother said Mike Lyle wasn't very bright. Let's hope she's right.

"Melody's pregnant." I don't know where that one comes from. But it works.

Mike swallows. "She is? She is not. Are you sure?" He looks like a bone is stuck sideways in his throat.

"Are you?" I blow a smoke ring at him. "Yeah." I laugh. "Pretty soon that vanity plate will be on a used minivan just like Mrs. Grimshaw's. 'Viper.' And that's the closest you'll get to it, Mike. Grimshaws come by the dozen, you know. Lots of little vipers." I tap the ashes onto the floor and take another drag.

Mike turns around and looks through the window at his car.

And I see the way forward. I'm going to take his upward mobility away from him, and then I'm going to sell it back to him at a very high price. When he turns to me again, he's frowning. I answer his next question before he can ask it.

"She sent me a postcard about it. How do you think I knew where to find you? She wants to go home." I blow smoke in his face. "But I don't." He studies me, and then a slow, crooked grin softens his face, as if now he understands what the problem was all along.

"Why?" he says. "You want to go in the bedroom and fool around?" In the bathroom, the dryer buzzes. I brush by him. I turn around in the bathroom doorway, put my arms over my head, for my final pose. His mouth is open.

"I don't fool around with other women's guys," I announce. In his breast pocket, his cell phone rings. It startles him, and he fumbles for it. It's Grimshaw. I can hear her demanding to know where he is. He doesn't answer her.

"It'll be my first time," I sort of breathe at him. "Let's make it special." And then I go into the bathroom, close the door behind me, and lock it. I put my forehead against the mirror and close my eyes.

"Help us God, help us God, help us God," I pray.

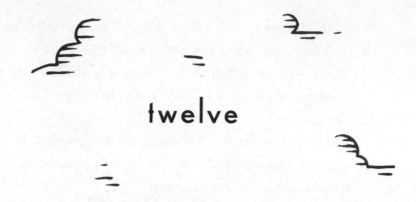

twelve

THE NEXT DAY, GRIMSHAW AND I are out on the Golden State Freeway with our thumbs out. I'm holding up the word EAST, which I drew on the front inside cover of my upward mobility notebook. Within minutes, a vintage Chevy pulls over and stops.

"I can't believe he did that," Grimshaw says, picking up her suitcase.

"It's amazing all the old cars you see out here," I comment. "Ruby would love it."

"He didn't even explain!" She shakes her head. "He was the one with all the plans for us. Big dreams." I can see two soldiers sitting in the front of the car, all dressed up in camo gear. "He was gonna manage me," she says. "All the way to the top."

I hold open the rear door of the Chevy for her. She stands there, still talking.

"He comes in, I'm, like, with a customer. He calls me a liar—right in front of the guy! Jesus. That is so unprofessional. I tell him we'll discuss it later—" Before I get in the car, she hits me on the arm, demonstrating how hard Mike had hit her. It wasn't very hard. "Because I was talking to this guy," she continues. "A customer! So it really wasn't that cool at all."

We get in the car. "He thinks he can get away with throwing his weight around 'cause he's the manager. But he's wrong. There's an owner, too."

We pull out into traffic. The soldier on the passenger side turns around. "What kind of music can we play for you ladies?"

"Jazz," I tell him. "But not too loud."

That shuts them up. A thick silence settles over us, which will last for the rest of the day, punctuated every twenty minutes by a sharp sigh from Grimshaw. She doesn't say any more about Mike or about the events of last night. She doesn't know what happened between me and Mike. I want to tell her—I tried to tell her. The body stocking, what he was ready to do to me. But I'm not even sure what happened myself. At one point, she checks her watch.

"I should be at work right now," she says.

"Don't think about it" is my only advice.

We stare out our respective windows. I don't know why I didn't tell her about what happened with me and Mike. I meant to. I mean, for her own sake, I should tell her that he intended to—I don't even know what he intended, to settle some old score, maybe—then what would have happened? But the Over Easy was so weird—I ran the whole way there, and when I walked through the door, there was a girl that at first I thought was Grimshaw in a wig, up in a little fenced-off stage wearing nothing but high heels and a big smile. The place wasn't what I expected: lots of chairs upholstered in green velvet, little Frisbee-sized tables, a few men sitting alone close to the stage staring intently at the girl, and a couple more men not really looking at anything. I'd been in bus stations with more atmosphere than that. But I didn't stop to stare. I strode through the place like I knew exactly where I was going. Down the length of the room, according to her drawing in my upward mobility notebook, through a door to the left of the stage, down the stairs, take a right, down four more stairs, walk toward the light and through a beaded curtain. Grimshaw had told me where the dressing rooms were. Sure enough, she was in there, alone, wearing a bathrobe, sitting in front of a mirror, putting the finishing touches on her makeup. When I walked through the door, she jumped up with another big hug for me. Before I could tell her what happened with Mike, she started telling me how motivating it was that I came. She still had the same dreams, she said, and she was feeling settled enough in her new life that she was going to start looking for studios and a teacher. It was her private dream, she said, apart from Mike, so—she stopped talking and got this faraway look in her eyes. "I still have to figure that part out." She started putting on this tiny gladiator outfit, with straps and rivets, and tiny patches of sheer camo material in all the places you'd expect.

"That's not what the girl upstairs is wearing," I said.

"I'm developing an act," she said. "That's how you get a following. That's why I like Monday nights. They're lousy for tips, but you get a chance to try new things. This place used to be nothing much, but it's getting a lot classier now that Mike's running it. They'll wake up when I go out there—you watch. Some say I'm the best in the city. They say I should go to Vegas. You should see it in here on weekends." She stood in front of me holding her hair up, and I tied two ties, one at her neck and one down her back.

"Busy?" I asked.

"Insane." While she put on her shoes, each one of which needed to be laced up to the knee, Grimshaw chattered about the money and opportunity and fascinating people that the Over Easy had brought into her life. The dressing room was long and rectangular. Gunmetal gray lockers, just like the ones at Colchis High, lined two walls. Mirrors lined the other two. A cigarette burned in an ashtray among the pots and tubes of makeup, adding to the tobacco smoke already embedded in the air. The smoke got into my brain and clouded it over, and I couldn't remember anything or make sense of anything. Even if I did tell her what happened, there was no guarantee that she wouldn't take his side, like she did before. Nobody had invited me out here, after all. All I got was a postcard with an address—the rest was my doing. When I sat down on a metal folding chair, all the coffee that had been artificially holding me up drained out through my feet and into the floor.

Grimshaw told me how much I inspired her by challenging myself at school. "You just did it," she said. "You just decided and did what you had to do. That's actually when I decided to leave, when you made the high honor roll like that. I thought, wow, I guess that's how you do it."

"So it was your idea to leave Colchis?" I asked.

"Mine. I said to Mike, let's go."

The smoke in my head cleared enough to let one thought through: *Go home.* "Could I use your phone?" I asked.

"When Mike comes in," she said. "Mike has it."

When she said his name like that, twice, it came like a one-two punch. I felt so defeated. All I wanted to do was go to sleep and wake up in my own bed in Colchis.

I had just enough strength to say, "I hope you're not giving him all your money."

"So what if I am?" Her mouth tightened. "It's still my money. Dreams need investment. That's what he says." She glared at herself in the mirror and took another drag on her cigarette, carefully, so as not to smear her lipstick. A speaker crackled on the wall. A male voice said, "Cinnamon—you're on in one."

"Gotta go," she said brightly.

"Cinnamon," I said. "Is that you?"

"You're not allowed to use your own name," she said primly. "Because of stalkers." She checked herself in the mirror, front and back.

The girl I had seen out front came in, kicked off her heels, put on a bathrobe, lit a cigarette, and put her feet up on the makeup counter. Grimshaw introduced me as her best friend from home.

"Hey," the girl said to me. "I'm telling Mike to close on Mondays. It's like dancing in a cemetery."

"He won't," said Grimshaw.

"Shit," the girl said. "I'd rather dance for my goldfish."

"Well, I'm on now." She turned to me.

"Is there any place here where a body could sleep?" I asked.

Grimshaw pointed to a pile of clothes in the corner. "There's a mattress under there." I lay down on lumps of sequins and feathers that smelled like sweat and other bodily fluids and sank immediately into sleep.

It takes a long time to get out of LA, but eventually we make it to the edge of the city and the beginning of nothing. The National Guard lets us out in front of a SPEED LIMIT 65 sign, where we stand until just before nightfall. Traffic is sparse.

"We've gotta get out of here," Grimshaw says. "At this time of night, rattlesnakes come out of the ditches to lie in the road because it's still warm."

"It doesn't sound like anything I'd do if I were a rattlesnake."

"Mike says they do."

A truck approaches. She runs out in the middle of the road waving both arms. It stops, and we're picked up by a guy in an F-350 hauling a horse trailer. He's a rider on the Indian rodeo circuit, he says, and his horse is named Mud. He takes us to a bar where Grimshaw lays five dollars on the edge of a pool table, lights a cigarette, and waits.

I sit at the bar and watch. Many eyes from the shadowy depths of the bar follow her every move. She has all the attention in the room. She looks so confident, it's hard to believe she was ever stupid enough to be with a guy like Mike Lyle. Soon enough, there's another five on top of hers, put there by a guy with long sideburns and a leather vest and a red scar on his cheek. She chalks her pool cue. As she leans over the pool table to break the triangle, she shoves her hair back and it catches the light. She lifts her eyes to meet mine and winks at me. I smile back at her. This is going to be good. I spent many hours in the basement of her little home by the highway, watching her play pool. Of all her brothers, Ruby was the only one who could ever beat her.

All of a sudden, it hits me: I won. We're gone, and Mike Lyle has no idea where we are. We're safe now, and we're free. I went way behind enemy lines, and I won the whole damn war. I harpooned the white whale, and now I *am* the white whale. A sense of victory washes over me that is so pure and so sweet and so unfamiliar that I'm not really sure how to handle it. For me, this is the high honor roll. I turn around to face the bartender.

"You might want to turn that smile down a couple notches," the bartender observes. "You don't want to get in trouble."

"I'm not afraid of trouble," I tell him, still smiling.

"No?"

"I'm not afraid of anything."

"If that's the case, there's a guy at the end of the bar who wants to buy you a drink."

"Okay."

Soon a man named Smokey is sitting on the stool next to me. Smokey is not young. Smokey has a very large black cowboy hat, which when he lifts it up to say hello, reveals a very shiny bald head. His hands are so smooth and brown they look like they're carved out of wood.

"You two not from around here?" Smokey asks me.

"No."

"Travelin' through?"

"Basically."

"Your friend sure knows how to handle a pool cue."

Smokey and I watch Grimshaw sink the eight ball, and then

another guy puts a ten on top of the fives that are now hers. I get my groove back for my independent study and ask Smokey a couple of questions about upward mobility. He says his parents were wheat farmers in South Dakota and as soon as his feet could reach the pedals, he was running a combine fourteen hours a day, and as far as he's concerned, it's been upward ever since. I try a guy a couple stools to my right, but he just shakes his head. At closing time, our rodeo rider takes us to a double-wide trailer, gets his mother out of bed, and she throws sleeping bags for us down on the living room carpet. When we get up in the morning, there are about half a dozen kids around the kitchen table, and one old man asleep with his chin on his chest. Grimshaw and I squeeze in, and Doris—that's the mother's name—feeds us fried rice and fried eggs and fried bread. I think she even fried the coffee.

Grimshaw looks up at Doris from across the table and smiles. "I'm from a big family, too," she says. "I'm the youngest."

The old man wakes up. He lifts up his cup of coffee. He clears his throat. "Here's to Mother," he croaks. He raises his coffee cup. I reach across the table and touch cups with him and Grimshaw.

After the children are gone, we have another cup of coffee, take showers, have another cup of coffee, and then Doris drives us out to the road, a two-lane highway threading through the Lone Pine Indian Reservation, which is where it turns out we spent the night. The road is empty in both directions. Our shadows stretch halfway to the horizon. The hills to the west have snow on them. The sun coming in low paints them gold. Grimshaw faces them with her hands on her hips.

"I wish Mike were here right now," she sighs. "Can you believe it? I really miss him."

Maybe it's because it is so unexpected, but the sound of his name has a profound physical impact on me. I see the black body stocking coiled around his hands like a rope, and the victory I was celebrating last night turns to ash. She wouldn't go back with him, would she? I hear a roaring in my ears, and all the blood drains out of my head. I have to bend over with my hands on my knees to keep from falling down.

"I'd give anything to hear his voice right now," I hear her saying, as if through a long tunnel. Her back is still to me. "You gotta admit it, Mike has a very sexy voice." She sits down on her suitcase. "Especially in the morning. He can sing, too. I love it when he sings."

I stand up. The blood comes back into my head with a rush. My vision fogs in from the edges, leaving me a circle to look through. There's a crow sitting on the dead branch of a pine tree in front of me. I watch it until the dizziness clears.

"I don't know," she says. "It's just how I feel." A trailer truck comes over the hill. I watch the crow flap slowly away, cawing. Grimshaw stands up.

"This one's ours," she says. The truck goes by with so much force it almost knocks us over. A long time passes before a green Dodge Ram stops, brand-new, one of those big ten-cylinder diesels that short guys like to drive. We throw our stuff in the back. He's a feed salesman from Indio, California, driving to a five-day convention in Kansas. It takes me an hour of failed attempts at conversation to get that much out of him. By Mono Lake, I'm completely drained. Hours and hours of sagebrush later, punctuated by billboards advertising slot machines at the next exit, he stops for a bathroom break at Boomtown, Nevada, a casino on Interstate 80.

"You girls wait right here," the feed salesman says. He locks up the truck, hikes up his pants, and heads into Boomtown. As soon as he's out of sight, I grab Grimshaw's suitcase out of the back and throw my backpack at her.

"We have to get away from him," I hiss.

"Why? He says he's driving to Kansas. That's, like, halfway home."

"But he was so boring," I groan.

"You find something better, fine," she says. "I'm not standing out there on that highway again."

"Okay," I say, backing away from her. "Take our stuff, go in there, and gamble or something. Just don't get back in that pickup." She rolls her eyes, picks up our stuff, and walks away.

A warm wind blows cigarette butts and dead leaves across the parking lot. Tractor-trailer trucks are lined up, snoring like a herd of sleeping buffalo. I head into the thick of them. I find a short, potbellied man standing next to a tank truck, tamping tobacco into a pipe. The name embroidered on the patch on his shirt in red thread is Bob.

"And what can I do for you, missy?" he says when he sees me. He's completely bald, with bushy brown eyebrows, mustache, and tufts on his earlobes.

"Bob, I'm headed east," I say breathlessly. "With my friend.

And we need a ride. But the thing is, we want to, you know, be able to have a decent conversation."

"You want a talker."

"Yes."

Bob squints at me, nods sagely, lights a match, squints at the horizon, and takes the first pull on his pipe. "I think I got a candidate. Can you wait?"

"Sure. I can wait." Bob climbs the ladder up into his truck. Soon, a voice comes through the speakerphone, and an exchange of code words gives way to an uninterrupted monologue, punctuated by Bob's laughter. Whoever Bob is talking to goes on and on and has a twang in his voice like I've never heard. He sounds more enthusiastic about life than you would expect a trucker to be, then they sign off.

"Yup," Bob says after a while, looking down at me through his open window. "Bo's a talker."

"He says he should be here in forty minutes or so," he informs me. "An older black Kenworth with a new flame job comes in, that'll be him. He'll wake me up when he gets here." Bob disappears into the recesses of his cab. I lean against the front bumper of Bob's truck and watch the girders of a high-tension line turn pink in the sunset, count the pigeons on the wires, and listen to the blues come crackling out of Bob's open windows. Night falls, trucks pull in and out of Boomtown, the evening star appears, fat and yellow, next to a fingernail of a moon, and then more stars come out, until the parking lot lights blink on and wash them out. Old people get off tour buses and file slowly into Boomtown, pushing walkers. Old people come out of Boomtown and get back on the buses.

I think about the guy whose voice I heard and wonder what he looks like. It seems like a lot more than forty minutes ago since I heard his voice. It occurs to me that Bo the Talker might not get here at all, and if he doesn't, I'm going to have to look for another ride. I feel a stab of disappointment about that, more than you would expect I would feel about someone I've never met before. I don't even know what direction he was coming from. I look as far as I can see to the west, where the daylight lingers in a purple glow in the sky. For a long minute, the highway is empty and silent. A pair of headlights comes over the horizon. I follow them with my eyes until they turn into a truck, which slows down and pulls into the Boomtown parking lot. It's a black Kenworth with an extensive orange and yellow flame job licking out from the wheel wells. It squeals around the entire perimeter of the parking lot at Boomtown before slowing down and then coming to a full stop in front of Bob's tank truck. The door opens, and a young guy swings down. He has long hair that goes past his shoulders. His green ball cap has a patch that reads IF IT AIN'T A CAT IT'S A DOG. He takes it off. He wears a flowered shirt, like the pattern of old-fashioned wallpaper. It's untucked on one side and unbuttoned enough to reveal a medallion against his chest, a little carving that looks like a cow horn. He's vain about his hair and scrunches it back up where the ball cap flattened it. If I had his hair, I'd be vain about it, too. I think it might be Bo the Talker.

We stare at each other for a minute. He shifts his weight to the other foot and hooks a thumb over his belt.

"This Bob's truck?" he asks me.

I recognize the banjo twang, but it's slower than when I first heard it on Bob's radio. It is Bo the Talker. It has to be. "Yes. He wants you to wake him up."

"You the one going—east, was it? 'Cause I'm going as far as Iowa."

"Sort of. But I have to go get my friend." I back away. "We'll be right back."

Boomtown smells like a nursing home. It has that thickness in the air that comes from trying to hide what a place really smells like. I walk by acres of slot machines, almost deserted except for a couple of old people feeding in quarters. I find Grimshaw by the card tables, standing with her arms crossed, staring intently at a game of blackjack.

"I could work in a place like this," she says when I come up to her. "I'd consider a career change."

I tug on her sleeve. "Come on."

"Not that I regret, you know, what I did. Experience is always a good thing."

"I got us a ride, a good one. Quick." I shoulder my pack, grab her suitcase with one hand and her with the other, and drag her through Boomtown again and out to the parking lot. When I see the Kenworth, I stop. Bo is standing in the headlights of his truck, next to the tank truck, talking to Bob.

"That's him," I whisper. I study her face for her reaction to him. "The tall one. Bo. What do you think?"

She whistles softly through her teeth. "Nice work, Serena. You found a young one. Very impressive. Any teeth?"

"Teeth?"

She shrugs. "Sometimes they go."

"He's says he's going to Iowa."

She keeps nodding and assessing. "I can see that I taught you well," she says.

"I got him on my first try."

"Don't tell him how far we're going, though," she whispers. "In case he's a psycho."

I take her arm, but she stays put. She's studying Bo. "He looks like a nice guy," she says. "I like the way he stands. You can tell a lot about a guy from the way he stands. Do you like him?"

"I just met him. Come on."

She still doesn't move. "Do you think he's smart enough for you?"

"Grimshaw! He's just a trucker. But I think he's smarter than he looks." I remember the long monologue I heard on the radio. "He has a lot of interests."

She nods. "Iowa's not that far away."

"It isn't?"

"Tell him—" She speaks slowly. "Tell him if he brings us all the way home, you'll give him the best kiss he's ever gotten in his life."

"Oh, come on. Do you even think that'll work?"

She just smiles that Mona Lisa smile of hers, picks up her suitcase, and walks toward them.

"Grimshaw!" I hurry after her. "Don't *you* try it, okay? Let me."

Once we get going, Grimshaw takes the passenger seat, gets nail polish remover and cotton balls out of her suitcase, and starts doing her nails. Boomtown has cheered her up. Maybe I'll never have to tell her about Mike. Maybe she'll just forget him. I sit on the hump in the middle. As advertised, Bo's a talker. When he first got out of the Marine Corps, oh, about a year and a half ago now, he worked for a big company and had a regular route, and he couldn't stand that, going the same place over and over again. He's an independent owner-operator now and can go where he wants, more or less. He's hauling rolls of synthetic rubber to a gasket factory in Iowa. He talks about gaskets for a long time, that same kind of flood-burst of words I first heard on Bob's radio, as he stares straight ahead of him at the white dotted line in his headlights. Gaskets are everywhere, it turns out, places you'd never expect—engines, tanks of all kinds—and made out of just about every kind of material you can imagine. Without gaskets, life would be a leaky, god-awful mess.

Maybe the feed salesman wouldn't have been so bad, I think. I'm not sure this guy notices that anyone else is in the truck with him. I steal a glance at Grimshaw, to see what she thinks of our gasket lesson. Her feet are braced against the dashboard, and by the light of the open glove box she is painting her fingernails blue. When she's done, she cracks the window and holds her hand up in the breeze. We watch a billboard go by, advertising slot machines.

"I've never gambled," she announces. "I have a feeling I'd be good at it."

"There's nothing to it," Bo says. "You put your money on the table, and they take it off. It's a very simple process."

Up ahead, a gas station sign floats in the darkness. Bo gears down, and the truck shudders to a stop. Inside are two one-armed bandits and a blackjack table. Except for a blonde girl in a tank top playing solitaire on the counter, the place is deserted. We stand next to the blackjack table and wait for her to notice us, which she appears to have decided not to do. She's chewing the biggest wad of green bubble gum I've ever seen. I notice a sign that says we have to be twenty-one to gamble.

"Hey!" Bo snaps his fingers at her. She looks up at him with flat blue eyes and blows a bubble half as big as her head. She snaps it back into her mouth and pushes herself away from her cards. She slaps across the floor in shower slippers.

"Three dollar chips," says Bo.

When Grimshaw and I take stools at the blackjack table, two men I hadn't noticed before materialize out of the magazine rack and join us. It takes me three cards to lose my chip, but Grimshaw wins and keeps on winning. She gives Bo his chip back, he slides it over to me, and I lose that one, too. Grimshaw's time in Boomtown obviously stood her in good stead. She has all the moves down—scratching the table with a card when she wants another one, holding her finger up when she's down. She never takes her eyes off the dealer. The girl wears press-on nails with rhinestones, which flash under the lights as the cards fly through her fingers. She keeps blowing those insolent green bubbles, though, until I can't stand it anymore. I go outside and watch the traffic, a line of diamonds and rubies strung across the dark country, under a sky that's twenty times more huge than any sky I've ever seen, with twenty times as many stars. Bo comes up and stands next to me.

"I don't blame you for wanting to leave Nevada," he says. "It's a rotten state."

"It feels like we've been in Nevada for a week."

"Yeah," he says. "Nevada's like that."

"I've never seen so many stars."

"When I was in Hawaii," he says, "you could see stars like anything." He points out the constellations, the dippers, the North Star, Orion going down, Hercules coming up.

"Where I come from," I tell him, "you have to look up to see the sky. The sky is like a river of stars between the trees."

"East? That's where I figured you were from. Where I grew up, you couldn't see 'em at all. Too many refineries."

"Oil refineries?"

"Oil. Petrochemicals."

"What's a refinery look like?"

"It's like you take all the lights in a city and compress them into one factory." He demonstrates the compressing motion with his hands. "But you can't really explain it. You just gotta see it."

"Where are you from again?"

"Texas. Not one of your garden spots. You never seen a refinery?"

"No."

"Never?"

"Never."

"Christ. Where you been?"

"Nowhere. I hardly know where I am right now."

"You better look at a map," Bo says. "I got a map for you to look at. Stay right there."

I watch him walk to his truck. He wears cowboy boots, and the denim on his back pocket is faded from where he sits on his wallet. I think about what Grimshaw said about how a man stands. He comes back with something rolled up under his arm. On the pavement under a streetlight, he spreads out an atlas of the United States, and we crouch over it.

"Here we go," Bo says, turning the pages. "Nevada. And there's Winnemucca. That's us. That little dot right there." As he talks, I watch his hands move across Nevada. It looks like all the grease of the world is under his fingernails and worked into the nicks on his knuckles. The pages of his atlas are soft with use and covered with arrows and circles in black and red ink. He tells me he has a thing for old iron bridges and he likes to visit them when he can. As he turns the pages of the atlas, I watch the world open up. All roads lead to all other roads, and I start to feel this intense curiosity about following them the way he does.

Grimshaw pokes her head out of the door. "They're closing," she calls to us. "If you want anything."

"Your friend must be winning," Bo says. "Otherwise they'd stay open." We go inside. Grimshaw is at the counter, counting out her chips.

"How much did you win?" I ask her.

"Enough," she says airily. "I'm definitely going to work in a casino. I wonder how much they pay."

"I think they hire dancers in casinos, too," I suggest.

"No. I'm going to be a real dancer from now on. I just have to figure out how to live." We walk across the parking lot to Bo's truck. An hour of winning at blackjack has put Grimshaw in a good mood. She chatters about her upcoming career, how she needs more training before she moves to New York. She looked into it some in LA and realized how far away she was from the precision and training of real dance, but when she's ready, she thinks she'll have something of her own to bring to it, her own perspective on it. While she talks, I study Bo's hands, wondering what they'd feel like on my skin and what my chances are of finding out. Grimshaw would know, if I could find the right moment to ask. By the Utah state line, though, she's asleep.

Across the Bonneville Salt Flats, Bo entertains me with his favorite moments from the call-in radio shows he listens to while he's driving across the country at night, psychic shows and religious shows. He says he gets ideas for songs from them. I tell Bo the plot of a play I started about a guy who murders his best friend and gets away with it by making it look like a motorcycle accident. But it turns out the murdered guy was an organ donor, so the murderer gets driven crazy by the thought of his frenemy living on in the bodies of all these grateful people, and he has to kill them all.

"I'm going to be a playwright," I tell him. "Or a speechwriter. I can't decide which."

"Either way," he says. "You got a future."

At a truck stop near Salt Lake City at midnight, the parking lot is full of VW campers and we buy veggie burritos from some cave hippies with dreadlocks and bones through their noses who offer to read our auras for twenty dollars apiece. From Salt Lake to the Wyoming border, the highway is dark, and the trucks are lit up like circus wagons. Bo tells me more stories, and I tell him more of my plots.

At sunrise, Bo can't drive anymore, and we check into a motel. We drag Grimshaw out of the truck and get a room with two double beds and all sleep past noon.

When I wake up, Grimshaw's in the shower and Bo is sitting on the edge of his bed arguing on the phone with his dispatcher.

"California!" he shouts. "I can't go to California! All right, I won't go, then. Either way. Tennessee. That's better. Give me Tennessee."

After breakfast, we get back in the truck and head east across Nebraska. The earth has just been plowed, and it's black and kind of heaving with fertility. Nothing's green yet, but you can feel it coming in the air. It pours through the open windows of the truck. We drop the rolls of synthetic rubber at the edge of a city in Iowa. We go into Missouri to pick up a trailer from a truck that broke down hauling potatoes to the Pringles potato chip factory in Jackson, Tennessee. Bo's been to the Pringles factory before, and he describes the Pringle-making process to me in detail, what they do to mountains of potatoes to make them stack in a can.

"God, that sounds really cool," I tell him.

"The place looks like a nuclear power plant," Bo says. I eye Grimshaw, wondering if she'd go for a scenic detour through Jackson, Tennessee, and decide to wait to bring it up until she's in a better mood, but the farther east we go, the gloomier she gets. Her every-twenty-minute sighs are back. At sunset, we drive into a truck stop next to a tank farm. Grimshaw crawls into the sleeper cab. She hasn't said a word all day.

"Come on." Bo holds out his hand to me as soon as we jump down from the truck. "I got something to show you." He tows me across the parking lot toward the trees. We head into the bushes, which are dripping wet from a recent rain. It's getting dark, and I stumble over rocks and almost trip a couple times, but he keeps pulling me forward. We break through the trees onto an asphalt path and turn right.

"Where are we going?" I pant.

"This way."

Around the next bend, we stop before a padlocked chain-link fence with thick iron bars that curve up over our heads. Bo grabs the bars of the gate.

"What is it?"

"Chain of Rocks," he says. "Nineteen twenty-nine." I peer through the gate, but all I see is what seems to be a bridge, a long iron bridge. I can't see the other side. "Here we go." Bo jumps, chins himself up on the bars, hooks a boot heel over, and then reaches down for me.

"Um . . ." I begin. "I don't think . . ."

"Just do it," he says.

It takes me three tries to get over the gate, but I manage it, and we drop down to the wooden deck of the bridge.

"There was a murder here last year," Bo explains. "A couple guys pushed a girl over the edge. So now they lock it up at night." He takes my hand and we walk out over an expanse of water. "Route 66 crossed the river here," he says softly, putting a hand on a girder and looking up at the web of steel. "Over a mile to the other side." The night is soft and warm. There are no lights along either side of the river, but a glow past the trees to the south provides a soft light.

"That's St. Louis," Bo says, pointing at the glow.

We walk a long way out to the middle of the bridge, where there is a scenic overlook hanging out over the water. I am just about to ask Bo about the name of the bridge when I notice just that, a chain of rocks, stretching across the river, partially submerged, creating a wake with a soft, rushing sound. I point at it.

"Is that the chain of rocks?"

"That's the chain of rocks."

"So what river is this?"

Bo looks at me and smiles. I smile back. "You can't guess what river this is?" he asks.

"No."

"That's St. Louis." He points at the glow above the trees.

"Yeah."

"Missouri."

"Yeah."

"And that's East St. Louis." He points at the glow on the other side of the river. "Illinois. And whatever river this is, it must be damn big, because the Chain of Rocks Bridge is a mile across."

"Yeah. So what river is it?"

He smiles and shakes his head. "You take your time. It'll come to you. We got all night."

"This bridge is a mile long?"

"That's right."

"And that's St. Louis, Missouri?"

"Yup."

"So this is . . . the Mississippi River?"

"Yup."

"Wow." Suddenly, I feel like weeping. I lean over the railing and let the tears drip off my nose. I wipe my eyes and my nose on my sleeve and stand up.

A barge glides by underneath us, a silent black shape followed by the rattling sound of a tugboat engine.

"I love how the river smells."

"What's it smell like?"

I inhale. "Mud. Oil. Tar. Faraway places. Like the road, a little, only different. On a river you can smell the whole world. A river smells like a big wet dog."

Bo laughs. "Good image," he says. "Maybe you smell me. I never did take that shower this morning. I was so worried the dispatcher was gonna send me back to California I forgot all about it."

"Have you always had a thing about bridges?"

"Always." He tells me old bridges inspire him, it's where he goes to write songs. Sometimes he sings them into his phone, sometimes he writes them down and then finds the tune later. We stay on the bridge for a long time. When I tell him the plot of *Huckleberry Finn*, how Huck and Jim probably went right past here on a raft, his arms are around me. When he tells me about his old-timey family in Texas, how he grew up singing in church, my ear is against his chest and his words sink into my skin. I ask him to tell me more about how he turns the stories he hears on call-in radio into songs, he says that everything you see and hear goes into a big hopper in your mind, and you can never tell what's going to come out in a song.

When we kiss, it's awkward at first. We don't really fit together right away. Fortunately, other forces are working in my favor. Going around the bend, a tugboat blows its horn, lonesome and romantic. The wind picks up and sighs through the girders of the bridge.

Just on the other side of the trees, trucks on the interstate hum east and west, and below us the river quietly flexes its muscles. Bo pulls me in close, and suddenly everything fits, like two halves of a broken bowl.

"Damn," he says. He takes a step away but leaves a hand on my back. "I wasn't going to put the moves on you."

"Why not?"

"I don't know." He sighs. "I don't like one-night stands. I always feel empty the next day." He brushes his hand up and down my back. "When I first saw you leaning against the bumper of Bob's truck, I thought I must be dreaming. I thought, *There is no way that anyone that pretty is standing in a parking lot in Boomtown waiting for a ride.*" He looks down at me. "I like you," he says. "A lot, but—you're so . . . educated."

"Hardly."

"Hardly," he mimics. "See? You been to college?"

"No."

"Me neither. You finish high school?"

"No."

"GED?"

"No."

"I got mine in the corps." He sighs. "I guess I'm kind of conservative that way." He holds my face in his hands, his forehead to mine. He looks off at the river. "I don't know," he says. "I've never met anybody like you."

"What am I like?"

"You're so sure you're right." He puts his arm around me, and we walk off the bridge back to Illinois. We take the bike path up the steep riverbank and then find the parking lot again through the underbrush.

And then there's the truck.

Is that it? Isn't he supposed to take charge, somehow, of something? Isn't that the deal? That's how it always worked with Grimshaw. All she had to do was be pretty, and they figured out the rest. But Bo is just walking toward his truck. I hurry ahead and step in front of him. He stops. My hands start flailing wildly. "I, I—" I stammer. "I just want to—" I look at him, wanting him to guess what I want. He puts his hands in his pockets and waits. "I want to sleep with you tonight." It comes out loud and wrong, a desperate cry clanging against the softness of the night and ruining the rightness of everything that's happened so far.

"Yeah." Bo nods. "I want that, too."

I run to get my backpack out of the Kenworth while Bo rents us a room.

"Sst, Grimshaw," I hiss into the dark cab. No response. "Grimshaw!" I repeat, a little louder. Silence. "You got a condom?" The curtain flings open.

"Se-*re*-na!"

211

"Well, do you?"

"With a *trucker*?"

"Why, are truckers beneath us now?"

She coughs her disdain.

"Just give me the damn condom." The curtain shuts.

"Grimshaw . . ." I plead. Out comes the condom. I snatch it.

"Slut," she says.

"Bitch," I hiss back. I slam the door as hard as I can. Bo comes walking toward me. We meet in the middle of the parking lot. He tosses me a key attached to a big wooden stick. It looks like the restroom key to a filling station.

"Room thirty-three," he says, walking toward the truck. "I gotta go get my gym bag."

I hold up his gym bag. "I got it."

He stops and slowly pivots around to face me. "You got it," he says.

"It was on the front seat." All I can see is his silhouette. We walk toward the strip of doors, staying about five feet apart.

"You sure this is the right thing to do?" he asks.

"No." I find room thirty-three and jam the key into the lock. I jiggle the handle and kick the door. The room smells like mildew, urine, Lestoil, and stale tobacco, covered over by artificial strawberry air freshener. There are two huge beds. I throw Bo's gym bag on the first one, my backpack on the second one, go into the bathroom, strip, and get in the shower. I lean my head against the shower wall and let the water beat on my back. The water is so chlorinated it makes my eyes burn. When I put my clothes on and come out into the room, Bo's looking out the window at his truck. Without saying a word, he picks up the gym bag and goes into the bathroom. The shower starts. The wallpaper room features little amoebic shapes with specks in them, like magnified germs. The drapes and bedspreads are green. The carpet is orange. It's the ugliest place I've ever been.

Bo showers for a long time. I'm staring up at the ceiling when he comes out. He's rubbing his head with a towel. He has blue jeans on and no shirt. I close my eyes. When I open them, he's looking out at his truck again, through the slats of the Venetian blinds.

"I don't even know where you're headed," he says.

"New York."

"City?"

"State. We started in LA."

"She doesn't seem very happy."

"She's not."

"Are you a dancer, too?"

"No." I tell him the story of me and Grimshaw, which leads to the part about her wanting to be a stripper, which leads to the part about Mike Lyle and LA and the postcard and the bus trip out. I take him right up through how Melody left me asleep on the dirty laundry pile in the dressing room at the Over Easy.

"Was your plan—to try to seduce the boyfriend to get him to break up with her?" he asks.

"It was more like survival than a plan. But, yeah. I guess that was the plan."

"And it worked?" he asks.

I nod again. "She's out there in the truck." Bo comes over and sits across from me on the other bed.

He jerks his thumb at the window. "Does she know? About your plan?"

"Are you kidding me? If she knew . . . oh my God. But she doesn't know. No, she's not going to. I was going to tell her about it, about what happened. I tried to. But it's too late now."

Bo shakes his head. "It's a dangerous game, saving people. Usually, they hate your guts for it. I should know."

"I didn't mean to save her."

"So did this guy do anything to you?"

"Well, not exactly. I left him thinking something would happen later, after he broke it off with her. At the club, I was asleep in the dressing room, out cold, and Grimshaw comes storming in with her suitcase, talking about how she's always hated his guts, and she throws my backpack on me and says, 'Let's go, we're going home,' and by then it's early morning and we're out on the road, and that's pretty much the end of the story." The only part I leave out is that Grimshaw and I are still in high school, or at least I am.

When I stop talking, he's quiet for a long time. At first, I regret having told him anything. I wish he still saw me as this educated girl stranded on the shores of I-80. I feel dirty, like the whole thing's just too sordid. Then I think through the whole scenario again, starting with Grimshaw's postcard. I think about what would have happened if I'd gone straight home from Western Civ that day, if I'd not pilfered my mom's wallet, not gotten on the bus, not showed up at Grimshaw's gate, and not provoked Mike Lyle. Nothing, that's what. Something is better than nothing.

It has to be. This is America, after all. So I don't have anything to worry about, morally.

"You're still in high school, aren't you?" Bo finally asks.

"I'm a senior. I'm on my spring vacation."

He nods. "That notebook should have tipped me off."

He sits on the edge of the bed. He takes my hand, opens it up, and traces the lines with his fingers.

"You're a good friend. See? Right there."

"That one? It ends."

"I'm just kidding around. I don't know anything about it. I just wanted to hold your hand. But you don't have to know how to read palms to know you're a good friend."

"That's what everyone says," I sigh. "Everyone but her."

"Yeah," he says. "That's usually the way." He climbs over me and lies down next to me on the other side of the bed on top of the covers. He puts his hands under his head. I turn toward him under the covers.

"You have skinny arms," I tell him.

"Yup." He holds them out. "Long and skinny. My old man always says that's why God put pockets on blue jeans."

"Are you ticklish?" I ask.

He slaps his arms down to his sides. I have an intuition that the small of his back is vulnerable. I attack it under the covers. Bull's-eye. He screams, I mean, literally screams with high-pitched laughter. So I keep it up. He attacks back, but to no avail—I am the least ticklish person in America. We roll around laughing and wrestling and yelling. We end up on the floor between the beds wrapped up in the covers like a burrito, with only one thin layer of blanket between us. Somebody bangs on the wall next to our heads. Bo grabs two pillows off the bed for us and props his head on his hand.

"So you've tried saving people, too?" I ask him.

"Yeah. And I really screwed it up."

He starts telling me how stupid and mean and lazy his brother Jason got after he quit school. The marines wouldn't take him because he didn't score high enough on their test, he was too proud to work in fast food, and he couldn't get a real job because nobody was hiring dropouts, although his father pulled every string he could at the refinery. So he got in more and more trouble, out of boredom. Finally, Jason seemed to get it together. St. Luke's, the hospital in Beaumont where he had a temp job doing maintenance, hired him on full-time. He got a car and a steady girlfriend.

"Priscilla," Bo says, and then stops.

One day, Priscilla shows up at the high school and wants to see Bo. It's important. She's running away, and she wants Bo to tell Jason why. Remember that story in the papers, she starts, about the crack addict who was found half dead and tied to the bed in an Econo Lodge? Well, that was Jason. He did it. He traded crack for sex, and then afterwards the girl told him she had HIV. She thought it was funny. Jason grabbed her by the hair, she kicked him in the nuts, and then Jason lost it. He wasn't used to smoking crack. He came home and told Priscilla everything. For a long time, they thought the girl was brain-dead, but now she was coming out of her coma. She was still hooked up to tubes, but she would be ready to talk to the police as soon as the doctors thought she was up to it. She's at St. Luke's, Priscilla said. Jesus, Bo said. You don't think he'd do anything, do you? Talk to Jason before his shift starts, she begged. Tell him. He won't listen to me. Why would he listen to me? Bo asked her. I'm just his kid brother. I don't know, I'm too scared, Priscilla said. I can't deal with shit like this.

"So I turned him in," Bo says. "Before his shift started, I called the cops. And it turns out the girl was so messed up already, she didn't remember a damn thing. All she remembered was getting soda cans out of the machine to make pipes. When he sat in front of her in court, she had no idea who he was."

"Maybe you thought he'd get help," I suggest. That makes Bo laugh. Not in Texas.

Nobody in his family has spoken to him since that day. Not even his old man, not even after Bo joined the marines.

"Stubborn son of a bitch," Bo says.

"I think they're making a terrible mistake."

"I stabbed him in the back. My own brother."

"Yeah, but—"

"But nothing."

"But—"

"No buts."

"But—"

He rolls on top of me and stops my mouth with a long kiss.

"You want to defend me," he says.

"Yes."

"Defend my honor."

"Yes."

"Say I did the right thing."

"You did—"

He kisses me again.

"Just because I'm a nice guy," he whispers in my ear, "doesn't mean I did the right thing. Remember that now."

I push him off me and sit up. "You think too much," I tell him. "Riding the roads all day and all night, brooding on the past."

"Well," he says, "I just met someone who's as big a fool as me." He puts an arm under his head. "So now I've got something else to think about."

I look down at him. "You don't think I did the right thing?"

"Sure," he says. "You did the right thing. Take it to the bank. But it's like you said, you set bigger things in motion, things you can't control. Yesterday I was hauling gaskets to Iowa, wondering if I could stand the boredom for another day. Today I'm in a crummy hotel in East St. Louis, talking to you."

I try to get back that feeling I had that first night out from LA, while Grimshaw played pool and I drank whiskey at the bar, the feeling that I had won, and that I was right, and that everything was going to work out. But the feeling isn't there anymore. Grimshaw is out there in the truck, certain that the closer she gets to Colchis, the farther she's getting from her dream.

"We really don't know very much, do we?"

"We sure don't. The smart ones know how stupid they are."

"So they can forgive themselves?"

"Maybe."

Against the white of his skin, there is a triangle of chest hair. I put my hand on it. I slide my hand down his chest and feel his stomach muscles tighten. In the shadow his eyes reflect an unseen source of light, and they're fastened on me. In this swirl of right and wrong, good intentions and bad outcomes, there's only one thing I'm sure of right now. Only one thing is certain. And that's what I want.

He reaches his hand up to me. I pull him off the floor, and we get into bed.

Next morning, I come into the truck stop diner, wearing Bo's white T-shirt and his leather jacket. He's on a pay phone somewhere, having a big argument with his dispatcher about whether someone else can take the potatoes to Tennessee so that he can secretly drive us the rest of the way home. I walk up to Grimshaw, who's in the back of the restaurant. She rips open a packet of sugar and slowly stirs it into her cup of coffee.

"Hi."

She raises her eyes and fixes me with a hostile gaze. A guy in white with a paper hat on his head goes by behind me, dragging a mop and a garbage can on wheels. I lean forward to get out of his way. She watches him walk by. I sit down.

"Here. Have another one." Grimshaw flips a condom across the table at me. She jerks her head at the janitor. "In case he wants to do you behind the dumpster."

I feel like I've been socked in the stomach. "Jesus," I say when I get my breath back. "I didn't even use the first one. We didn't do *that*." I dig the condom she gave me out of my pants pocket. "Here. You can have this one back if you want it."

"Do you have any pride?" she asks. "Any? Any at all?" She's almost spitting at me. "Where is he, anyway? I want to go. He better drive us home now."

"Pride? I can't believe who I'm hearing this from."

"At least I didn't drag you around behind every little thing that stuck to the bottom of my shoe."

"Your boyfriend"—I lean over the table and speak slowly— "is *scum*. I wouldn't have him on the bottom of my shoe." Grimshaw, who has never lost a staring match, looks away.

"And he thought you were so innocent," she says finally.

"He did *not* think I was so innocent."

Something about the way I say that snaps her attention back to me. Grimshaw looks at me very closely for a minute and narrows her eyes. Her lips get very thin. This time I look away.

"I think we're getting a ride the rest of the way," I say quickly. "So that's good news. We just have to drop this load of potatoes. Bo's calling his dispatcher now and—"

"What did you tell him?"

"Who?"

"You know who I mean."

"Mike? Nothing!"

"It was you, wasn't it?" she says.

"No!" I protest.

Grimshaw gets up and walks out of the restaurant. "I didn't tell him anything!" I call after her. My voice is high and squeaky and guilty as hell. I follow her to the door and watch her walk to

Bo's truck. A waitress comes and leaves a coffeepot on our table, so I sit back down to wait for Bo. My hands are shaking so bad it's hard to open the little creamers. I put six of them in my coffee, until I run out of room in the cup. A few minutes later, Grimshaw comes back, and she's carrying those stupid rose flannel sheets, and she dumps them on the table in front of me. My coffee spills down the front of Bo's T-shirt.

"I was making money," she says. "Real money, my own money. I was about to start taking dancing lessons. Real dance. For the first time in my life. Not that shit you saw, but the real thing. In a studio. Nobody cared that I was a Grimshaw. Nobody knew the church paid for me to see the dentist. For about three months, I had a life. And then you came."

"I didn't know the stupid church—what does it matter?"

"I'm leaving." She jabs her finger in my face. "You can sleep with anyone you want—go back and do Mike if that's what you did, but don't you dare follow me." She stalks out as I sit there gasping for air. I grab my backpack with one hand, the sheets with the other, and run out into the parking lot, dragging the sheets through the cigarette butts and the oil spills. She's climbing into the cab of the worst-looking rusted wreck of a Mack truck I've ever seen. The motor's running. The truck driver gets in, grinning. When he sees me standing on the running board, the grin disappears. He pushes his hat up and scratches his forehead.

"You didn't tell me you had a friend," he says.

"I don't," she says.

I push the sheets through the window, open the door, and climb in. Bo's truck is next to us, engine running. But he's nowhere in sight. So we ride into the eastern third of the US in silence. Although we're wedged together in the front seat, Grimshaw makes sure she doesn't look at me, speak to me, or touch me. I ball up her sheets and stuff them under my feet. In the pocket of Bo's jacket, I find a jackknife and a comb. When I woke up this morning, less than an hour ago, I was lashed to his side like a lifeboat with those long, skinny arms. My body feels different than it's ever felt. It's like he woke it up. So now I'm the one who's sighing and sniffling, and Grimshaw is stiff and silent. The truck we're in is so old it has a CB radio. For hours across Illinois, the driver whistles tunelessly, plays sentimental hits on the radio, and makes wretchedly sexist comments about us to other drivers on the road. Just when you think you've met the all-time loser of the universe, another contender comes along. His CB name seems to be Two by Four.

"Hey, buddy," comes through the static. "Can ya handle it?"

"I figure I'll just watch first."

He uses this line on several different passing trucks, and it always gets a laugh.

"They don't talk much," he says to one trucker.

"Jesus, that's beautiful."

"Don't brag, now."

"The one is pretty cute, but the other one looks like she's been fed rat poison."

"Let her sit on the gearshift. That'll perk her up."

"I'll let her sit on *my* gearshift," Two by Four giggles. He catches me looking at him and waggles his tongue at me. Grimshaw sits between us and stares straight ahead of her.

Midwestern towns and Midwestern fields roll by, looking even flatter and dingier than they did from the bus. At a rest stop in Indiana, I put the sheets in a dumpster. At four in the morning, we pull in to a warehouse in Toledo. I spend an hour unloading boxes of champagne glasses and giving them to guys with hand trucks, while Two by Four watches and treats us all to a monologue on life and race and politics in America. Grimshaw stays in the cab. We spend half a day's agony in a truck stop near Pittsburgh, Pennsylvania, waiting for him to get another trailer. He locked all our stuff in his cab so we can't look for another ride.

During this whole time, I say one sentence to my friend: "Once we get going, we should be there soon." They're the first words that have passed between us since Illinois, and she ignores them. When we do get underway again, Grimshaw falls asleep. Two by Four sits so he can look down her shirt while she sleeps. His left hand is down the front of his pants. I take off Bo's coat and flex my muscles while I slick back my hair with Bo's comb. I tuck the comb into the pocket of Bo's blue jeans. Then I take out Bo's jackknife and push my cuticles back. It's alpha male behavior. I'm hoping it'll register subconsciously, I don't want to have to actually knife him. He's wasted enough of our time already. For most of the night, I fight off sleep—unsuccessfully, because I wake up just as we're driving past a large brown sign that says DELAWARE WATER GAP. I look up at leafy cliffs silhouetted in blue mist and backlit by the first pink rays of dawn. I'm still holding the open jackknife. By the time Grimshaw wakes up, we're puttering through suburban side streets, which are slowly filling up with weekday morning commuters.

223

"Where the—"

"You ladies get some beauty sleep?" the driver asks.

"Hell?" she asks.

"New Jersey," I tell her. "The license plates."

She blinks at me. "New Jersey?"

"You know," our hero says as the truck shudders up a hill, "I took a big risk taking you ladies on. It's ee-legal for you to even be sitting in this truck. So I figure I'm about due for a little, ah"—he grins and winks—"compensation."

"You know," I observe, "if you'd try downshifting, your truck might not stall." His grin disappears.

"You telling me how to drive?" he asks.

"No." I study my fingernails. "It was just a thought." As we crawl forward, the truck starts to shimmy and clack.

"Damn load's too heavy," the driver mutters. We hear a horrible grinding noise, and then a huge crack underneath us. "Jesus," he says. "I hope that wasn't the u-joint." The truck stands still for a minute and then it starts to move backward. Behind us, about twenty cars start honking their horns. I look out the side-view mirror, and a long hill stretches behind us, heading into a busy intersection. I grab the door handle with one hand and Grimshaw's sleeve with the other.

"Grimshaw, jump!" I shout.

The driver cranks the steering wheel, hard, and the truck jackknifes, swerves, tips up on a curb, and stops.

"You wait here!" he barks at us. "Close that door!"

I'm standing on the running board, pulling on Grimshaw's arm. "Grimshaw, get out."

"But he said—"

"Come on!" I yank her out of the cab. The wheels of the trailer are on the sidewalk and the back end of the truck is about two feet from the front door of a little white church. Grimshaw looks dazed. I get her suitcase out from behind the seat. It's a lot lighter without the sheets. I hoist my backpack and take her by the hand. On the other side of the street, a line of commuters in trench coats and sneakers are holding up their phones. We run across the street and get in line behind them just as a bus pulls up.

"Where are we again?" Grimshaw asks. I point at downtown Manhattan, pale blue in the early morning haze.

"That's New York City," I tell her. "You made it." Her eyes open wide. Just as we're about to board, Two by Four boils out from behind the bus.

"Did you steal my wrenches?" he yells. "Let me look in that suitcase!"

I give him the finger and push Grimshaw onto the bus.

"Lezzies!" he screams.

The bus is warm and humid, and the motor makes a soothing grumble. The last thing I remember telling Grimshaw is that the daffodils are out in New Jersey already. At the Port Authority Bus Terminal, she needs to shake me awake. We get in line to purchase two tickets to Colchis. Having to backtrack like this gives me a strange feeling of completion. If we had stopped at Buffalo without going all the way to the East Coast, I would have felt like I had written a long, long sentence and then never punctuated it. The problem is, we only have Grimshaw's winnings from Winnemucca to pay for two bus tickets, and eighty-five dollars only buys a ticket and a quarter. She pulls a fifty-dollar bill out of her shoe and passes it through the window.

"My last tip," she says.

After a long wait, a change in Albany, another long layover, and another night spent traveling, the bus pulls in behind Al's Superette. The obvious thing for me to do is walk over to the school. Grimshaw picks up her suitcase and walks straight-backed from the bus to Ruby's pickup truck, which is waiting for her with its motor running. She must have borrowed a phone and called home while I was asleep. I have enough pride, barely, not to stand on the sidewalk and watch the back of her head and Ruby's taillights disappear.

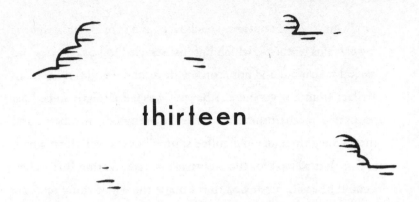

thirteen

IN THE WEEK THAT I was gone, Colchis has changed utterly. It now looks like an abandoned movie set with the facades propped up by sticks. It's shrunk to about half the size it was before I left. When I climb the steps of the school and open the front door, I'm surprised to find the lobby on the other side. But it seems to be real. There are the closed doors of the auditorium, the junior high corridor to the left, with handpainted signs for upcoming dances and fund-raisers, the stairs leading to the administration offices to the right. I climb the stairs and walk into math class a minute after the bell rings.

"You're late," Mr. Rallis barks at me.

I look up at the clock. My classmates are sitting motionless with their textbooks open in front of them. It's my turn to say something.

My usual chair waits for me in its usual spot. I walk to it and sit down to the same graffiti on the desk. Mr. Rallis stays focused on me. I look up into his small, glittering eyes.

"Did you bring your textbook to class, Serena?" he asks.

"Um . . ." I zip open my backpack, and sure enough, there is my calculus textbook, which has just traveled to Los Angeles and back. I take it out and put it on my desk, and we all stare at it, an artifact from a bygone era. I haven't washed my hair since East St. Louis, haven't brushed it since the bathroom in Albany, and there's a big three-day-old coffee stain all over my T-shirt, which is Bo's. If it weren't for the fact that I'm also wearing Bo's jacket, I could be easily persuaded that I made the whole thing up.

"Take out your homework," Mr. Rallis directs.

"Homework," I repeat. I can see that everyone else has their homework out, just like they do at the beginning of every class.

"Miss Velasco, did you *do* the problems that were assigned to you over spring break?"

While Mr. Rallis stares at me, I spool through my spring break. It flows through my mind in no particular order, the long miles of America through the dirty windows of the bus, the club in LA where Grimshaw worked, the guy at the bus station in Chicago who told me that people in St. Louis murdered each other for twenty bucks.

"No, I'm afraid I didn't get to it, Mr. Rallis."

"Nine days of vacation, and you couldn't manage sixteen math problems?"

"Um, no, I didn't get to it. I'm sorry."

"Don't feel sorry for me, miss," he yells, clumping up and down aisles. "I'm not the one getting a zero. You're not off to a particularly good start, here. You don't want to get knocked off your perch, do you?"

"I can get it to you tomorrow," I offer.

228

"Ah." Mr. Rallis stops and puts his finger in the air. "Aha. Tomorrow, she says. *Mañana.* So. Ten days is the magic number, is it? X equals ten. Not nine, but ten. Ah yes, the precision, the exactitude, of math. If only vacation were ten days long instead of nine, there would be no problem. Is that it?" His sarcasm washes over me and sinks in like the next wave on the beach.

"Mr. Rallis, I don't think I'm the one with the problem."

He spins on his heel and stares at me. He points at the door. "Get out!"

So I go to the girls' room to wait out math class. I sit on the windowsill and close my eyes. I'm trying hard to hang on to what Bo's face looked like, but it's already fading. Another bell rings. I walk down the hall to my mother's office instead. She's in there with the chairman of the school board. I watch them through the plate glass door to her office. Before Mrs. Kmiec can stop me, I open the door and walk in.

"Hi, Mom."

The chairman frowns at me. "Can you excuse us, please?"

"Serena!" My mom comes around her desk and runs toward me. She hugs me—not a stiff hug, not a conditional hug, but a real hug. Both of her arms get involved. "Oh, Serena. Thank God you're back. What an odyssey." She holds me at arm's length. "Look at you." Tears are in her eyes. "It changed you."

"It's the jacket," I tell her. "It makes me look tough. Were you worried about me?"

She smiles. "Well . . . yes and no. I knew God was watching, and He's pretty tough Himself. I prayed a lot. What else could I do? But I am glad you're back." She keeps an arm around me as

229

she turns back to the chairman. "Dick, thanks for coming by. I need to take my daughter out to eat. She looks like she hasn't had a square meal in a week."

It takes her so long to arrange to leave the office for breakfast that it's lunchtime when we pull up in front of the diner. She orders each of us a Reuben sandwich.

"So what did the chairman want?" I ask.

"Oh, the chairman," she scoffs. "His digestion is off because . . ." She sighs. "He's actually in a very fragile position these days. He's running for state assembly this fall, but he's got this young guy to his right—telegenic, handsome, full of zeal—creating problems for him in the primary. The chairman's trying to stick to the issues, but he needs the school to be a platform."

While she talks, I squint at her. She's been snarled up in school board politics for so long she thinks it's reality. There's something different about her, though. I can't exactly identify it. The suit's the same, the earrings, the hair color, the wrinkles are in the same place, but there's some—nervousness—around her eyes that seems new. Our Reubens come. We both take big bites.

"Oh!" She spits her first bite out into her napkin. "Grace." She reaches across the table, seizes me by both my hands, switches into her prayer voice, and thanks the Lord for bringing me home safely. That done, she talks school board politics straight through lunch. When the Reubens are done, she's ready to listen. She orders a cup of coffee, and I have another Reuben.

"Now tell me about your trip," she says. "How's Melody?"

So I sketch in the basics—the postcard, the bus trip, LA, how we got home.

"And she's in a relationship with Mike Lyle, I understand? How is that going?"

"Well, he's actually really crude and—"

She takes a sip of coffee and holds up her hand. "I just think we should be really careful not to project your own cultural expectations. Mike, and also Melody, haven't been exposed to—well, let's call it the finer things in life. They do the best they can with what they have."

So I leave out the Mike Lyle part. I leave out Bo. I don't mention Two by Four. I tell it like it was a big, inconsequential adventure, and by the end of the story, that's what it is. I might as well have gone to Disney World. "Except that halfway across the country, Grimshaw got mad at me, and now she won't speak to me," I finish.

"Oh, that won't last," Mom says.

She tells me a story about her best friend Judy, whom I've never heard of, about how they were roommates in grad school and then had a falling-out over a misunderstanding and how devastated she was. And how she spent years trying to patch things up and then finally Judy had a baby and ever since then they've exchanged Christmas cards.

"So things have a way of working themselves out for the best, honey." She squeezes my hand. "Never underestimate the healing power of time."

Honey? Since when have I been "honey"? I look at her closely. She's on something. She starts telling me that when she was young she had no role models, and so she learned to have faith in life, that life itself was her greatest teacher, and to learn from it sometimes you just have to live in the world on the world's terms, and that's what I was doing, and while I was gone, she kept having to decide to live in faith rather than fear, and she thanked me for that opportunity to reaffirm the power of prayer.

"Well," she says brightly. "I have an appointment at three with the superintendent. Oh—Allegra's home! For a week. It was a total surprise." She tells me the school year ended early and she came home with a friend.

"They got here a few nights ago."

When I get home, the first thing I see is my bike. It seems like the most natural thing in the world to swing a leg over it and ride to the cemetery, where Grimshaw will be waiting for me, except I know that she won't. An icy feeling clamps onto the small of my back. For the first time, it occurs to me that I might have done something very wrong. Not the kind of wrong you can apologize for, but a permanent wrong, an irrevocable wrong, a wrong someone doesn't have to forgive you for. An adult wrong. The feeling follows me into the house and upstairs to the portico roof, where I find Allegra and her friend sipping what looks like minted sun tea out of a mayonnaise jar. When I climb through the window, Allegra sits up and shades her eyes.

"Saints preserve us," she says lazily. "If it ain't the teenage runaway." She lies back down and closes her eyes. "Serena, Robyn. Robyn, Serena."

"Hi, Robyn."

"Hi, Serena. Nice jacket."

"Tea?" asks Allegra, holding up the mayonnaise jar.

"No, thanks. I had a big lunch with Mom."

"Have you been sucking up to the principal again?" Allegra asks.

"You know I've always been a suck-up. That's what explains my success in life." I take off Bo's jacket, shirt, and pants. I ball his coat up into a pillow and put it under my head. Trading dirty clothes for sun is good.

"There are actually two jugs of tea," Robyn explains. "Virgin, and experienced."

"What's it experienced with?"

"Bourbon," says Allegra.

"I'm from Kentucky," Robyn explains.

"Where is everybody?" I take a sip from the mayo jar of experience. "Damn. This is really good."

"Aaron's playing ultimate Frisbee somewhere," Robyn says. "Spending the night with a friend. Zack's at extended day care with Nora."

"Which reminds me." Allegra puts a hand on Robyn's arm. "We better not get too drunk. We have to pick him up at six o'clock."

"I'm not that drunk," Robyn says. "I'll get him."

I eye Robyn and frown. For a newcomer, she seems awfully breezy, somehow, with family information.

Allegra sits up. "I'll stop drinking, too," she announces. "I'll cook." She pulls on her T-shirt.

"I'll stop, too." I take another sip.

"Since we've been here, Mom and Scot don't have to come home much," Allegra explains. "Robyn and I act as the collective soccer mom."

"When do you go back to school?" I ask her.

"I don't. I quit."

"You quit *college*?"

"Mom didn't tell you?"

"No."

"The whole thing reminded me way too much of what I went through last summer in Maine," Allegra says. "I was out of my league with those summer people. They weren't real friends, not like I have here."

They exit through the bedroom window.

After they go, I keep sipping the tea. The sun goes down and the tree frogs start trilling and a warm breeze wafts off Mizerak's fields, bringing the smell of turned earth. The moon is a few days bigger than it was over the parking lot at Boomtown, Nevada, and it seems like a different moon. I never even found out Bo's last name. Bo from Texas. That's all I knew about him. Now that's all he'll ever be. I get up to go inside and I jump when I see someone standing over me, waiting for me, silhouetted in the window. It's Allegra.

"You scared me," I tell her. "How long were you standing there?"

"I was thinking about college," she says. "I didn't know who I was there."

I look down at my notebook. "I don't know who I am here."

"We're really different, aren't we, that way?" she muses. "Anyway, we're going to go downtown to get some food." After they're gone, the streetlights blink on over the empty house lots, and I start writing in my upward mobility notebook. Even if everything that happened was a dream, it's still a dream I don't want to forget. One week in my life when I really lived, when what I did, for better or worse, actually had consequences.

Many pages later, Robyn and Allegra have long since come back, and Nora and Zack are bouncing on Mom and Scot's bed and screaming a shrill song about underwear. I shut the notebook and go inside to take a shower.

After the kids go to bed, I sit down in front of some cold pizza and start telling Allegra and Robyn about my trip, starting with the postcard. By eleven o'clock, I've just gotten to the part in Grimshaw's kitchen where I shut the door in Mike Lyle's face. When Mom comes home, the three of us race upstairs and dive on my bed.

"Serena!" Allegra hisses. "You seduced Mike *Lyle*?"

"I didn't seduce him exactly," I explain. "I just took advantage of his reptilian brain."

"Who is he?" asks Robyn. "Is he famous?"

"Only within about twenty yards of the football field. He was big stuff back in the day."

"One of those," says Robyn. "The savior of the high school, Jesus for a year."

"I wish I hadn't done it, though," I tell them.

"Except your friend would never have left him if you hadn't provoked him," points out Robyn.

"Except my friend didn't want to leave him."

"Then why did she?"

"He sort of broke up with her, and she left. She's very proud."

"Then he's a prick and you did her a favor."

"Except now she hates my guts."

"She'll get over it."

"You don't know Grimshaw."

It occurs to me that the sharpest image from that whole event is the one I haven't told anyone about, the black body stocking stretched like a rope in between Mike Lyle's hands. It still has the power to scare me, even safe in my own home, even with him all the way across the country.

"He actually sort of threatened me," I blurt out. "For real."

"Well, you're very provocative, Serena," says Allegra. "You know you have a big mouth."

"Still, threatening is not cool," says Robyn. "Did he literally threaten you, with words?"

"Well, not exactly with words, per se."

Allegra turns to Robyn. "Do you have any idea how many times I've wanted to kill my sister with my bare hands?"

"Not the same," she argues back.

At one a.m., Scot comes home, and I've just described our night at the Lone Pine Indian Reservation. He knocks on Allegra's bedroom door, kisses my forehead, tousles my hair, and leaves without saying a word. We go into the bathroom to brush our teeth.

"What's up with Mom and Scot?" I whisper. I turn on the water so my voice won't echo.

"Nothing," Allegra says.

"Is Mom on pills or something?" I ask. "She seemed weird today."

"She just got off them, you idiot." Allegra drops the toothpaste cap on the floor and bumps her head on the sink standing up. "She *went* on them after that fiasco you perpetrated last summer."

The three of us go to bed. Allegra's in the middle. "Turn out the light," she says. I turn out the light. "And don't talk anymore."

"You don't think Scot's having an affair?" I ask into the darkness.

Allegra rolls over with her back to me. "Serena, go to sleep. Just because your life is a melodrama doesn't mean everybody's is."

"What about Nanci Lee?" I ask.

"What about her? She lives with that cop. Now shut up."

"What cop?"

"The one that fixes Mom's speeding tickets all the time. The weight lifter."

"Oh." I think about the time I surprised Scot in the Crossways Tavern, and how he seemed much more relaxed with Nanci Lee than he's ever seemed here. I have an image in my mind of the two of them, how they fit together comfortably on the bar stools, reading the paper. Maybe some people just fit together—their broken edges fit together and make them whole again—like Bo and I did for just one night. The fact that Mom and Scot don't fit together probably matters more than any affair he might be having.

"Scot sold another lot," she says. "So he works during the day and does contracting at night. He's not having an affair. He's too busy."

"Oh."

"Sorry to disappoint you."

"I thought they were having an affair," I tell her. "I better rewrite that part of my upward mobility notebook."

"Your what notebook?" Robyn asks.

"I keep a notebook for Western Civ, as part of an independent study, and it sort of turned into a lot of other things. It made the trip to Los Angeles with me."

"That sounds interesting."

I turn on the light again, zip open my backpack, find my notebook, and show it to her. She leafs through it, reading parts, and for some reason none of this bothers me.

"Very picaresque." Allegra puts the pillow over her head. "Who's—" Robyn turns the notebook upside down. "William John Pabo?"

"Who?"

Allegra sits up and snatches it away from her. "From Beaumont, Texas?" she reads.

I take the notebook from them. On the back inside cover, in Grimshaw's handwriting, is the name and address of William John Pabo, from Beaumont, Texas, complete with zip code and telephone number. I put my face in my hands.

"So who is he? William John Pabo?" Allegra smiles. "Tell."

I tell them the rest of the story. To get from Boomtown through New Jersey all the way back to Colchis takes until three in the morning.

"So," Robyn says when I'm more or less done. "That's Bo's leather coat, then."

"Shit," Allegra says, reaching for the notebook and looking

at the address again. "Now that you know his address, you'll have to have a moral crisis about whether to send it back to him."

"Allegra," Robyn says, "look at her."

I'm still staring down at Grimshaw's handwriting, wondering if I'll ever see her again. Allegra puts her arms around me. "You're in love," she says. "I don't believe it. Our little girl is growing up."

There is about a month left to the school year. In Western Civ, we're well into the twentieth century now, talking about fascism and communism and the Cold War. French IV is still the best. Mlle. O'Shea has started calling it French 4 Fun. We play games, we cook, we go on picnics, we listen to her rhapsodize about Paris, and we learn French. There's just me and the teacher and the exchange student from Kenya and two quiet girls who are going to be doctors when they grow up.

Mom's first year as principal is coming to a close, so she's a little less agitated. Aaron is pitching for the baseball team and spends his spare time with his friends building skateboard ramps on the unused driveways of Versailles. Robyn leaves, and Allegra has started to help Scot with the business, lining up subcontractors for a new house that's going in. She looks impressively professional when she's on the phone. She sits there at our kitchen table and purses her lips and gets quotes on loads of fill for the new site. Scot gives cocktail parties on the patio in the backyard for prospective clients and pays me to hostess. The new Serena, I'm happy to announce, is post-ironic. I smile and pass around cheese cubes and smoked almonds and say how marvelous it is that Nora and Zack have so many sand piles to choose from, and Scot's prospective clients beam at me and say isn't it nice to see a young person with real manners.

I see nothing of Grimshaw, of course. She lives less than a mile away, but she might as well be on a different planet. Rack and Angel are off living their new lives, but I have no more idea what Grimshaw is doing than if she did live in LA. I know one thing, though: the rising star of the Over Easy isn't going to put up with chasing Whitney and Dallas through the junkyard for very long. Past that, I don't know.

I don't like to think about it, but the memory intrudes. It wakes me up in the night, and I try to keep it away from my throat. I lie there with my heart pounding. I should have told her everything in LA.

"How's the independent study going?" Mr. C. asks me one day as I'm leaving his class. "The due date is May twenty-fourth, remember. That's Monday." He had no idea I'd hitchhiked across the country during my vacation. He gets really excited about it. He says hardly anyone under thirty-five even knows what hitchhiking is anymore.

Although my conversation with Mr. C. makes me less than a minute late for my next class, I get sent to the principal's office for a late pass, so I just walk out of the school and sit by myself on our old bench and wait for the bus. There's about half an hour left until the end of school. In my upward mobility notebook, there is one blank page left. I turn to it and start writing a letter to Grimshaw. I describe what happened that day in that hot kitchen in Los Angeles. No interpretation, no justification, just the facts. I can see that any danger to me is in the past and many miles away. But it's real, and I should have told her.

There is space at the bottom of the page, and I have time, so in the lower margin, I finish the letter by sketching in the suitcase with the bumper sticker for Niagara Falls. And then on top of the suitcase I draw my old friend Irony Man.

I hear a sharp whistle. It's Prof, looking at me through the side window of the bus.

"You coming?" he yells.

"Hang on," I yell back. As I hurry through clumps of Colchis High kids, people say hi to me and I respond, but I'm basically back to being the semi-invisible character I've always been. Nobody knows exactly what I did during my spring vacation, but it has gotten around that it was a little past the edges of accepted middle-class teenage behavior. I carry with me the whiff of the open world, and my peers draw back from it as if they're afraid it's contagious. I climb on the bus and sit in our usual seat. It occurs to me that Prof probably misses Grimshaw, too. She chatted with him every day for all those years, and now she's gone. He watched her grow up. He watches everyone grow up. Even me. I lean forward.

"Are you looking forward to summer?" I ask him.

"You know it," he says.

"What do you do during the summer?"

"Garden." He holds up two fingers. "This many acres big."

"Flowers? Or vegetables?"

"Both. Don't you know my farm stand?"

"I go away every summer."

"Summer is a very blessed time," he says. "I think this Valley might have the most fertile ground in the country."

We roll through the streets of Colchis. It's the moment in spring where the little leaves are sticky and pale green and look like clouds of confetti. In the cemetery, the azaleas are out.

"You want to put some music on?" Prof asks.

"Sure." I go up and look through his shoe box, but nothing speaks to me until I come to the last one in the box. "Who's John Coltrane?" I ask.

"Put it on," Prof says. "You'll find out." So I put it on, and today the bus ride home has a jazz soundtrack. Normally, spring afternoons on the bus are pretty rowdy, but today the music has everybody, even the seventh graders, staring contemplatively out the windows. We know the doors on every house we pass by. We know every bend and rise in the road. When we get out into the country, I know the shape and lay of every pasture. I know every rock and maple tree in the windrows that separate them. Watching it all roll by one more time, accompanied by saxophone music, makes it not exactly new, but neutral, separate from me. I see it as if I've already moved far away. It's just land; it was here before we were, and it'll still be here after we're gone. It's not limited by anyone's experience or opinion. The story's not over. Anything could still happen here. I catch Prof's eye in his big rearview mirror.

"This music is good," I tell him.

"It never gets old," he says. He turns onto my road and downshifts for the last rise. "So," he says. "You went to find her. You brought her back. You saved her."

"Maybe, but . . . she didn't really want to be saved." At this, Prof throws back his head and laughs a good one.

"Yeah," he says. "They say that's been going on for about two thousand years." We're approaching Versailles. We're the last stop on Prof's route. He swings open the door. Coltrane is still playing.

After I get off, I turn around and wave through the door. "Bye, Prof. See you tomorrow."

"You take care, now," he yells after me. Even after the bus disappears over the rise in the road, I can still hear the saxophone coming to me through the open windows and over the trees.

When I get home, I tear the letter out of the notebook and fold it up and put it in my pocket. I get on my bike and pedal to Grimshaw's, down the dirt road, out onto the highway to coast the half mile down to her house.

The junkyard has a deserted feel, like nobody's been there for a long time, although I can hear the television on inside. The blackberries are in bud. I push my bike through the tall weeds between the junk cars, lean it against a lobotomized Toyota, and knock on the front door. After the heavy noise of her slow approach, the door opens just wide enough for me to see that Mrs. Grimshaw doesn't have her teeth in. When she sees that it's me on her front stoop, her face gets so red and angry I think she's going to reach out and clobber me. Over her shoulder I can see Whitney and Dallas watching a soap opera.

"I have something for Melody," I tell her. "It's important."

"He came and got her again," she snaps at me.

"He did? Mike?"

"Well, it sure as hell wasn't Santa Claus." The door shuts in my face, but I do something that surprises both of us. Right before the door closes, I stick my foot in it. She squeezes my foot and then opens the door very slowly and stands in the afternoon sunlight that slants across the field. I stand there on the stoop for a minute. I open my mouth, but no words come out. There are too many.

"I—I—" I stutter on the first sound. "I—I'm sorry." It takes such an effort to get it out that I practically holler it at her. What am I sorry for? "I'm sorry I didn't come sooner," I stammer. No, that's not it. So I keep going. "I'm sorry I was so . . . stupid. I didn't mean to be."

Mrs. Grimshaw's face changes a little. She nods. Neither of us thought I was going to say that. She steps back and turns away, leaving the door open. I can see into the house, see the trash spilling off the counter and onto the floor, the potato chip bags and juice boxes and plastic spoons and broken toys. People always said the Grimshaws lived like rats in this house, that it should be condemned. I never knew what they were talking about. I came here day after day, and I never saw any trash. All I saw was people. Now I see the trash. A heap of garbage bags leans against the house, dating from when Whitney and Dallas were in disposable diapers. It's been gathering for years. Then I hear a window slam shut and the TV goes off. The only noise left is the slow bang of a shutter in the wind.

I stand there on the stoop and listen to the irregular rhythm of the cars going by on the highway, and every now and then the Jake brake of a truck already stuttering for the ride down the hill. So this is the end of the story. She went back to LA for a second shot at leaving all this trash behind, and there's nothing I can or should do about it. At least now I know where she is, and I can think of her again, developing her act at the Over Easy.

Grimshaw's gone. She's really gone this time. I can feel it. And why wouldn't she go? Why would anybody come back here? There's nothing to come back to. So she's gone. She had her choice, and she made her choice. And this time I don't have to go get her. I ball up the letter and throw it on top of the trash.

About a week after that, I'm in French 4 Fun, listening to the foreign exchange student attempt to use French to describe his life in Kenya, and Mrs. Kmiec shows up at the door of the classroom and knocks.

"*Oui?*" Mlle. O'Shea says to her.

"Mrs. Pentz would like to see Serena. She says it's important."

Mlle. O'Shea looks at me sadly, her hands clasped in mock disappointment, and asks me what I've done now. "*Oh, ma fille. Qu'est-ce que t'as fait maintenant?*"

"*Sais pas, eh, moi?*" I shrug, getting up out of my chair.

Mlle. O'Shea laughs and claps. "*Très bien fait!*" We've been watching French films, and I've been practicing my gestures in class—the shrugging, the hands, the attitude. It's almost the end of the period, so I gather up my books and bring them with me. I follow Mrs. Kmiec down the hall, as if I need her to lead the way. We go past the open doors of the classrooms and hear the teachers' voices droning like bumblebees in the summer, and we go past the miles of empty lockers, down the stairs, around the corner by the vending machines where the portraits of all the past principals of Colchis High hang, all the way to Mr. Van. When I come into her office, Mom is facing the window overlooking the parking lot.

"You should put your portrait up there," I tell her when I come in. "Next to Mr. Van's." She turns around, and her face is puffy and tearstained. She's twisting her wedding ring around and around. "What's wrong?"

"Oh, Serena. Something really terrible has happened." She starts to cry. Her tears don't instinctively alarm me. She's always cried fairly easily, and what is terrible to her is rarely terrible to me. I prepare myself to fake the shock of learning about Scot's long-standing affair with Nanci Lee, although why she had to pull me out of class to tell me, I don't know. I'll tell her what I've learned recently about Grimshaw, that some people fit together and some people don't, that absence and loss can either be an ache or an opportunity.

"Look at you," she cries. "I wish I could express how very proud of you I am."

"Why? What happened?" I ask.

Gripping the back of her chair, she closes her eyes for a few seconds. "Amen," she whispers. She opens her eyes. She sits on her couch and pats the cushion next to her. I sit.

"Serena. It's about Melody. Grimshaw." She takes a breath. "Melody Grimshaw is . . ."

"Dead." We both say it at the same time. I don't know why I

say it, because it's obviously not true, but it just seemed like how that sentence was going to end. So I stare at my mother, waiting for her to tell me what's really going on. She stares back at me. She takes both my hands and tells me that there was an incident in a motel room. She starts talking to me about shock and grief and bereavement, about counselors and all the help that's there for me, while I'm still waiting for her to break the news about Scot and Nanci Lee.

I take my hands back. "Can I use your phone?" I ask. "I know where she works, in LA. I went there. I'll call her."

Mom moves in close. "Oh . . ." she breathes. She takes my face in both her hands. Her palms are cool and dry. I'd forgotten how they felt. "My darling, precious child. My sweet girl."

I take her hands down and then I get up and go to the office phone on her desk. It was a mistake to let the silence last this long. "It doesn't matter if she still hates me," I tell my mother. "I mean, I know you have to let people go sometimes, but I let her go too easily, just because she got mad at me. Being mad—that's not the end of the world, is it?"

"No," my mother says. "It's not." Tears are running down her face.

"We'd get mad at each other," I explain. "She gets sick of me, sick of my big mouth and bad attitude, just like you." I pick up the phone and stare at my mother, who stares back at me. She takes the phone out of my hand. She leads me back to the couch, and we sit down.

"Her body is being flown back today," she says.

"Whose body?"

"Hers. Melody's. Melody's body."

I pull away from her again, move over to Mr. Van's leather chair, and put my elbows on my knees. My head fills with this rushing, ringing noise. My hands cover my ears. My mother kneels next to me. A gale-force wind starts blowing through my head. Then a sound like rattling metal takes over and gets louder and louder until that dies down, too, and all that is left is a harsh note in my ears that repeats itself over and over in a familiar way. It was the crow, I realize, the crow on the Lone Pine Indian Reservation, that morning when we stood by the side of the road together and all we had was each other. Then I hear her voice, talking about Mike, so clear it's like she's standing in the room. I push it away, and as I do that, I realize I will never hear it again. All that's left is the cawing noise, over and over. That doesn't go away. I open my eyes.

"Her dead body?" I ask.

"Yes."

"From Los Angeles?"

"No," she says. "From Las Vegas."

"Las Vegas?"

Mom brings a chair over next to me. "I called Allegra. She's coming down. I'm taking the next two days off." A long silence stretches in which my mother starts crying again and my mind is full of useless thoughts, thoughts like *I bet those are Mr. Van's African violets over there by the window.*

"Was it an accident?" I ask. The minute the question comes out, I know the answer. I knew it before I asked. There has never been a moment in my life where I didn't know.

She shakes her head. "No."

In the time it takes me to ask the next question, the clock ticks, the phone rings on Mrs. Kmiec's desk outside the door and she takes a message, the bell rings, the noise of passing students fills the hallway and then subsides. The longer I wait to ask the next question, the more time I have for it not to be true. I think I'll let so much time go by before I ask it, that I won't ask it until we're all dead and the answer won't matter.

I clear my throat. "Was she killed?"

"Yes."

I remember those hands, that thing stretched into a rope, those empty eyes. I saw that she didn't love him and how weak he really was. I remember Scot telling me about football: where the enemy is vulnerable, they are dangerous.

"Was it Mike Lyle?" I ask.

She nods. "He strangled her." She starts to cry again. "With a pair of panty hose." She blows her nose and offers me a Kleenex. I shake my head. She takes about four. "The chief of police wants to talk to you. I told him not today, though."

"Okay." I remember him coiling up the body stocking in his hand and then stretching it. I can see his eyes, standing before me in that little kitchen, and I can hear his voice. How come I can remember him, and not her?

"I'm sorry, Serena." She's crying so hard she can't talk.

"It's okay, Mom. You can cry for both of us." I give her more Kleenex, and she dries her eyes again. She sobs out another apology, and I tell her again that it's okay. As I watch my mother cry, I wonder how I got to be a thousand years older than she will ever be. There's not a tear in me. Everything is dry and empty and old. There is some ratlike feeling scuttling around the edges of my brain, but I don't pursue it.

"I knew they were a couple," she says. "But I didn't know—how long were they together?"

"About a year."

"Jesus." She stops crying and stares at me. "A *year*? Why didn't—" And then she stops herself. "But—is that why she was in California?" I nod. "And that's why you went out there?" I nod. "You were worried about her?" I keep nodding, even though I have no idea if it's true. "Worried about her . . . with him?" she asks.

I open my backpack and take my upward mobility notebook out, find Grimshaw's postcard, and hand it to her. It's been in there since the day I got it. She looks at the front and then she reads the message on the back. *Freedom's just another word for nothing left to lose.*

"It's the one she mailed to the school just before April vacation," I tell her.

"Oh my God," she breathes. "Oh God forgive me."

"Do you know any of the details?" I ask her.

She falls apart again, and I have to wait for her to collect herself enough to tell me the rest of the story. Grimshaw had left Mike and Los Angeles, applied for work in a casino in Las Vegas, rented a motel room, alone, and Mike found her there, probably after looking for a while. They know she had left him once already, and it may have sent him into a rage when she did it again. There were people in both adjoining rooms, but nobody heard a thing. She hands me a business card.

"The police chief thinks you may be in danger. We'll go down to the station tomorrow."

"Mom." I lean forward and throw the chief's card into her wastebasket. "I'm not in danger. What do you think her brothers would do to him if he came back here?"

Mom starts to cry again and pounds her knees. "I could kill him myself," she says. "I really wish I could."

"Is there going to be a funeral?" I ask.

"Saturday. At ten. Pastor Don's been with Mrs. Grimshaw since they found out." The door to the office opens, and Allegra walks in.

"That's nice of him," I say. "But I doubt she wants him there."

"Serena, I'm really sorry," Allegra says. She's been crying, too. She comes forward to give me a hug. I get up and suddenly feel dizzy. All the blood drains out of my head, and I totter backward a few steps.

"Mom," Allegra says. "Look at her. She needs to lie down."

"No, I'm okay," I tell them. "I just want to go."

"I need one more minute with Serena," Mom says. "Serena, wait a minute." She waits until Allegra goes. "Mrs. Grimshaw has requested that—" She sighs. "That you not attend the funeral." The ratlike feeling pokes its head above the white surface of numbness and grins at me. I feel ice-cold. The gale in my head starts again while my mother explains that for some people when the pain is too great, they turn it into anger and look for someone to pin it on.

"Mrs. Grimshaw never 'requested' anything in her life."

"You're right. It was harsher than that. But it needs to be respected."

"Don't worry, Mom. I'm not going to crash my best friend's funeral."

"It turns out that Melody called from Las Vegas. Her mother wouldn't take the call because she was still too angry with her. That woman has a lot to live with."

Suddenly, all my blood rushes back into my body and I feel hot.

"She could have called me."

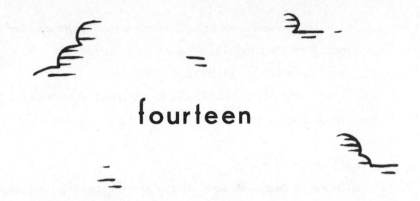

fourteen

THE FIRST NIGHT AFTER THE news of Grimshaw's death, nobody at home knows what to do with me or for me or about me, so to spare us all, I just go to bed. I feel like I'm lying in a coffin looking up at a closed lid. I'm not looking forward to waking up, either, but when I do, the sun is shining in my face and I have too many covers on. I remember right away about Grimshaw. There is no respite from this. I sit up and stare at my feet on the floor next to each other. I try to "get it," to pound it into my head that she's dead, my friend Grimshaw is now a dead body, lifeless, in a box, soon to be put in the ground forever, amen. I can't make myself believe it, though, and I don't feel anything, either. Maybe I'm the one who's dead. The girl I used to be had a friend named Melody. Neither girl exists anymore. That feels true enough. I take a cold shower, and then I turn it all the way hot, and then all the way cold again, but it doesn't help. I find my mother in Zack's room, sorting through old clothes and toys. Nobody else seems to be around. I sit down next to her, and she enfolds me in a hug.

"I'm sorry, Serena," she says. "I'm so, so sorry." Her eyes are still puffy from yesterday. I unwrap myself from her arms.

"My face feels odd," I tell her.

"Odd how?" She puts her hand to my cheek. It's not that I can't feel her hand; it's more like it feels as if it's on someone else's face.

"Numb. Rubbery."

"It's nearly noon," she says. "You're probably hungry. Let's eat some breakfast."

At the table in the breakfast nook, she sits across from me. The sun is bright against her back, and I can't see her face. She asks me a lot of questions, what did Grimshaw do in Los Angeles, what did Mike do in Los Angeles, how was he connected to her job, what was my relationship with Mike like, etc. She cocks her head and laces her fingers around her coffee cup. It's what she does when she's carved out time to listen. I can't answer her questions, though. The thoughts inside my head are clear enough, but conveying any of them to her seems impossible. Maybe I'm afraid all answers would bend back to me and what I did, and I don't even know what I did. I just don't feel ready for my own mother to find out how guilty I am. I chew on some of my breakfast—scrambled eggs and home fries and bacon—but none of it has any flavor. Even orange juice tastes dead. Mom watches me intently as I take a sip and then push it away. Coffee is good, though. She made it strong. That I can taste.

I follow the sound of her voice around all morning. It's like a cord towing me along from room to room as she sorts through drawers and closets, making piles of old things. She tells me stories from her life, what a jerk her father was, how she met my father, how I remind her of him. She apologizes for not telling me more about him, but what do I care about a dead girl's dead father? Her voice takes me from room to room, and I hang on to my mug of coffee with both hands. We go outside, and she takes a deep breath and tells me how much hope there still is in the world, even though it might take me a long time to find it again. I still have my whole life in front of me, and she'll help me think about college. Maybe the right thing now is to take a gap year before college and do something with my love of French. Maybe Mlle. O'Shea will have some ideas for us. We end up in the backyard, where the sun is young and strong and the sky is enameled blue and the new grass and trees throb with green. Mom is still talking, now about the garden Scot wants to put in back here. He tried turning over a plot last fall, but the sod is so thick that even his monster tiller couldn't bite through it. So we have to turn it by hand. I walk out into the middle of a patch of dirt clods and tufts of new grass. She wrestles a shovel out of the ground. It looks like it spent the winter there.

I drop to my knees, pick up a sun-warmed clod of dirt, and crumble it between my palms. The hard, winter-washed gray gives up easily to the cool brown dirt inside, and a dust-colored spider hurries away with an egg sac in its mouth. Mom starts turning clods over with the spade, and I come along behind her, breaking them up with my hands, picking out the earthworms, shaking the loose dirt out of the clods of last year's yellowed grass. We work through the afternoon. She takes a break once, and comes back out with hats and a jug of water. When Allegra comes home with

Zack and Nora, they join us. Allegra sets up her speakers on a folding chair next to the garden and baroque trumpet music wafts out over our backs as the sun goes down. Then Scot and Aaron pull in, home from baseball practice. Scot's brought two bags of Chinese takeout for supper, and he sets the boxes on the ground next to the garden and runs in and out of the house with blankets and drinks and dishes. Aaron stands next to me in his baseball uniform and glove, scuffing the dirt with his toe. Nobody knows what to say to me.

Everybody takes the next day off, except Aaron, who is starting pitcher that night in a game against Linerville. The garden is turned by early afternoon. I think we've turned over about five times more ground than anybody will ever plant, because nobody knows what to say to me when we stop. In the evening, we go to Aaron's game. We're not the sort of family who does things like this, and when Aaron sees all of us lined up on the bleachers, he gets stressed and can't concentrate. He walks so many batters his coach takes him out of the game, and Colchis loses.

On Saturday, Mom has to go to Grimshaw's funeral, so Allegra and her on-and-off-again boyfriend, Tyler, and I get in her car and drive for a long time. Allegra puts Italian love songs on. The day is warm, the windows are open, and the speakers are loud.

At some point, I lean forward. "Where are we going?"

"Anywhere we want." Allegra holds up a credit card. "Scot's. He just sold another house lot."

Tyler turns around. "Niagara Falls okay?"

"I guess so."

When we get there, Allegra and Tyler go down to the bottom of the falls for a boat ride. I stand in the viewing area and watch the thundering wall of water and think what a tiny life Grimshaw had and how little difference it makes that she's gone. People keep going to Niagara Falls. House lots keep selling. Water keeps pouring over the edge.

Although my mother's books on adolescence and grief counsel otherwise, I don't go to school for a week. I do my physics and calculus at home and send it in with my mother. Scot treats me like a cancer patient. He'll be watching a baseball game, yelling at the TV, and pounding the arms of his chair. I walk by, and he mutes the volume and looks sorrowful. He hopes I won't talk to him. A lot of people are like that. They don't want to feel inadequate.

When I do return to school, the kids leave a four-foot buffer zone around me, as if they're afraid they might catch it. But then by day two, Grimshaw's murder gets eclipsed by the prom. It's an all-night, nonalcoholic, locked-in-the-gym affair, and the halls are abuzz with schemes for smuggling in alcohol. In the ten days since her death, I still haven't cried, and of course Mom is worried. So she sends Pastor Don down to get me out of class so that we can "talk." It means getting out of school before lunch on a nice day, so I go along with him in his car to the church.

"It's too nice a day to be inside," Pastor Don declares. "Let's take a walk."

"I know a place we can go," I suggest. We drive in silence past the drinking places and all the former dairy farms. I show him a place to pull over, and we cross the road and thread through rusty barbed wire and walk up the edge of one of Mizerak's alfalfa pastures. At the top where the woods begin is a deep little ravine cut by the same stream that runs behind Grimshaw's. From here, it goes past all the party places in the gorge and on down through Colchis, and keeps going until it ends up in the Mississippi River. We stand at the top and look into the ravine. Down near the bottom, there's still the crusty remnant of a snowbank.

"My goodness," says Pastor Don. "Snow. In June! I had no idea." We sit on either side of a big flat rock. A silence sits between us, like a third person that was already there before us. But he is here for me, and he needs to be talked to, otherwise my mother will send more specialists after me. I decide to make it easy for him.

"So," I start. "Do you want to know how I feel?"

"Yes," he says. "I do."

"Okay, I'll tell you. On one condition. Nothing you can say, no Bible verse you can quote, no heartwarming anecdote you can relate, will make me feel any different. So don't bother. Agreed?"

"Okay," he says doubtfully. He waits for a minute. "So," he prompts, "how do you feel?"

"Guilty."

"Is it . . ." He speaks carefully, holding his fingertips together the way he does on Sunday mornings when he's making a fine theological point that he knows nobody will understand. "Is it guilt that you're alive and your best friend is . . . dead?"

"No. It's guilt that had I not done the things I did, my best friend would not even be dead."

"I see." His shoulders sag. Real guilt. He wasn't counting on that. "Can you say more about it?"

"I could, but . . ." I shake my head. We watch a flock of starlings move across the sky. It moves like a single being, stretching out, then bunching up, then getting absorbed into a tree. "How's Mrs. Grimshaw doing?" I ask after a while.

"Well, she actually feels somewhat like you do. She won't talk, and she can't pray, so I just try to be there with her."

"She doesn't like anyone in the house who's not family. It makes her uncomfortable."

"Well, the church has done a lot there recently, cleaning it up, hauling away the . . . stuff. She seemed to appreciate the help."

A heavy bass booms out, and a minute later, Allen Mizerak goes by on the new John Deere, CD blaring, rear tires flinging clods of manure all over the road.

"The Mizeraks must be planting now," I comment. The sight of Allen makes me think back to the day after homecoming, when Grimshaw and Angel and I did the milking together for Rack, and then did it again in the evening. We seemed wiser then, wiser than we are now. It seems to me that the real mistake we made wasn't just mine, but all of ours, and that we made it right around that time, maybe that very day. It was so easy being together like that, then it was just as easy to throw it away. We didn't value the best thing we had, which was each other.

"Serena," Pastor Don says suddenly. "Can I pray for you?"

Asking my permission to pray for me? This is a new courtesy. "Okay," I agree. "Not in my presence, though, okay? I always found that really rude."

"Fair enough," he agrees.

"I don't understand prayer, anyway," I blurt. "I mean, my mother prays when she ought to be paying attention. She just turns everything 'over to the Lord.' As if He knows her problems better than she does."

"Maybe she prays so that then she can think."

"Maybe," I concede. "But I doubt it."

"A wise man told me once that when he prays, he doesn't ask God for any particular outcome. He just says thank you."

"What would the point of that be?"

"Well," Pastor Don says patiently, "for example, if you were moved to pray for your friend, you would just thank God for her. For her life." In front of us, the same flock of starlings has reappeared. We watch them fly to the horizon, wheel around, and come back. "It may take you a long time to figure it out, Serena, but she was here for a reason. Whether or not you even do figure it out, her life was important. Just start there. That's faith."

I wipe my nose with my sleeve. "Are you trying to make me cry?"

"No, but I'd pray right now," he offers. "With your permission."

"Okay," I say slowly.

He clasps his hands, hangs his head, and frowns. With no introduction, he starts telling God all about Grimshaw. Pastor Don tells God about her childhood and her long friendship with me, and then he goes on and tells Him about the rest of her family, too, each brother and her mom and the dead father, about whom I know very little. It's as if God is sitting on a branch of the maple tree above our heads, listening to us, interested, hidden by the new leaves.

It's a long prayer. My butt goes numb from sitting on that cold rock for so long, but still, I think it's good somebody told God what was going on.

We're pretty close to Versailles, and Pastor Don drives me home. Nobody's there. As I walk through the front door, I hear a man's voice on the answering machine. It's the police chief of Colchis, telling us that Mike Lyle was arrested in Nogales, Arizona, for driving off from a gas station without paying. He's being held in Nevada, without bail.

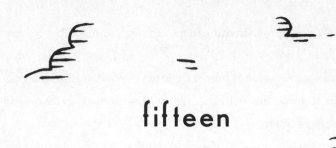

fifteen

AT THE FRONT DESK OF *another motel, she explained her situation to another manager. She'd left her boyfriend, she had no money, nothing, but she saw the* HELP WANTED *sign in the window, and she was willing to work for a room. She was going to look for a job as a croupier tomorrow. Night was falling. Her feet hurt, and she was losing her voice. She had done this at least ten times so far today, but she couldn't think of anything else to do.*

While she was talking, this manager kept his attention on his computer screen. When she was done, he nodded. "Jobs all over the city." He put a key on the guest book and moved it toward her. "Sign here." She took the key, and he watched her sign her name.

"Friend of mine's in personnel at the Alhambra," he said.

"Really?"

He wrote a name on the back of a business card and slid it across the counter to her. She couldn't read it because of the tears in her eyes.

"Thank you," she whispered.

He shrugged. "No need to cry. Everyone needs a hand sometimes."

* * *

The man in personnel was from Buffalo. He knew where the Minnechaug Valley was. He asked her if she could start immediately. They were short-staffed. He said there were opportunities for dancers, as well, but she wasn't interested in that. Back at the motel, she borrowed an iron from the front desk and laid her clothes out on the other bed, the uniform she'd been given against her first paycheck and panty hose. The last thing she thought about before she fell asleep was the phone call she would make tomorrow after she started the job. She smiled and shook her head, thinking about her friend. No, maybe she wouldn't call until she started a dance class, which she would do once she had some money. She would start to dance, finally, real dance. What was this feeling, though, this vibration in her chest? Maybe it was confidence. She had always been jealous of her friend's confidence—what must it be like to walk around with that? It wasn't really a feeling, it was more like a knowing. It was knowing that if you did one thing for yourself, you could do the next thing, and so on, until it got you where you wanted to go. And she had done it. And it felt good. People would help you, that's what she'd never realized. Before she fell asleep, she got out of bed and double-checked the locks on the door one more time.

Tomorrow was hers.

She was so tired that she didn't hear the knocking. It had to penetrate slowly into her sleep. Once she sat up, it took her a minute to remember where she was. She put on a sweater to answer the door. It was his sweater, because she had nothing of her own that was warm. It still smelled like him. She stood in front of the door. The knocking came again.

"Hello?"

"It's me. Open up." She leaned her forehead against the cold steel.

"It's me, Mel. Open the door." The door had a peephole and a sliding chain lock. She ran her fingers over the dents in the steel. "I just want to talk," he said. "I'm on my way back to LA. I just wanted to say good-bye."

She had just done her nails, and she watched them come up to the chain. He heard a small sound when her fingers touched the knob. He waited, but he didn't hear the slide.

"I been doing a lot of thinking in the last couple days." From the way his voice cracked, she could tell he was crying. "You don't need me anymore. I know that. Shit, you're on your way. I'm on my way, too. I just wanted to say good luck."

She slid the chain out of the slide. He tried the door, but it was locked. "You gotta open it from the inside," he said. "Mel? Open the door." She turned the doorknob.

The force blew open the door. It knocked her on the floor between the beds. He lifted her up and threw her on the bed. She lay there, limp, expecting the worst. She wouldn't resist. She held on to the thought of tomorrow. She didn't want anything to get in its way. But nothing happened. She didn't know where he was. It took her a minute to realize that he was next to her, sitting on the bed with his elbows on his knees and his head in his hands.

He had left the door ajar. She rolled over and dove for it. With one hand, he caught the back of her sweater, and with the other, reached out and swatted the door. It closed with a quiet steel click. He held her by the collar like a kitten.

"You're not going nowhere," he said. "We gotta stick together, you and me. I've told you and told you and told you, but you don't listen.

You can't just split off and go—this world will eat you alive. You don't know that yet, because you haven't been anywhere."

He was breathing hard.

"For two days now, two whole days, I been riding around, visiting one motel after the other. I knew I'd find you, because we're meant to be. You know what else I knew, though?" He chuckled in her ear. "I knew you'd sign your own name." He was holding the collar on the sweater so tight she couldn't get her fingers inside it. "I offered you mine, but you wouldn't take it. You didn't want it. But you're no better'n me. You're dirt. From nowhere. You're nothing."

"Mike," she whispered.

"Say it," he insisted. "'I'm nothing.' Say it once. Then we'll forget this whole thing ever happened. We'll start over."

"I can't breathe."

"Say it." He loosened the collar. "Say it."

"Okay," she gasped, sucking air back into her lungs.

"Say it."

With one motion, she twisted around, grabbed the telephone by the bed, and hit him with it on the bridge of his nose. She sprang off the bed for the door. Her hand was on the doorknob, but in another second, she was on the floor again. His knee was against her throat. His whole weight was on her chest.

"Bloody my nose, you piece of shit."

She tried to push him off, but it was like being under a building. He was just too heavy. A blow to her face, and she was choking on blood.

"You piece of white trash." He hit her again. She heard popping, cracking noises in her head.

"I was taking you places." He hit her again. Sharp objects cut the inside of her mouth. Her teeth.

"I was going to make you something."

She started to cry. When he wrapped the panty hose around her neck, she didn't resist.

Another night of horrible sleep. Toward dawn, I get up.

I put on my bathrobe, go downstairs, and make a pot of coffee. I go outside and wait for the sun to come up, but it doesn't. It just gets paler and paler gray.

The framers of the new house come at seven. The crew offers me a donut, and I sit on the tailgate of one of their pickups. They take out chop saws and nail guns and air compressors, and set up sawhorses. They spread orange extension cords around the foundation, scratch the stubble on their cheeks, look up at the sky, and discuss when is it going to open up and pour, and whether it's worth it to even start. After seven, Scot stumbles out of our house, tying on his nail apron. I have to get ready for school, so I go inside.

My uncle Hugh calls Sunday morning as everyone's leaving for church. Allegra probably told him what happened and ordered him to talk to me. He called from his car.

"Everybody's worried because I'm not crying," I shout at him. "I feel kind of pressured by it."

"Life will always provide opportunities to cry," he shouts back. "You can count on it for that."

"Hey, Hugh?" I holler. "Are we rich?"

"You need money?" he shouts.

"No. I mean, is there any, like, family money? I'm just curious."

"I see. There was, but . . . Well, the fact is, your father gave it all away."

"He did?" I shout. "Away to who?"

"To the people who he felt had earned it. It took him some work, a little time, but those were his beliefs, so that's what he did." Hugh and I are silent for a while. "So it's all gone," he says finally.

"All of it?"

"Every dime."

"Wasn't anyone mad when he did it?"

"Your mother was pretty irritable for a while. My family, of course, wouldn't speak to him again. They wanted him to give it back to them, but he didn't think it was theirs any more than it was his. None of us earned it. He was the oldest son, and the way trusts work, the rules were written a long time ago. The money owns you more than you own the money, and that's not what your father was about." Hugh's voice thickens when he says that, and he has to stop talking for a few minutes. Then he clears his throat. "So he had a lot more than the rest of us. The girls got the silver, and the house. The stuff. He got the cash. I'm the youngest, of course, so I got the good looks. And the charm." He laughs.

"The silver? Like . . . monogrammed silver?"

"That's right."

"You mean there are lots of little *V*'s somewhere, on sugar bowls and teaspoons?"

"That's the idea, yes, only they're little *P*'s. My mother's name was Pond. His father wasn't around long enough to leave an impression on the silver."

"Where—"

"She married five times."

"Do you think he did the right thing?"

"Yes, I do, in the end. But he could have done it differently, I think. There was a way to handle it better than he did."

"Was it a lot of money?" I ask.

"It was a fortune."

"Wow."

"It was after you kids were born. He didn't want it to land on you three."

"I don't know what it would have done for us, anyway."

"Well," he says. "Money is opportunity. It could have sent you guys to boarding school, gotten you the hell out of—what's the name again, the town you live in?"

Suddenly, I can't speak around the huge lump in my throat. I have to swallow a couple of times. "Colchis," I whisper.

"Right," he says. "Not much to work with there. You could have made friends with people who had more going for them."

Then we talk about my graduation from high school and the beginning of adulthood and what I want as a present. He asks me if I want to come out to where he lives. "I come and go," he says. "You could hang out, do some thinking, figure out what your next step is."

He tells me his plan is to be in Maine in the early part of the summer, so I can meet him there and go to Europe with him, if nothing better comes along, and after that he'll stay in Europe, and I can check that out, too, if I want. Just like that, my future opens up. Easy. I thank him for his offer and then stand there on the front lawn for a long time after we hang up.

"Pond," I say out loud. The word tolls somewhere inside my brain like an ancient, unused bell, and pronouncing it like that, the world shifts a little under my feet. Suddenly, I understand a lot that I never understood before. *Hey, Grimshaw*, I want to shout into the empty space she disappeared into, *you were right; I am from a rich family*. I remember what she said about the spaces between people. She was saying something about rich people that day, about the space between rich people and everyone else, something specific that I can't remember, but it feels like it pertains to me. I get a powerful urge to get on my bike and go to the cemetery to wait for her, so I can find out what else she thinks about it.

I look down at the phone in my hand. It turns out my father was a real person. Whoever he was, I feel a sense of pride that he did something that everybody thought was so stupid. Whatever I know, or don't know, I'm glad I learned it myself, instead of having it bought for me with someone else's money. I could cry about that, but that wouldn't be crying about Grimshaw.

The next weekend, Angel asks me if I want to go out with the cheerleading squad. On the spot, I can't think of any reason why not, so they pick me up and we go to the gorge. It's still light. Nobody's built a fire yet. I sit with a bunch of cheerleaders in the backseat of someone's car, passing around cans from a six-pack of beer. Nobody mentions Grimshaw. It turns out that a lot less than a thousand years need to go by before a person ceases to matter. It doesn't even take a month.

The big news is that Junior Davis has announced he's going to the prom. Rack is now great with child; she and Junior are not together anymore. The cheerleaders are all talking about how they would never, ever, under any circumstances go to the prom with Junior Davis, they don't care how hot he thinks he is. I'm sipping on my beer, sitting halfway out of the open car door, half wondering what it would be like to go to the prom or show up at the gorge with a guy, your own guy, to belong with somebody like that, to have the terrible space between you and everybody else go away for a minute. One of the last things Bo said to me on the morning I left him was that the minute he heard Bob talk about me on his CB radio, he knew I was someone special. I was just out of Sacramento, you know, he said. Man, I drove fast. I didn't know who you were, but I didn't want you to leave before I got there. What did Bob say about me? I asked him. Oh, he said, just that you were a girl going east and you had a friend.

I take another sip of beer. I wish I could be that girl again.

Suddenly, all the cheerleaders shriek and pile out of the car, even the ones in the front seat. I'm left there, alone. A firecracker lands in the car at my feet and goes off.

I hear somebody say, "She didn't even move."

I look to my left and see a small crowd all focused on me. Tonight, it's mostly older guys out drinking, guys that graduated from high school a few years back. I pick Lance Hoffman to focus on. When we were in ninth grade, he was the football hero. He's got a ponytail now and the beginnings of a beer gut. Junior Davis is with him, along with Lars Madsen and Marty Gerard. The cheerleaders are standing off to the side. I hear the fizz of another firecracker near me and then it goes off. I guess that's what made the girls get out of the car. After all Grimshaw went through, I don't think I'm about to freak out over a firecracker. I take the last long swig of beer. When I turn my head, everybody's still looking at me. I look back at them.

"Having fun?" I ask.

"Ooh . . . somebody's not afraid of firecrackers," Marty Gerard says.

"How about my big stick of dyno-mite?" asks Lars. Nobody says anything after that.

"Hey, who's got a beer for me?" Junior yells. That breaks the spell, and the party starts up again. After a minute, Junior walks over to the car and gets in next to me on the other side.

"What are you doing here?" I ask him.

"This is my car," he says.

"Oh." So Junior and I sit in the backseat of his car and drink another beer and talk about the football coach who won more football games than anybody else in the NFL.

"Winning isn't everything," Junior tells me somberly. "It's the only thing." Junior says he's patterned his life after the guy. Then he drains his beer, crumples the can, and throws it out the window. I ask him how algebra is going. Terrible, he says, and this is his last chance. If he screws up this time, he's out of college, out of a scholarship, out of luck, stuck in the Valley for life with the rest of these losers. He pulls his math book out from under the front seat. He's been stuck on the quadratic formula since before spring vacation. I offer to help him with it. He tries to kiss me. I push him away. It starts to rain, and we roll up the windows. I ask him about Rack, and he brings up Grimshaw. I start to tell him about how we met this guy Bo that I think about all the time, but Junior's attention span isn't that long. He tells me he's always been in love with me. I tell him not to be stupid, and he tries to kiss me again. The windows steam up, and I draw the quadratic formula in the fog on the window and tell him if he memorizes it, I'll give him the best kiss he's ever gotten in his life.

"Repeat after me," I command. "X equals."

"X equals."

"Negative b . . ." And so on, plus or minus the square root of b squared minus 4ac, all over 2a. I've read my mom's books on learning styles, and Junior is definitely kinesthetic. He doesn't understand the plus-or-minus part. I explain to him that since negative times negative equals positive, the square root of any number can either be positive or negative.

He looks amazed. "Nobody ever told me that," he says. "That actually makes some sense."

We repeat the formula rhythmically, over and over. He gets it down cold and writes it in the steam on his window. And then I take charge of the situation, put my lips on his, and give him the best kiss he's ever gotten in his life. I pretend he's Bo and that Grimshaw is alive. For a minute, I feel like a real person again. But it doesn't last.

Junior sits there for a minute, stunned. "That wasn't the best kiss," he says. "That was only the second best. You better try again."

"I'm going to get another beer." I get out of the car and look for the cheerleaders. They are crowded into a van with the side door open.

"Are you, like, going to the prom with him?" Raven asks me when I approach.

"With who?" For a minute this wild, irrational hope takes over that Raven knows something I don't, that Bo's about to pull in with his truck and take me to the prom like I'm Cinderella.

"Oh, Miss Innocent," one of them says.

"Well," says another. "We just want you to know that if you go to the prom with Junior—" I reach for a beer from a case on the ground.

"We think it's unethical," Raven finishes. "She used to be your friend, you know."

When she says that word, I realize that's what I've been waiting for, that judgment. Guilty as charged. It's kind of a relief to finally hear it. Inside my head, I hear a noise of falling glass. It feels like my insides have turned to glass and then shattered. A sound like a waterfall continues in my ears. It lasts for a while. I never get to the beer. I just stand there with my hand outstretched listening to the sound in my head. I walk away from the cheerleaders. Junior is still in the backseat of his car. His math book is open on his knees. I get in next to him. He's excited to see me.

"Hey," he says. "I think I got it! It was the plus-or-minus part that screwed me up. I never knew you were supposed to get two answers."

I watch him do a few problems. "You know," I tell him

eventually. "You're actually pretty good at this stuff. If you concentrate on the math and forget about the word problems,
you'll probably pass."

"Don't even mention word problems to me," he says. "I have
bad dreams about word problems." He looks at me. "You don't
believe me, do you?" he asks. Junior Davis has beautiful blue-green
eyes, the color of the sea. He looks back down at the math. I put
my hand on his head. His hair, which I had always thought was
wiry, is actually very soft.

"Hey, Junior, will you go to the prom with me?" Everyone
will hate me, but I deserve it.

He stops calculating and considers. "Will you give me another
kiss?"

"No. But I'll help you pass your math final."

"Okay," he says. "I was planning on asking you, anyway." The
look on his face is so sincere that I can tell the thought has never
once crossed his mind.

Mom is too busy to take me to get a prom dress, and so Scot takes
me. Mom tells him to spend some money, and we get a skinny,
shiny red thing. Allegra helps me put my hair up, and sure enough,
the Serena impersonator looks much better than the real one
ever did.

Nobody tells me that we're supposed to match, and a week
later, Junior shows up at my front door in a powder blue tux and
a corsage in a clear plastic box with a rubber band for my wrist.
Nobody is around except Aaron, who monopolizes him with football talk. He and Junior are deep into the early career of Vince

Lombardi when Scot pulls in. Scot is excited about Junior's car, a 1974 Plymouth Duster. We all troop back outside to talk about it.

"I learned to drive on these cars," Scot says, pumping Junior's hand. "Automatic?"

"Manual."

"What's it got under the hood?"

"Three sixty."

Scot whistles. "No kidding. That's a monster."

"It was my grandfather's," Junior says. "He died about a month after he got it customized."

Scot shakes his head about the tragedy of it all. "It's always the way."

The conversation segues back to football, and I leave them in the driveway. I put the corsage in the fridge and poke around the kitchen for something to cook. I find a lump of meat in the freezer, nuke it, and open cans for chili.

"Serena." Aaron is standing behind me, looking concerned. "Does your boyfriend, like, know how to read?"

"He's not my boyfriend. And he's in twelfth grade. Of course he knows how to read."

"He was showing us something from his Vince Lombardi book, and he didn't get it right. He mixed up words like *sacrifice* and *success*. But he kept acting like he was reading it. He was faking. I could tell."

"Vince Lombardi's a god to him, Aaron. He knows that book so well he has it memorized. He doesn't need to read it."

"But he's taking ninth grade math for the fourth time! He's in my class!" Aaron looks like he's on the verge of tears.

"I know. He has to pass it, or he can't get a football scholarship."

"You have to help him, Serena."

"Why don't you? You're good at math." I take off my apron and hand him a small stack of bowls. At that moment, Scot and Junior come in, still talking football, so Aaron just scowls at me, grabs the bowls, and takes them into the living room. By eight o'clock, the chili is gone, the beer is gone, and all the males are in front of the basketball playoffs. I strap the corsage back on, which consists of one dyed-blue carnation and a silk butterfly on a spring. It's eight thirty by the time we're back in Junior's grandpa's Plymouth Duster heading for the prom. I drive. The beers have wiped him out, so the conversation isn't exactly sparkling.

"Hey, Junior," I say into the darkness.

"Hmmm." His head is rolling around.

"Can you read?" I ask.

"I get by," he mumbles as he falls back asleep.

Junior snores all the way down to Colchis. His head is thrown back, and his mouth is open. When we get to the gym, the couples are like statues, clutched in a slow dance. Everybody perks up when Junior gets there. His nap has given him a second wind. First, he walks on his hands between the couples and then he capers around the gym, whisking tablecloths off tables. Dixie cups of punch and frilly basket of mints go flying. He says it's an army trick his father taught him. He's the life of the party. Nobody speaks to me, of course, being immoral. Toward midnight, I'm sitting alone on a dark corner of the bleachers, wondering when I should start walking home. I look around, and there is Rack, standing in the gym doorway by the trophy case. She looks fat and pregnant. She's wearing a tight maternity top that shows the outline of her belly button. Junior is now fully out of control. He has lowered the gymnastic rings and has put Lars Madsen's feet in them, and is aiming him like a huge wrecking ball into the middle of the dancers. I catch up to him just as the missile is about to be launched, and lead him away by a pinch of blue cloth.

"Look who's standing by the door," I hiss in his ear. He looks.

"Jesus Christ," he says.

I push him toward the door. "Go talk to her."

"I can't."

"You have to."

"I can't do it." He walks away from me, holding his hands in the air. "I'm a football player, not a farmer."

I stay right behind him. "You're not gonna be a football player if you can't pass algebra."

He turns. "College isn't everything," he says hotly. "I can always play semipro." He puts his head down, shoulders through the dancing couples, and escapes through a swinging door into the boys' locker room. I follow him in. I don't think she's seen us. The cool air of the locker room is a relief after the stale heat of the gym. It's dark, except for the murky red light from the exit sign. It smells like feet.

"You can't hide in here," I tell him.

"Yes, I can," he says. "I do it every day."

Junior body slams a locker and sinks to the ground. Smoothing my dress underneath me, I sit on the floor next to him.

"It's not that I don't care about it," he announces. "I mean, I think about it all the time. But she told them before she told me! She announced at dinner. *Both* of her brothers were there. Just like that, in front of all of them. 'Junior, honey,'" he mimics. "'Guess what? You're gonna be a daddy!'

"I didn't know. I had no idea. Jesus. I about swallowed my fork. Mr. Mizerak points at me with a steak knife and says, 'Son, you can finish high school, but by God, you'll marry this girl, and then I'm gonna teach you how to drive that new John Deere.' I said, 'Yes, sir,' ate my pie, and walked out the door."

"Never went back?"

"Nope."

The red from the exit sign outlines the angles of his face and neck, and lights up the ends of his hair. A shower drips in the murky depths of the locker room. In the gym, the band is still playing.

"I'm sorry about your friend," he says. "I never got a chance to tell you that."

"She wasn't just my *friend*," I tell him. "She was a lot more than that."

Junior nods. "You really miss her," he says. "It's like you miss yourself."

I sigh. "I guess so. I can't really feel anything. It's like all the switches got turned off."

"I know how to do that," he says.

"Is that why you started drinking?" I ask.

He asks me if I remember that game against Minnechaug where he sacked their quarterback twice and then messed up his hand and they taped him up and put him back in the game.

"Broke two bones in my hand," he says. "But I only missed one play."

"You didn't used to drink. You were the only one who didn't drink because you were—"

"I *know*—" He smashes the locker to his right with his elbow. "Jesus Christ. You think I don't remember that?"

"Don't do that. You'll break another bone."

"So what? I don't even care."

"Junior, I don't know what the right thing to do is. But—you can't just leave her out there all alone by the trophy case."

"Oh, shit," he moans. He swallows, wipes his hands on his tux, and stands up. "I wish I had a beer right now."

"Go talk to her. She usually has two."

"Really?" This interests him. "Okay," he says. "If she's still out there, I'll talk to her, okay? But she's probably gone." I reach up, and he pulls me by the hand. There's so much strength in his arm I practically float up.

We stand very close together. The air smells like fifty years of sweaty socks, of games lost and won in the youth of men's lives in a factory town by a river where the Iroquois used to make raids. From out in the gym, we hear the faint strains of two people being crowned king and queen of the prom. Last year it was Junior and Rack. He leans his forehead against my shoulder. I put an arm around him, and he starts to breathe raggedly, long, shuddering breaths that sound like they hurt, emotions with one-way barbs that are going to feel twice as bad coming out as they did going in.

But other people's feelings go off like firecrackers at my feet.

279

I'm just not that connected. Maybe it's that great space between me and everyone else. And all the switches that got turned off. Eventually, he lifts his head, and the light from the exit sign illuminates the tears on his face. I pick up the hem of my dress. We walk back out of the locker room. Rack is still there.

"Come with me," Junior says. "Maybe she's got three beers."

"No." I point him toward Rack and give him a push. "I'm going home."

Finals come and go. I go in after my last one, and Mr. C. is at his desk, correcting tests. He stands up when I come in. I give him back all the books I've either stolen or borrowed over the past two years, and he hands me my upward mobility notebook.

"Quite a journey," he says. "I was honored to read it. It would appear you're a wonderful writer. And you have something original to say. That's a combination with a future."

"Thanks," I mumble. The future is one thing I don't enjoy discussing, so I pretend I'm interested in what he wrote in my notebook. He's left checks and comments and question marks in the margins, all in red ink, but I guess that would be my fault, for not typing it into an official report. He watches me flip through the pages.

"I think about her a lot," he says. "Your friend."

"You do?"

"We all do. I don't think anybody knew what her potential was—probably she didn't, either, but—"

"She knew," I interrupt.

"Well. Then it's doubly a waste." He turns to the window. He leans on the radiator on his fingertips. He turns his head toward me. "She did know?"

For some reason, that remark about her not knowing anything makes me really, really angry. "It was already there for her!" I shout. "She was a dancer! It wasn't just a dream! She was doing it! God damn it! In Los Angeles! More than me, more than you, more than anybody, she was not just dreaming about it, she was living it!" Mr. C. holds out his hands to protect himself, but it's too late. "Melody Grimshaw from the trash up on the hill and all the brothers in jail, and she's not doing it anymore. That's the tragedy! And nobody gets it!"

He bows his head. This was supposed to be our big conversation about capitalism and the class system, in which I defend my year's work and tie it all together, since I failed to do it on paper. But Mr. C. is tearing up. His face has turned red. I know I should apologize for taking it out on him. It's not his fault. Mr. C. takes off his glasses and wipes his face with a pocket handkerchief. He blows his nose and clears his throat.

"I picked up your yearbook for you," he says. "It was the last one there, and we had to close up."

He hands it to me. It's gold with the letters *CHS* in lavender in the upper right-hand corner. I flip through to the seniors to see if I can find Grimshaw's senior picture. They were taken in November. She wore her cheerleaders' uniform.

She's not in there. I look up at Mr. C. He was the yearbook advisor.

"The news came too late to commemorate her in any way," Mr. C. says. "Or we would have. It was already at the printer's."

I turn the pages and find Angel's picture, and then Rack's. "How come Claudette Mizerak is in here, and Melody's not?" I ask him. "They left school around the same time. The same day, actually."

"Well, Claudette, you know, made arrangements, and she'll get her diploma along with the rest of you."

"Did Claudette pass Western Civ?"

"No," Mr. C. says quietly.

"I see."

I stare at him. Does he really not get it? No. There's too much to get. You can't get any of it, unless you get all of it, and if you get all of it, you just want to blow the whole thing up. So unless you're prepared to blow the whole thing up, you're just sorry.

"Yeah. I'm sorry, too."

Mr. C. taps the cover. "I took the liberty of signing yours."

"Where?"

"Oh, you'll find it." He holds out his hand for me to shake, and I take it. I don't want the yearbook, of course—the document that officially makes my best friend nonexistent forever, but he looks so miserable and guilty that I can't bring myself to leave it there. It's not his fault. He walks me to the door.

"Whatever your next step is," he stammers. "Whatever you decide you want it to be, just let me know, and I'll do whatever I can to help you achieve it." His voice is choked. "Not that you need it."

"Thanks, Mr. C."

I turn around and wave good-bye to him, walking backward. "I'll be here," he calls after me.

And then that's it for me and high school. On my way out, I open the envelope with my grades in it. Six As, in a vertical row, like a monogram, like an inheritance. I should have known. Now they don't seem like the result of a year's hard work. They seem like the inevitable product of the monogrammed silver. Now that I know about the *P*'s on the silver, it seems that there's nothing in my life that they don't explain. Or Grimshaw's.

I put the yearbook and my grades in a trash can at the end of the hall.

Next to the trash, there is a window that overlooks the town of Colchis. Before I go down the stairs and out into my rosy future, I stop and put my forehead against the glass. The trees create a solid quilt of green that covers everything in the town—streets, houses, cars, the park, the people . . . Under it, everything is hidden, at least from here. I could be angry at this town, I could make a case that it killed her. I could hate. I could hate Colchis, hate Colchis High School, hate Mr. C., the church, Scot, Nanci Lee, the cheerleaders, Mike Lyle, my mother, even myself . . . but there's no point. What erased her is so much bigger than all this, bigger than all of us. Behind me the high school is filled with the silence of summer, which also erases everything. Hating is stupid. What do I have to be angry about? I'm one of the winners, if I want to be, and like Junior Davis says about Vince Lombardi: winning isn't everything. It's the only thing. It's all up to me.

But I'm still angry, and I still want to do something.

I pick my grades out of the trash, tear them into confetti, and let them fall from my hands down the stairwell. With my foot, I start pushing the trash can toward the stairs. I inch it closer and closer to the edge. When it gets to the tipping point, it hangs there for a minute and then seems to make up its own mind. I watch it bounce down the stairs; the echo reverberates through the empty halls of Colchis High. It comes to the first landing, rolls, and the top comes off and bounces down the second flight of stairs. I close my eyes and listen to the soft sound of crumpled paper spilling down the steps. Mr. C. hurries out of his room, sees it's me standing there, looks worried.

"Serena?"

We look down at the paper on the stairs. He puts his hand on my shoulder, and I let him steer me down the stairs.

"I just did that."

"We'll go clean it up," Mr. C. says. "We'll do it together."

At the bottom of the stairs, a janitor is standing, looking up at the mess. He's the big one, the one with the limp. His hair is white, cut in military style. In his breast pocket is a pack of Salem menthols.

"Just a little accident, Mike," says Mr. C. "We got it."

"No," the janitor says. He climbs the stairs heavily. "It's my job, not yours." Halfway up the stairs, he's out of breath and stops to get it back. By that time, I've picked up the trash bag and have put the yearbook back into it. He takes it from me. I don't want to let it go, but he pulls it out of my hand. It's Mike's father, the one who hurt his back falling off a ladder. I look into his pale blue eyes, almost colorless, into the hatred I thought would never shock me again.

"Do me a favor," he says. "Just get out of here."

When I get back home, Allegra and Tyler are studying one of Scot's accounting textbooks.

"I'm not going to graduation," I tell Allegra. "So we can pretty much leave for Maine any time. Tomorrow, if you want."

"Serena." Allegra says my name in a calm, soothing tone of voice, like she's become the undertaker of my life.

"What now?"

"We're not going to Maine," she says. "Or at least I'm not." I look from her to Tyler and then back at her.

"Scot bought another field from Mizerak," he explains. "So he's broke again. He can't afford Nanci Lee anymore, and we're going to manage Pentz Homes for a while, get some experience running a business, and maybe go into business for ourselves someday."

I look at Allegra. "What's he talking about?"

"Serena," Allegra says, "I'm at a point in my life where I can't organize my existence around running off and having fun all summer."

"A point in your life? Jesus, Allegra, you're not even nineteen!"

"So?" she says.

Mom comes in. She looks happy. "Guess what, Serena?"

"What?" Allegra and Tyler say in unison.

"Great news! About your friend!"

I hold up my hand. "I don't want to hear—"

"Claudette Mizerak got married yesterday! To Junior Davis!"

"—it," I conclude.

"Praise God!" Mom warbles. "Her baby's due any time, and it'll have a father. That makes such a difference."

"Allegra?" I ask. "I think we need to go to Niagara Falls again."

Allegra looks sideways at my mother. "Mom?" she says. "I think this is your moment."

"Oh!" my mother exclaims. "Serena! We're—Scot and I—giving you a car! Straight As!" She hugs me. "We always knew you could do it!"

It turns out that Scot needs a new pickup truck, for the turn his business is taking, and rather than trade in his car, the BMW is now my reward for a year of hard work and accomplishment.

"So now you're free!" Allegra says. "You can hit the proverbial road!"

"See the world!" Tyler choruses, not looking up as he leafs through the pages of the accounting book.

"But come back by noon on Saturday, though, okay?" my mother says.

I leave the next day and stare at Niagara Falls for a long time—all day, in fact—but it doesn't do any good. So I just drive. I drive until the gas tank is empty, and then I fill it up again and keep driving. I have a sleeping bag and Scot's credit card, so the only reason to go home after a couple days of driving and listening to the radio is that I only brought two pairs of underwear.

When I get back to Colchis, I don't tell anyone I'm home.

I go to the cemetery. It looks like some kids have discovered it. One of the slates is tipped over, and there are beer cans and cigarette butts scattered around. I stand up on the Helmers, the way Grimshaw used to do when she was practicing her dance moves. From here, you can see the entire Minnechaug Valley. It looks like a quilt rippling over a bed, with its patches of pasture and woods and corn in different colors of green and gold. Colchis is tucked under the next ridge, so when the leaves are out, all you can see of it from here are the smokestacks of the Arms and one church steeple. On the other side of the Valley, the highway cuts into the hillside. Trucks crawl by, and the sun glints off the girders of the overpass where it soars over Linerville, right before the exit that leads down into our hometown.

I get a bag out of the car and start cleaning up around the gravestones. I find a condom wrapper. Next to it in the grass I find a jagged piece of granite. They've broken a chip off a corner of the Helmers' stone. It's thin and sharp, and about as long as my hand. I sit up on the Helmers with the piece of rock in my lap, fingering the edge of it.

There will be no experience that will set the world back the way it was. The way I feel now, an alloy of anger and guilt fused together, is probably permanent, so I just have to get used to it. I've been acting like Grimshaw's murder is a movie I'm watching on TV. I've been waiting to cast myself in the right setting with the right script, and so have my catharsis, sob my too-long-held-in sobs, shine my tearful smile of healing, learn my spiritual lesson, which I then channel for the benefit of humanity.

Then I understand that everything happens for a higher purpose, even a murder, which in the end serves its own purpose, as long as somebody expendable dies. I've been waiting for the TV movie to end. I've been waiting for her to come back.

I press the edge of the granite into the flesh of my arm, and then I keep slowly adding pressure, harder and harder. I find a threshold where I can't stand the pain, and it brings a cool sense of relief. Exactly one tear slides down my cheek. No more follow. When it gets dark, I get Aaron's sleeping bag out of the trunk of the BMW and spread it out on the grass so I can sleep where I belong, among the Helmers, the Getmans, the Purdys, and Mr. Sprague.

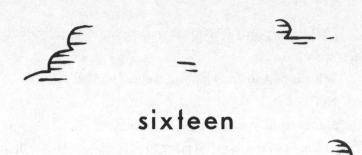

sixteen

WHEN I GET BACK TO Versailles on Saturday, there's a sign over the gate that says CONGRATULATIONS SERENA in capital letters. A big party is going on in the back, the noise bubbling up over the house. I lean my forehead on the steering wheel. I can tell without even getting out of the car that there is going to be nobody here that I want to see or talk to. But I don't have anywhere else to go. So I dig out the mascara that has been in the bottom of my backpack since my cheerleader days. Looking in the rearview mirror, I paint on a little makeup and a little smile. As I get out of the car, Allegra comes out to greet me. She's in bartender garb, complete with a garter on her arm.

"Hi."

"Hi," she says. We gaze at each other, new adults, across the wide expanse of asphalt.

"I guess I'm the dead body at the funeral," I say finally.

"Yeah," she says. As I get closer to her, she says, "Um, Serena?"

"Yeah?"

"I have a surprise for you that you might, like, really, really hate me for."

"What is it? A summer job with Pentz Homes?"

"No."

"A gift certificate to Crossways Tavern?"

She laughs a little. "I'm just going to tell you." She takes a deep breath, holds it, and exhales and shakes her head. "I can't. Come on." She takes me by the elbow and leads me around the house. At the last minute, she stops and turns around.

"Serena," she starts. "I just want you to know that if you do hate me, it's okay. I understand. I still, like, love you." She puts her arms around me while I stand there stiffly. She turns away from me, and I follow her into the backyard. The party is what I would expect—Scot's clients, the school board, people from the church, all with swarms of children, who have fanned out all over the semibuilt homes of the development. The volleyball net is up. Scot is burning steaks on the grill.

I turn to Allegra. "What is it?"

"Over there by the punch," she says.

"All I see over by the punch are people."

"Keep looking."

I notice a guy who stands a little apart, ill at ease, like he doesn't know anybody, surveying the crowd between the top of a plastic glass of beer and the brim of a dirty green ball cap. He has a big pewter belt buckle, the kind nobody I know wears, and one thumb hooked in his watch pocket. In my memory, riding high in that Kenworth, he looks like a movie star. He doesn't look like a movie star at Versailles. He looks like a trucker. It's Bo.

"Jesus Christ." I look at my sister. "What did you do?"

"I called his number." Her face is white. "The one in your notebook. But I didn't think he was gonna come."

"Jesus Christ." I grab Allegra's arm. All the blood rushes to my head. "What did you do?" I whisper.

"Omigod," she babbles. "I am so, so sorry. I should never have—"

Bo sees me.

"Jesus Christ," I say a final time.

He walks over. I cross my arms and watch his feet approach. They stop about three inches in front of mine. I can't look at him.

"Your sister called and told me everything that went down," he says. "So I came."

I forgot about his voice. All the times I thought about him, I tried to remember his face, or his hands, or how he walked, but not his voice. That place that I thought was impenetrable, that nothing would ever reach again, his voice slices right into the middle of it. I watch as big wet splotches start to fall on the dusty toes of his boots. I wrap my arms tighter around myself. I still can't look at him.

Then it all surges up in a ball into my throat. I clap both hands over my mouth, but it comes out anyway, in waves so strong they feel like they'll break my ribs. I sound like I'm throwing up, but I can't stop it. He puts his hands on my shoulders, and I lean against the faded blue of his T-shirt. His presence makes it all real again. He makes her real again.

I'm not sure if I cry for ten minutes or ten hours. When I stop, the world looks newly washed and so beautiful that it's unbearable to look at. Past the edge of the development, Mizerak's corn is about a foot high. For a second, the world comes back to me the way it felt when Grimshaw was alive. Suddenly, I can almost see her walking toward me through her favorite crop, a girl who wanted what she wasn't supposed to have, which was her own life. I don't know how long I've been crying, but apparently it was enough to clear out the backyard. I look around the remains of my party. It sounds like the guests have gone to the other side of the house.

I look into Bo's face. "Where's your truck?"

"I lost my truck."

"No truck?"

He shakes his head. "I couldn't make payments and repairs," he explains. "One or the other I could swing, but that truck was old. I ain't a crack-shot mechanic to keep it runnin' on a dime."

Those trucks are high-shouldered buffalo roaming the paths of the prairie in single file. At night herds of them sleep together in parking lots, keeping the West alive. Bo doesn't have one anymore, though. He walks like a cowboy, but he isn't one. Ain't one. The truth is puny, next to the romantic version, but it has more possibilities.

"If I could have driven twenty-four hours a day, I could have done it," he says. "But—they don't let you do that."

His hat is now folded up and stuck into the back pocket of his jeans. I take it out. It's the same one he was wearing in the parking lot in Boomtown, Nevada.

"If it ain't a cat it's a dog," I read.

Bo nods gravely. "Words to live by." For some reason, that

makes me laugh, and that feels familiar, too, like it is something I used to do, and I didn't know my face would still remember how to do it, and then I start crying again.

Eventually, I take his hand. "Thanks for coming." It comes out in a whisper.

"It's okay."

When I look into his eyes, I see the same expression there as Grimshaw had the first time she looked at me in the cafeteria in sixth grade, wondering if I had what it takes to get across that great space in between us.

"Do you want to go see her grave? I haven't seen it yet."

"We could do that."

"I have a car now."

"That's good," he says. "'Cause I don't."

Grimshaw doesn't seem like much for two people to have in common. If he had a truck, I could leave Versailles and ride around the country with him. I could visit factories where they make gaskets and potato chips, and stand on the bridges that staple a continent together and look down and watch history flow by under my feet. I could be a tourist. Nothing at stake. Just looking, just passing through. But he doesn't have a truck. That's what this road is about. Crying, giving your money away, that's the easy part. As for the rest . . . maybe only people with no other choice have the courage to get across, and we should leave it to them.

But Grimshaw is dead, so that means I have to do it.

acknowledgments

Thank you to the many friends, readers, and fellow travelers for reading, commenting, encouraging, and generally hanging in over the course of the creation of this book. To Cowboy, the taxi driver in St. Louis who squired me to the Chain of Rocks Bridge on the fourth of July and gave me some of the best lines in the book. To my students over the years for getting me to teach what I needed to learn. To my family for being such good storytellers. To the people of the Mohawk Valley of New York State. To the New Hampshire State Council on the Arts for their early support. And, most especially, to Wayland.

Thank you to my agent Sorche Fairbank for finding the book such a good home. A thank you to Christy Ottaviano for seeing the story's potential, to Jessica Anderson for helping shape the book, and to them both for their belief in it. And thank you to the rest of the team at Henry Holt Books for Young Readers.